CALL YOU Mine

THE BAKER'S CREEK BILLIONAIRE BROTHERS SERIES

USA TODAY BESTSELLING AUTHOR
CLAUDIA BURGOA

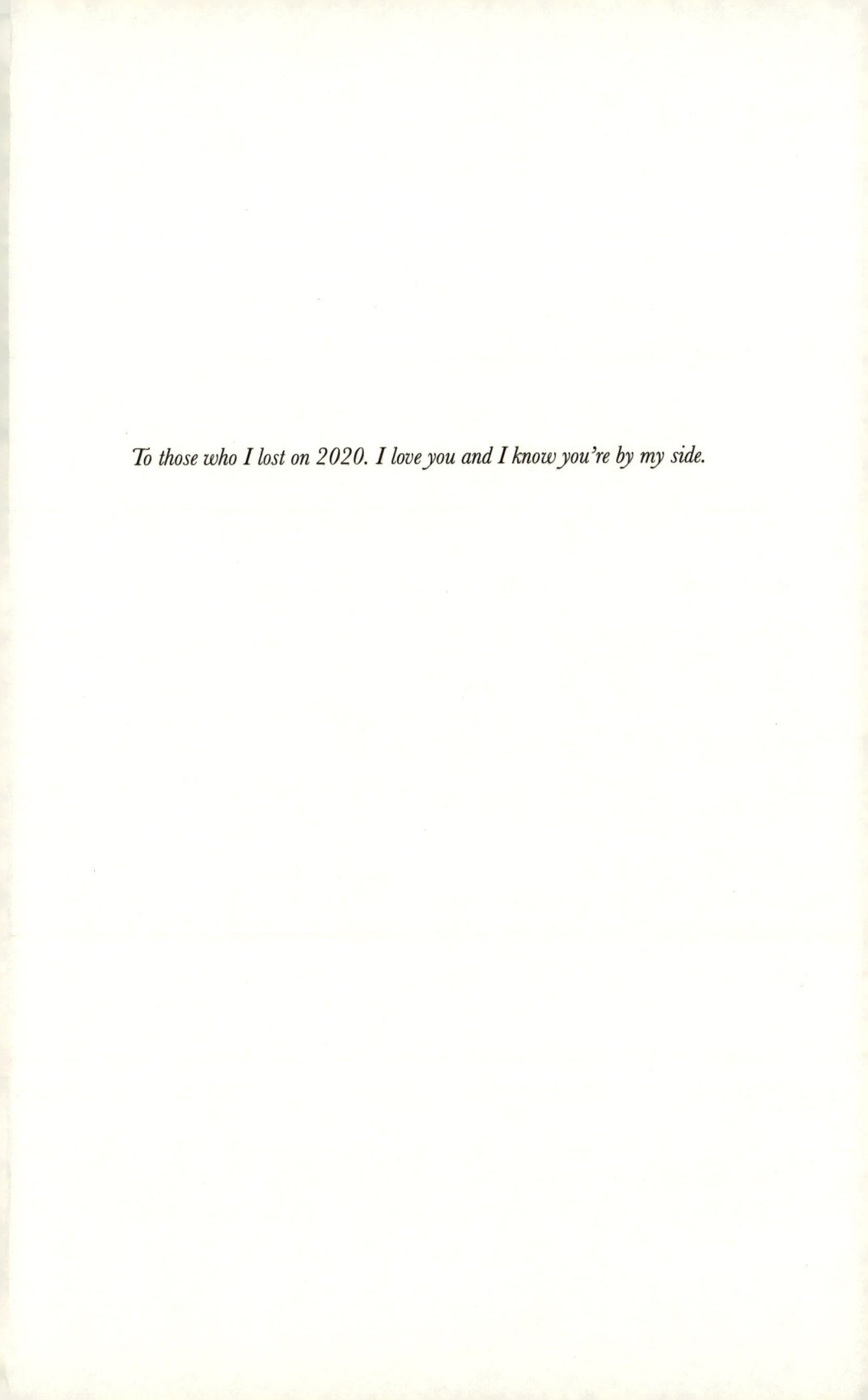

To those who I lost on 2020. I love you and I know you're by my side.

"I love you without knowing how, or when, or from where. I love you simply, without problems or pride: I love you in this way because I do not know any other way of loving but this…" —Pablo Neruda.

Grace's Prologue

I've known about the Aldridge brothers all my life. I'm best friends with the youngest, Beacon Kirk Aldridge. We've known each other since…well, I wasn't even born when he moved to Mercer Island, Washington, where *all* of my family lives.

You could say we've been inseparable since the beginning of time. We're talking about having embarrassing pictures of the two of us covered in finger paint, swimming in a kiddie pool, and taking naps together. There are videos of us playing music together. Well, it's not music. It's just noises a two-year-old—that'd be me—and a four-year-old can make at that age.

Summers together were the best, except for that one week when he had to visit his father. I missed him so much. He'd come back talking about his brothers. They were older. He wanted to bring them home so they could be a family. When I think about that boy asking, "But why can't we live together?" my heart shrinks. He wanted them to be a part of his life. He looked up to them until they stopped going to Baker's Creek; and it was just him.

Who are his brothers?

He likes to categorize them by assholiness. I'm not kidding. That's how he does it. Number one is Henry. The guy owns one of the best hotel chains in the world. Number two is Hayes. He's one of the best orthopedic doctors in the world. Number three is Pierce. He's a lawyer—*bloodsucking asshole*. Number four is Vance. He's a former Delta Force. Number five is Mills. He's not really an asshole—or maybe he lost his title because his son, Arden, is super cute. We adore him.

Number six is Carter. He died when he was twenty-one. Carter was his favorite brother.

I'm not a fan of those guys—or his parents.

His dad dying and leaving a will where he forces his sons to spend eighteen months in Baker's Creek was bad. You know what's worse? Beacon doesn't like nonsense. Good luck keeping him in one place for that long.

While he's gone, I'm taking this time to find a boyfriend. Without the man around who likes to swat away any prospect like a fly, I might be able to finally meet *Mr. Right*.

Beacon's Prologue

When I was twenty-five, I was named the Sexiest Man Alive.

Is it true? Nah, but there are things said about me that I don't care to control. The rest—I keep a tight grip on what the media prints, publishes, and posts about me.

On the outside, I'm a free-spirited man who doesn't give a shit about the world. That's how I want everyone to see me. As I mentioned, I regulate the narrative of my life.

I'm also called one of the most influential figures of alternative rock. That is the one I care about. I work hard to be number one. I live for what I do.

Music is one of the most important and powerful things in the world.

Music is my life.

A life I fill with melodies, harmonies, and lyrics. Without it, my existence would be pointless.

She's been a part of me since I can remember.

I started playing music as a young child. Although I composed and wrote lyrics when I was a teenager, my career didn't take off until my friends and I formed Too Far from Grace.

We could go on and on about how my career began. But I'm sure you're not here to hear about my epic band, our success, or how millions of fans idolize us.

You want to know more about me because I'm one of the six Aldridge brothers.

So let's do this with style, unlike my brothers.

The name is Beacon.

One name. I'm a mononymous person, like Plato, Molière, Bono, Sting, and Beyoncé.

Most know me as the front man and lead guitarist of the punk rock, alternative band Too Far from Grace. I formed that band when I was twenty-one after graduating from Juilliard. My best friends and I planned it while growing up.

It was all set, except one of them said, "Thank you, but I play solo."

Maybe she said, "I'm too cute to be with a bunch of disgusting boys."

Nah, I'm kidding. Grace isn't a diva. She's my closest friend. It's because of her and her mom that I found my love for music.

When we were forming the band, though, she was already a famous cellist getting requests to play worldwide. She's the Bach of our time.

When you're that famous, why would you want to play for an unknown band?

Also, she doesn't like to deal with crowds. She'd rather be in a conservatory playing for a few stuffy people than in a stadium filled with thousands of fans chanting out her name.

I know her better than she knows herself. She's a lot more than a friend. She's my person. You know, the one who understands you, and without a doubt will be there for you no matter how crazy your ideas are. She's that and more.

She claims I'm an attention seeker. I'd like to defer. If I wanted attention, I'd use my last name, mention my parents, or flaunt my grandfather's legacy.

I'd write a tell-all book. I'm not thirty yet, but I know tons of juicy stuff that I could leak to the press.

Things that they don't know about me: My grandfather is the late actor Kirk Fitzpatrick. My mother is the famous pop-star Janelle, who began her career at fifteen. She surrendered me to her parents before my second birthday.

My father never gave a shit about me after the paparazzi caught him with me, and he lost his wife and all of his mistresses.

I was raised on Mercer Island, Washington, but was born in LA.

The Decker-Colthurst family opened their arms to us and helped my grandparents raise me. Legend says that I was a handful.

Confession, I still am.

I had six brothers. One of them died, and the other five don't care much about me.

What do I do with my free time? Well…some secrets keep many safe, and that's how they'll stay—secret.

Everyone is always wondering about my love life and the part of myself that I protect from everyone.

I don't have any romantic relationships. The speculation that I'm dating some groupie that's always hanging out with the band is false. Grace isn't a groupie.

So, let's be clear. This is the only statement I'll make.

I chose *the job*.

If there's something I learned at an early age, it is to prioritize.

You can judge me. I don't care. I live by my values and put what matters the most before everything. Just remember, sometimes we only see what we want to see and let the illusions take over reality.

Chapter One

Beacon

IT'S the end of the last song—the second encore.
　The audience sings the lyrics along with me.
　I still remember when my fingers finally let you go.
　When I lost the right to hold you,
　The right to claim you,
　The right to call you mine.
　You're close, and so far,
　I lost the right to call you mine.
　If only I could kiss you once,

One last time before I become the ghost of your past.

I direct the microphone toward the audience. Everyone knows this song, loves this song, and empathizes with my pain.

The pain of losing my first love, the love of my life.

My forever.

This was the first song I wrote from the heart. It's inspired by one of the most painful experiences of my life. Everyone connects with it on such a deep level. It makes me wonder if humanity feasts on the despair of others, or we are all hurting. Maybe we're joined by loss, agony, and melodies.

I'm drenched in sweat, my throat is tired, and I'm ready to disappear. Thank fuck, the tour is over.

This is a big chunk of my life. Live concerts, fans yelling at the top of their lungs, and sharing the stage with my best friends—my brothers. I love everything, but to an extent.

It's loud, hot, and crowded.

I'm a huge contradiction. Before a concert, I'm pumped up and ready to give everything I have to my fans. During the show, I play and sing my heart out. Once it's over, I can't stand the masses.

I need to go.

Making a final bow to the applauding crowd demanding another encore, I jog off the stage with my guitar. Manelik continues drumming hard while I cross the hallway. One of the bodyguards and the rest of the band follow me. When the drums stop, the people begin to stomp their feet harder and faster.

They chant, "Encore, encore."

They need another song, another hour with us—more of Too Far from Grace. I hope Mane runs fast or the driver will leave him. Near the service door at the back of the arena, I spot Byron Langdon, our manager, who waits with towels and water for all of us.

"Where is Manelik?" Byron asks with annoyance.

"Behind us?" I ask, pulling the doors open and breathing the cool, fresh night air.

"Get into the car," Byron orders and then speaks to one of the security guys. "I swear if he's not here soon, I'm leaving him without a detail—or a ride home."

The clapping and stomping noise continues up until I make my way inside the limo. My mouth stretches from ear to ear when I see the best thing in the world waiting for me.

"Hey, G," I greet the most beautiful woman in the world—and my best friend.

Her grayish eyes look at me with amusement.

"Hi, stranger," she responds, moving toward the corner of the bench and fixing her long braid.

Today, her hair is different shades of pink with streaks of blue. Her beautiful face illuminates the entire night. She's wearing a tank top that lets me see her tattoos. They are black and white riffs, lyrics, and symbols. Looking at my arm, I smile; we actually draw each other's tattoos.

"Why do you always lose your shirt?" She rolls her eyes, handing me a clean T-shirt and another towel. The one Byron gave me is soaking wet.

Some artists need drugs, alcohol, or women after a concert. I just need her. Her presence, her voice, and her hugs.

"He's an attention whore," Sanford, the bassist, answers as he makes his way into the car.

"What's your excuse, San?" Grace exchanges a knowing look with me.

We love the guy, but he's full of shit.

"We're like a boy band," he responds. "Instead of wearing matching dorky outfits, we just don't wear shit."

"You're your own boy band, asshole," Fish, the keyboardist, complains and looks at G. "The fucking place is too hot to wear clothes. We keep our pants on just because our PR would kill us."

"What are you talking about, assholes?" Mane asks as he enters the car along with Byron.

The clunk of the car door seals away the outside noise. We all take our seats. Mine is right beside Grace. After I put on the shirt, I finally hug her.

"You okay?" she asks, hugging me back.

"And it's over," Sanford states as the driver sweeps us away.

It's time to go home.

"Did you catch the show?" I ask Grace, not letting her go. I need to absorb all her magic.

She's like an enchanted unicorn or a magical fairy who possesses the power to ground me.

In the past few months, we've barely seen each other. She's one of the most famous cellists in the world. This spring, she toured with The New York Philharmonic. Last week, she played a solo concert at Carnegie Hall to wrap her season.

She yawns and nods. "Uncle Jacob let me be backstage," she mentions our agent. "I was hanging out with him and Byron."

"At what time did you arrive?"

"Just as you guys took the stage. I told you I'd make it on time," she says, resting her head on my shoulder. "I love the new song."

My fans liking my songs is an accomplishment I don't take for granted. Her loving them is what I live for. I don't say a word and just watch as the car drives north toward home. For the next week, I don't plan to do anything but be at home with my friends, G, and our cat. The rest of the world can crumble, and I won't give a shit.

Chapter Two

Grace

CURRENT SITUATION. I'm in my parents' kitchen after what I can only describe as the worst date in the history of romance.

It's not an exaggeration. This was by far the most horrible date I've been on.

My plan of action is erasing the embarrassment and drowning my sorrows.

My method is eating frozen yogurt and drinking tea.

Thoughts of the day: My love life is either the result of bad luck, the fact that the men of my generation are defective, or there's something incredibly wrong with me.

"I should give up dating and men," I grumble.

"You're only twenty-seven," Mom says, as if that explains why I can't find a steady boyfriend.

Bringing up my age won't make me feel better.

She can't sympathize because the woman has been married for over thirty years to the love of her life. I don't remind her that Nathan, my baby brother, has been dating his girlfriend since they were sixteen. Six years of happiness. There are plenty of women and men who find love at a younger age.

Why can't I have that?

"You date douches," Nathan remarks, and I glare at him.

Who asked you, twerp?

And if his comment isn't enough, my brother Seth adds, "She mail-orders them from Doucheland."

"Original." I groan, rolling my eyes.

They both laugh at me, and I swear I don't kill them only because my parents are fond of them and might notice if they go missing.

Why couldn't I be an only child?

"Stop!" Mom orders as if we're younger and she needs some order before we start chasing each other.

So, I know what you're thinking. Why is she at her parents' and not with a friend drinking a glass of wine, eating popcorn, and streaming some sappy rom-com?

My best friend is in London. He'd be mocking me, just like my brothers. The rest are busy with their lives. The good thing is that I have my family. From a young age, I learned to confide in them.

I come from a big family that is close—too close.

We live on the same cul-de-sac where Mom's parents and her brothers live. Our backyards are connected. Our playground is the size of a park. My aunts, uncles, grandparents, and parents took care of us, the children, at the same time. My cousins and I grew up like brothers and sisters.

Even my great-grandparents used to live close to us. My chest aches at the memory of them. I still miss them so much. Gigi died when I was twenty. Great grandpa James died a couple of years ago.

Mom and I are pretty close. When I need someone to vent to, I usually call her or come by my childhood home to complain about the latest dating disaster. I'm prone to those. Today is different, though.

I'm here because Dad had to pick me up at the hospital where I drove my date. Well, it's more like he had to clear my name with the police because the doctors were accusing me of domestic violence.

Yep, that's how bad my date went.

"I'm still confused about how you ended up breaking the guy's nose," Nathan snorts.

"He must've said, 'You look pretty tonight,'" Seth replies. His hip is parked against the kitchen counter. He's drinking from a can of Dr. Pepper while he watches me with amusement.

I was hoping this incident would stay between my parents and me. These two are never going to let it go. Having two pesky younger brothers is every girl's nightmare and a woman's headache. Again, my parents should've just kept their family small. Only one child—me.

"I still don't get why Dad had to bring you along."

"It's poker night," he reminds me.

I groan because that means everyone in my family already knows about this mess. My uncles and Dad have had this tradition since before I was born. Every Thursday, they get together to play. It used to be video games, but over the years, it transformed into poker night.

From only four players, it's now up to at least ten a night—if not more. My grandparents, uncles, and cousins always gather in Uncle Jacob's basement. The night is open for whichever Decker is in town.

"I came to rescue you," Seth says and tsks. "Who knew it was the guy who needed me to save him from you."

"Har. Har, har, har." I glare at him. "We're all going to forget about this."

"Or…I'm going to hack into the city's CCTV system. It should be easy to find the footage where we can see your little stunt. I'll be streaming it everywhere by Sunday," Nathan teases me.

"You want to experience it yourself?" I show him my fist. "I can give you a live demonstration."

"You can try, shorty," he taunts me.

Mom claps her hands. "There won't be any demonstrations or fights," she warns us, pointing at Nathan. "We don't make fun of people's height just because you're a gigantor."

We all laugh at my petite mom.

I'm not short, but my five-nine seems small compared to my brothers, who are six-five. Not as small as Mom, who is five inches shorter than me. My uncles, her brothers, who are also tall, call her pocket size.

Nathan lifts his arms. "I wouldn't dare. You're the boss, lady." He winks at her.

"Flattery won't get you anywhere, Nathan Bradley," she says, and she narrows her gaze at him.

My brother stands up and pulls her into a hug. "I wouldn't dare to upset you, Mom. If you don't need me, I'll be in my room."

I glare at Nathan and say, "Aren't you a little too old to be living with Mom and Dad?"

"I'm just twenty-two." He grabs a yogurt from the fridge and searches for a spoon in the silverware drawer. "Just because you're some kind of musical freak who likes to go around the world showing off, that doesn't mean I should do the same."

"She's a prodigy, not a freak!" I jolt at the sound of the low baritone voice.

I'd recognize that sound anywhere. Turning around, I find him. Beacon Aldridge. His tall, broad body stands by the kitchen entrance blocking it. His dark hair is cut short on the sides and longish on top. The fringes almost cover his deep green eyes. His black long sleeve T-shirt stretches over his broad chest.

He's too handsome for his own good.

"Beacon, did you break into the house again?" Mom sighs and shakes her head, looking at the microwave clock. "It's almost midnight. A little late for visits—or break-ins."

He gives Mom his signature cheeky grin. "I wouldn't call it a break-in, as much as I decided not to disturb you guys since it's late, Mrs. B. I didn't trigger any alarm."

He saunters toward Mom and gives her a hug and a kiss. This guy is the one who taught Nathan how to get away with murder when it comes to Mom. Just a sly smile, a hug, and their ass-kissing words.

Nathan grunts. "Great. Dad's going to add another layer of security to the alarm because someone was able to hack it."

"You should thank me," Beacon says. "I'm keeping him entertained and off your case. Have you decided what you're going to do with your life?"

Nathan mumbles something under his breath and shakes his head.

Seth high fives Beacon. "Since there's someone to control our criminal, I can leave. Beac, call me tomorrow." He hugs Mom and kisses her forehead, walking out of the kitchen.

"Hey." Beacon sits on the barstool next to me and takes a spoonful of yogurt.

"How are you, stranger?" I greet him.

"You're just the person I am looking for," he says. "Heard you broke someone's nose this time. Nothing says, 'Let's go steady' better than a visit to the ER."

"Shut up!"

He bursts into laughter, and Nathan joins. They begin to mock me. Beacon is a big part of the family, like a brother. He's been around us ever since I can remember.

His mother and father didn't want to deal with him, so they gave him to his maternal grandparents who were too old to raise a child. They reached out to my grandfather Gabe. He convinced them to move to Washington, where their grandchild could have a life away from Hollywood and the paparazzi.

While growing up, Mom and Dad filled those places his parents didn't care to fill, and his grandparents couldn't because they were too famous and too old. He's my best friend, but he can also be a pain in the ass. Sometimes he behaves like the big brother I never wanted.

I cross my arms and glare at them both. "Are you done?"

Covering his nose, Beacon nods. "So, what did he do to piss you off?"

"You're not funny." I glare at him but tell him what happened. "He came up from behind and covered my eyes. I was outside the coffee shop waiting for him."

Beacon gasps. "Wait, let me get this straight. He saw a woman alone on the street and he thought covering her eyes was a good idea? What a fucking idiot. Why would he do that?"

I draw air quotes. "To surprise me." I sigh.

"Well, he got a big surprise, didn't he? Our Grace isn't just any woman. She works for the best high intelligence, private security company." He chuckles. "What did you do?"

"I went into survival mode, and I hit him with my elbow to get away. Then, as I turned, I kicked him in the face while getting ready to run away. He should be glad that I didn't break any ribs."

"You're such a romantic, G," Beacon teases, but he doesn't smile.

The tease is just an automatic response. He uses humor to deflect from him or his emotional state. That's when I realize that there's something wrong with him. There's a wave of lingering anger in his eyes.

I've been so preoccupied with Jonathan Wilson and the police that I forgot about Beacon. I tried to reach him earlier, before my date. He didn't respond to any of my calls. He's supposed to be in London. As a matter of fact, I just realized that he didn't call at midnight his time zone.

What happened?

"Do you want to go home?" I ask.

He bobs his head twice then smirks at Mom. "I'm taking your troublemaker away, Mrs. B."

"I'll call you tomorrow, Mom." I hug her and then squeeze Nathan's arm. "Don't cause any trouble while I'm gone."

"Says the black sheep of this family," he jokes.

Beacon drags me by the hand.

"Where is your dad?"

"It's the day of family emergencies," I answer. "My grandparents' sink broke. He's at their house helping them."

Rumor has it that my grandparents were having sex on top of it. Ew. I'm not sure who started it or if it's to give them a hard time, but I choose not to think about them doing more than holding hands.

"Never a dull moment around you." He chuckles.

His truck is right outside the house. As we drive away, he grabs my hand. He doesn't let it go during the drive, and neither one of us speaks. Twenty minutes later, we're at my place, which happens to be right next door to his. Once we make it inside, he hugs me tight. His chin rests on my shoulder.

"What happened?"

He doesn't answer. His hands tap my back lightly. It's a slow rhythm at first that switches to a fast tempo a few seconds later. It's hard to understand what's the motive. All I know is that he's working his emotions through music. We're so similar in that way. I'd rather be playing my cello than talking about what's happening to me.

I stay quiet for a while. In the meantime, I'm trying to figure out what's bothering him. He was in London scouting the place. We have a tour coming up next September. There's a lot involved in that European leg. He and the guys were using this time to meet with the members of our team who are already working undercover. If something had happened, he would've contacted Dad.

It's not until I feel like there's a pattern—a melody eager to be played—that I know he's ready to let it out. If not in words, through music.

"Do you want to go to the music room?"

He takes a deep breath and finally lets me go. His eyes still harbor some frustration. He's not ready to talk. I wouldn't be surprised if he goes for the drums and expects me to follow him with the cello or the violin. He's too upset and has a lot of pent-up energy inside of him.

At first, I'm shocked when he chooses the piano and tilts his head toward the cello. As he strokes the keys slowly, I understand. He's not angry.

He's sad and hurting.

Beacon goes to the recording console, turns it on, and grabs the remote. Then he starts playing, and I follow. We take a few breaks. He insists I go to sleep, but I disregard his suggestion. He needs this.

He needs to bleed through the music.

I won't let him do it alone.

It's almost six in the morning when we finally stop. His features are more relaxed, and his eyes have that calm I love. I set Camilla, my cello, in her stand and begin doing my hand stretches.

"Want to grab some breakfast?" he asks.

"Still not ready to talk, huh?" I yawn, stretch, and lift Mozart, our cat, from the floor.

He has been walking around since we arrived, patiently waiting to be the center of attention. This guy is pretty intuitive and knows when it's his turn to be demanding.

"There's nothing to talk about," Beacon counters and takes Mozzy from my arms. "What have you been up to, Mozzarella? We should feed you while we're in the kitchen."

"Beacon."

His eyes find mine, and he sighs. "My father's lawyer called. William Aldridge is dying. He'd like to see me." He shows me his hand as if to stop me from ranting. "No, I won't be visiting him. It's just fucking frustrating that he can reach out just when he's about to die. At least he isn't like my mother, calling to see if I'll sing a duet with her to revive her career."

"Did she call again?"

He nods once.

I don't usually hate people, but I loathe his mother. What kind of coldhearted bitch abandons her son with her parents when he's not even two? Oh, but now that he's famous, she's been trying to figure out how to use him and make a comeback.

Bitch.

I hate his father too. I met him when we were living in New York. He was charming with most people, but cold with his son. His parents have ignored him since he was a kid, and even though he has five older brothers, only one is part of Beacon's life.

"Have you heard from Mills?" Mills Aldridge, his brother, is the star defenseman for the Vancouver hockey team.

Beacon shakes his head. "He's traveling with the team all week. He'll call me when he's back." He grunts. "I told him to quit. This is the second time he's injured that knee. The third time is going to end more than his career."

"He should go to a specialist. We'll find him the best. If he moves in with us temporarily, we can give him a hand with his son," I suggest.

"If my fucking brothers weren't selfish assholes, he could go to Hayes."

I arch an eyebrow as I try to remember which one is which. He has five brothers, and it's hard to keep them all straight since we don't speak about them often.

"Is Hayes the doctor?" I guess, trusting my logic.

Beacon nods. "Best fucking orthopedic doctor in the world. Has he reached out and said, 'Hey, asshole, I heard you hurt your knee. I might be able to fix it' or visited him to check on him? No. We… maybe we should visit Mills soon and convince him to take a hiatus."

"We'll do that," I assure him. "Arden needs a break from that hockey life too. He's just a baby."

He looks at me and smiles. It's such a sad smile. I want to cry for him.

Even though Mills is older than him, Beacon is the one who is always trying to take care of his brother. Mills and Arden are what he has left of hope. I wish he would accept my family as his and forget about the assholes. There are so many things I can wish for, but I don't say a word because I understand him better than anyone else.

He lives with a guilt that doesn't belong to him. He wants to fix everything he believes he broke. He wants to protect everyone he loves. The only thing that gives him peace is his music. That's the only constant that we share.

Chapter Three

Beacon

"I HATE YOU!" Grace says as I cut the homemade sourdough bread into cubes.

"Good. I still love you," I say teasingly.

"You could just bring the frittata, but no, you have to make your famous cinnamon French toast casserole."

"It is famous," I agree. "It's become an institution during the Deckers' brunch. I can't just skip it because you can't eat it."

She glares at me while wiping the bread maker.

"If I promise to make you some special muffins tomorrow?"

She smiles at me. "Fine, I might like you again."

"Wow, I can't please the crowd. What does a guy have to do to get an I love you?"

She shrugs. "Keep trying, Aldridge," she jokes.

My phone rings. I pray to God that it's not an emergency because I don't have time to entertain nonsense. It's my time off with Grace. Everyone knows not to call on Sundays when I'm at home.

"It says Hayes." G shows me my phone.

"Great. Asshole number two is calling." I sigh.

"Answer."

"No," I say. "Just ignore it. I don't care if he needs me to go to New York. For all I care, our father can die, go to hell, and I won't be bothered."

"He's your brother. You should answer."

"Tell me something I don't know."

"Good idea," she says and slides her finger across the screen. "Beacon's phone, how can I help you?"

That snarky tone and the grin while she's answering are a turn on. I should be upset that she can't let things be, but how can I when she's so fucking adorable—and challenging.

"Is he available?" I can hear his voice from where I stand.

I shake my head. *Hang up the phone*, I mouth.

"It depends." She twirls a lock of her hair, which surprisingly is dark brown today—her natural hair color. "Why are you calling, asshole number two?"

There's a chuckle on the other side of the line. "Is that how my name comes up on the caller ID? He catalogues us as assholes, just like Mills calls us Fuckers."

She responds, "No," but she nods.

Because actually, yes. I categorize my brothers by the severity of their assholiness, which coincidentally matches their birth placement from oldest to youngest. No one is a super asshole like Henry. He is his own kind of fucked-up dickhead.

"It reads Hayes. However, when your name flashed, he just said,

'Fuck. First, a lawyer calls about my father, and now it's asshole number two," she explains further. Only G can make up that shit on the go.

She doesn't need me to have a conversation with my brothers. Grace knows how I feel about each one of them. If she could just not try to make a low male voice, we'd be cool. Her raspy voice makes me hot.

You'd think she's on my side, but nope. She knows the reason he's calling, and she's fucking logical. "I answered because I guess things are not going well with his dad, and he can only ignore him for so long."

"I can ignore him forever." I sigh and warn her, "Leave it alone, G."

"He's sick, and you have to at least say goodbye. It'll be good for your soul," she claims.

Leave it to her to try to find a good excuse to make me give a shit. She has a badass family. If anything happens to one of them, we're all there to offer support. I mean *we* because they've welcomed me as part of their family since I was a kid.

"I'm soulless, so it doesn't matter," I argue while she groans in response.

Baby, not everyone has a set of terrific parents like you.

I frown when she says, "Beacon's Jiminy Cricket."

Then smirk at her because she is like my conscience. The one who grounds me. The person who makes me be a better version of whatever the fuck I'm supposed to be.

"Just less green, sassier, and cuter," I correct and wink at her.

I extend my hand and wiggle my fingers, asking nicely for the phone. "Hang up, G."

She turns around, ignoring me. I hope she knows what she just got herself into. I'm getting that phone, and she's going to beg for mercy.

"What is it that you need to tell him? I'll convey the message."

"Fine." She sighs loudly and makes an entire production of tapping the phone. "Speak."

"Beacon, our father died yesterday morning."

The entire room dims. I swear my heart stops beating. Grace

rushes to hug me. I lean on her. Ever since Thursday, after the fucking lawyer called, I've been pretending that I don't give a fuck. He didn't care. Why should I?

But I do care. No one deserves to die alone—not even *him*. I spent the flight from London to New York wondering if I should stop by his house. I did. I sneaked into the penthouse without anyone noticing. I saw him lying on a hospital bed, unresponsive.

"I pray I don't end up like you," I said, kissing his forehead, and I left.

Only Seth knows about it. I haven't mentioned it to Grace. She's been by my side ever since I went to pick her up at her parents' house.

Well, I guess there won't be a family reunion to celebrate the miracle that the old man got better. I should just let everyone go. I don't need the fucking hassle of dealing with them.

"Tell him I don't give a fuck," I say, releasing her.

I pace around the kitchen. This isn't my problem anymore. Why should I give a shit?

"When is the funeral?" Grace questions. I look at the ceiling, not sure if I'm praying that she just hangs up or if I'm annoyed by her worry.

She shouldn't care either. *You care. Of course, she gives a shit. She's your best friend.*

"In two weeks, in Baker's Creek. We need him to be there—it's not optional," he answers.

Grace and I stare at each other. Baker's Creek is this small, picturesque town that we often visit since her cousin Tucker has a vacation home and family in the town. They don't know my father is from there. I'm technically Baker's Creek royalty—if it was a fucking kingdom.

"Hmm, I know where that is." Grace grins. I'm sure she's planning on inviting her entire family to the funeral. "You hear, Beac, we're going to Baker's."

"There's no fucking way I'm going to that damn town," I announce.

More like, I'm not going to the funeral, but we'll be there during the next Decker family reunion.

"Um, we were there just a couple of weeks ago."

Fuck, what is with her today? I charge toward her. "That's it, you asked for it, G."

She screeches, running away from the kitchen.

I catch her by the waist and begin tickling her as I shove her on top of my shoulder.

She's laughing, snorting, and yelling, "Stop! Put me down, Beac!"

"You know what to do."

"Uncle!"

I laugh, tossing her on the couch. She grabs my hand, pulls me to her while kicking me behind the knees, so I lose my balance. I end up on the floor and her on top of me. We're both laughing at the nonsense.

"You need to finish the call," she mumbles when we finally calm down.

"I don't."

She holds my face. "I know it hurts. Maybe it doesn't have to be a final goodbye but a new hello."

"No. I'm better without them, G."

I push myself up and help her stand up. We find my phone, and I say, "Look, asshole, I don't give a shit about the old man."

"We agree, Beacon. Yet, we're here trying to deal with his shit one last time."

Grace and I frown, looking at each other.

Mills? she mouths.

"Mills?" I ask, fucking confused.

G pulls out her phone and shows me his calendar. He's supposed to be in New York. The Orcas are playing the Rangers…right about now.

Why is he there? He could've called me. Actually, why hasn't he reached out to talk about our father?

"Yeah, and Henry is here, too," he responds. "Just do this once, okay?"

I want to say no, but I'm not leaving him alone with those assholes.

"Fine. Send me the info. I'll be there. Now, if you'll excuse me, I have family shit to do."

"Your wife?" he asks.

I laugh because wouldn't that be fucking amazing.

"Nah, I don't do that shit. My best friend invited me to have brunch with her family. See you later, assholes."

"I wish you had said goodbye to him."

"I did," I mumble.

"What?"

"On Thursday, we stopped in New York. He was unresponsive. I scanned his chart and sent it to Seth. He got one of the doctors to explain to me that he was about to die soon."

She nods. "You wanna skip brunch?"

If anyone would like to know the definition of the perfect woman, go no further. Grace Aiko Decker Bradley is it. She knows me so well. I do want to stay. It'd be easy to agree. I don't. She needs her family. These weekly meals make her happy. I wouldn't keep her away from her people. Never.

"Everyone is expecting Beac's French toast," I say, trying to let go of my dad and the call.

She rolls her eyes. "Just so you know, they'd love you even without your casserole."

"You get muffins tomorrow," I remind her. She grins. "Only if you stay with me for one more night, though."

She hugs me, and I absorb all of her while holding her tight.

"WHAT ARE YOU DOING HERE?" Mills arches an eyebrow and glances from Grace to me. "I appreciate all the presents, but can you keep it to just one per visit?"

"The last time we visited you ran out of finger paints," Grace answers. "I'm sure you haven't replaced them."

Mills smirks and says, "Sometimes I wonder if the toys and crafts are for you or my kid."

She grins. "I like to think it's for both."

Grace makes her way inside the house. When Arden sees her, he yells, "G!"

"He doesn't need all these presents, but I appreciate them," Mills tells me when I enter the house and hand him all the packages we brought. "Though, I wish you had called telling me you were coming?"

"So you could clean the place?" I glance at the living room that's filled with dinosaurs. "Lucky for you, I'm pretty good at the Jurassic and Crustaceous periods. We can handle this gig."

He rolls his eyes.

"Not that I don't like you to visit, but why are you here?"

"We were just passing by," I lie.

He laughs. "Really? You decided to take a drive and ended up in Canada?"

"Something like that," I confirm.

"I told you to call him before we dropped by," Grace claims.

"It's not like he's throwing a dinner party and we're interrupting him," I state, glancing around. "Unless you called *your brothers* to visit you, and I wasn't invited."

"I knew you were going to give me shit about it." He mumbles the last words.

"It's just weird that I wasn't invited to this brotherly reunion." I shrug.

Mills grunts. "It wasn't a reunion. Hayes and Henry texted me in the middle of the game to announce that our father died on Saturday. Somehow, they knew I was in New York. They asked me to join them at Henry's office. When I arrived, they were on a video conference with Pierce. Hayes is the one pushing for this reunion."

He looks at Arden and then back at me. "He's going through a middle life crisis of sorts."

"His dad just died…your father just died four days ago. It's okay not to be okay," Grace says. "How are you doing, Mills?"

"That 'okay not to be okay' makes zero sense, G," I argue.

"I'm coping," Mills responds to her, rolling his eyes at me. "She's right. How are you handling it?"

"He isn't," Grace responds. "The man is in denial. How about you?"

Mills shrugs. "I have an appointment with my therapist tomorrow. There's the usual anger, sadness, denial...I think we all have that ongoing. I spoke to Vance and he refuses to think about our father until the funeral."

He grabs a couple of beers from the fridge, and we go out to the deck.

"You okay?" I ask him, pointing at his knee. "While you were with Hayes, you could've told the asshole to fix your knee."

He shakes his head. "We grabbed some lunch after the calls. He seems lonely. We're all a bunch of pathetic losers."

I laugh. "Thank you. I always wanted my big brother to call me a loser."

Mills takes a sip of his beer, looks at the horizon and then back inside where Grace is laughing with Arden. "You're in love with her, yet you're *just friends*."

"Our lives are complicated."

"That's the thing. We just can't figure out how to coexist with another person. Henry is single. Hayes is still pining for Blaire—"

I whistle. "Good luck getting her to forgive the asshole."

He nods. "That's our problem, we fuck up all the time. Pierce is in the middle of a divorce. I only attract gold diggers."

I'm tempted to tease him and say, "You mean, puck diggers." If I do, he's going to tell me I don't take him seriously—like ever. Arden's mom did a number on him. The guy has trust issues.

"We can't find happiness. That curse our grandmother used to warn us about might be real, you know," he concludes.

Leaning against the railing of the balcony, I wonder what it would take to stop us from doing stupidities. Maybe we keep looking at our ancestors' failures. It's the fear that cripples our emotions and gets the worst of us. When I look at Grace, for the first time in eleven years, I wonder if I could make things happen for us.

Maybe someday?

Chapter Four

Beacon

THE AIR IS SLIGHTLY cold and humid. Sweat runs down my back as if we were under the sun—we're not. It's already dark. My jaw tightens. "What the fuck is taking so long?"

If this moment had a soundtrack, it'd be something composed by John Williams, and it'd sound close to the score of *Jaws*. While growing up, no one believed I'd be able to stay quiet in one place for more than a minute. If I have a target, it's easy. When I use one of my people as bait, it's fucking impossible.

"Calm the fuck down, Beac," Sanford says over the earpiece. "We've done this a million times."

He's right. We've been training for thirteen years, working for eleven. I've led missions for five years. We're professional musicians, and also agents for the best high intelligence agency in the world.

That doesn't make this moment any easier.

He can say shit, but his girl isn't in the line of fire, pretending to be a naïve college girl looking for the frat party everyone is talking about. Mine is. Fine, Grace isn't mine, but she's my reason to live.

It's about the same, right?

And no matter how many times we do this, it's nerve-wracking to wait, watch, and stay calm.

We can't fuck this up. I can't lose the girl or the assholes.

This is it. Our last chance to get a lead on the trafficking cell that has been kidnapping college girls in Portland. Classes are over. Everyone is in the middle of finals. In a few days, everyone is either going back home or starting a summer job. When that happens, these fuckers will disappear. They might come back when the next semester starts, or they'll move the operation to another big city.

It happened last year in Atlanta. We were so close. I don't want them to get away—again—but having Grace as bait is fucking killing me. I want to toss her over my shoulder and take her away from harm.

If she could hear my thoughts, she'd be so fucking upset. The woman knows krav maga, jiujitsu, and karate. She knows how to use a knife. That's her weapon of choice. They are easier to use than guns, according to her. She can take care of herself, but that doesn't take away my need to protect her.

"You know what would be easier?"

"If you shut up?" Lang responds. "I have at least seven different cameras to monitor."

He's in Seattle in his home office looking at the monitors on the wall. I bet there's one where he's playing a video game while we wait. As usual, he watches everything from a safe distance. The guy flies the drones.

The aircraft is several feet above Grace. It's far enough that no one in the ground can see it. The video technology installed in the drone makes it possible to film and take pictures of everyone around the quad. It should be able to capture the faces of whoever tries to take our girl.

"You know what we should be doing?" Fish asks.

"Recording an album, figuring out how to get Beacon out of his father's will, or playing video games," Mane answers. "Why did I sign up for this shit? I swear you said, 'We will form a band.' Not, 'We will be working as—' What are we? Some fancy look-a-like of a CIA-Interpol-FBI private agency with no retirement plan, dangerous working conditions, and a fucked up schedule."

San laughs through the communicator.

His question is complicated.

We've been friends for a long time—since preschool. Grace's mom likes to pair up people she thinks might have things in common, including music. One thing led to another, and we found ourselves learning martial arts with Mason Bradley. Several years later, here we are, working for him. I can't say that we do this during our spare time because sometimes we play in specific venues to scout or work on a mission.

Mane is right. There are times when it is confusing to understand what we do—even for us. Are we musicians or agents?

We can be both. Our band is renowned worldwide. We love playing—just like we love working for The Organization. They shouldn't complain about the working conditions. Today is a lot better than other missions.

"This reminds me of Moscow four years ago," San says.

Well, this is a lot better than being in the middle of Red Square having a red laser pointed at my chest. Back then, I was the bait and not in charge of the team. Yet, I feel a lot more anxious. G's safety is on the line. One mistake and…I don't want to think about what could happen to her.

My heart picks up its pace when I spot a guy talking to Grace. She tosses her head and laughs. Then she tilts her body just a bit to the right.

"That's the signal," I remind them.

Sure enough, there are two more guys close by watching their conversation. A prickle climbs the back of my neck as she nods and walks willingly with him.

"Got a few shots of the four guys," Lang says over the communicator.

"I only count three," San, who is on the highest point of the area with a rifle, announces. He's a trained sniper. "Where's the other one, Lang?"

Lang sends a text with the pictures of the suspects. One of them is the guy walking beside Grace.

"He's taking her to an alley. There's a van parked there," Lang alerts us.

Fuck, it's taking all of my self-restraint not to run and stop the operation. It's not because I don't trust her. I do. I'm just irrational.

"We get them, we pursue them...what's the deal?" asks Mane. He's the closest to the van.

"Follow her lead," I answer.

One of our drivers is ready to tail them if she decides to get in the van with them. I pray that she doesn't do it. The last time this lady let someone kidnap her, it was a fucking challenge to rescue her. It's not impossible, but I don't want a repeat.

Grace stops right in front of the restaurant that's next to the alleyway. The guy pushes her slightly. She steps back. He grabs her arm.

"Wrong move, buddy," San mumbles. "I'll shoot him if he tries something else."

"He's about to get his ass kicked," I murmur when he pulls her.

She takes off one of her hair pins. She stabs him in the side. Then, with gracefulness, she twirls, lifts her left leg, and kicks him in the shoulder. Once her feet are back on the ground, she lands a short jab square on his nose. This woman loves to break noses. The guy drops to the floor.

"Okay, we have the other three guys making a run for it and leaving their man on the ground," Lang alerts us.

"God, you have to stop talking so much," Grace complains as she starts walking away from the scene. "The guy is down. I swear I barely touched him. There are two more inside the van. I'm not sure if they are the ones we're looking for, but these guys are up to no good. I had time to toss a couple of knives to the tires. They can't go anywhere."

I text the team, assigning new duties for everyone. The police should be here to pick up the van and the guys in a few minutes.

"Everyone stays away from the scene. The cleaning crew is approaching. They're taking him into custody," I order.

"I can shoot the other guys," San announces. Knowing him, his finger is on the trigger and he's targeting one of them.

If this was an isolated place, I would say go for it and shoot the guys in the van. Since my orders were very specific and the quad is filled with people, I say, "We can't draw attention to them, or us. I'll let the boss deal with the rest—as he requested."

"G, walk away slowly," I command. "Get lost in the crowd."

"I'm not new at this," she protests.

She shrugs out of the black jacket she's wearing and hands it to a homeless person. She takes off the hat and wig, tossing it into a trash can. She pulls off the skirt she's wearing and shoves it inside her backpack. By the time she meets me, she's a different person.

She's now my G.

"Hey," I say, taking her into my arms. "You were going to get in the van, weren't you?"

When I release her, her gray gaze finds mine. She smiles, and there's so much mischief in her expression.

"You're either going to get me killed or give me a heart attack," I say, pulling her close to me and kissing the top of her head.

She takes off the earpiece, turning it off. I do the same, and she finally speaks, "You would've done the same."

"Probably," I answer, swatting her colorful braid.

Her hair is always a different color. Today it's teal. It amazes me how she can camouflage herself during a mission when she's so colorful.

"Let's go home. I'll cook tonight."

"Great, he's cooking," Fish says, joining us. "You heard that, Sir Byron Langdon. Drive your ass to Beac's."

"Just call him fucking Lang," I say, hoping his communicator is still on and Lang can hear me.

As we approach my SUV, I spot Mane and San leaning against it.

"Lang says that everything is under control." Mane fists bumps with G. "That was pretty badass."

"My favorite part is when you transformed from naïve student to"—San glances at her and shrugs—"you?"

"Let's go before people start recognizing us," I warn them, unlocking the car and getting into the driver's seat. "The plane is ready for takeoff."

"I thought you were driving," G says, pulling a granola bar and water out of her backpack.

"It's faster to fly," I answer casually, instead of saying, "Your father wants you back in Seattle, now."

"So, what's happening with your Dad's will?" Grace asks.

Could we avoid talking about parental units for at least a day or two? *I don't bring up your overprotective dad. You don't mention my fucking father.*

I blame her for answering the fucking phone when my brothers called. If I had ignored them…well, they'd have come to find me. Our father's will is too important to ignore. With a snap of his fingers, he can end the livelihood of thousands of people—and he's dead. Who has that fucking power?

William Aldridge.

But, if he's the Thanos to our world, I'll make sure to pull a Dr. Strange-Ironman-Antman move on him and avoid any destruction.

"Have they found a way to get you off the hook?" San asks.

"Nope. So far, the answer is I have to live in Baker's Creek for an eternity," I answer, driving toward the airport. "They're already building my studio. The contractors that will be building my underground home are already working on it too."

There's no way I'm going to share my space with them. I need a place where I can practice and another one where I can talk with The Organization in private. I'm still pondering how the hell I'll do my job. I'm the team leader. There's no fucking way I'll let my people go into a mission without me. That's like sending them to the grave.

"It's only eighteen months," Grace reminds me.

"We have work to do," I protest. "A lot is happening in the world.

I don't have time to sit back and relax—while dealing with my brothers. All five of them."

Knowing G, she has some kind of silver lining speech ready in case my brothers say, "There's no other alternative. You have to move with us, now."

"But—"

I shake my head. "Not today, G." I don't want to discuss my father, my brothers, or the stupid will. For now, I want to pretend it's not real.

Chapter Five

Beacon

"YOU DON'T PAY me enough for this," I joke when I enter Mills' place. "Can we discuss your relocation?"

His glare shuts me up. "What happened?"

"I think they're going to release me from my contract." He sighs.

For a moment, I'm speechless. What can I say that will make him feel better?

"My agent threatened to drop my ass," he continues. "It's the stupid will. I already told him I'm not going to live in Baker's Creek."

"We're not?"

After my father's funeral, the fun part began. His lawyer announced that we're inheriting all his shit. There's a catch, though. We have to stay in Baker's Creek for eighteen months, starting next week. Not only that, but we can't leave town. William Aldridge was insane, even though the bloodsucking lawyer swears he was in his rightful mind when he wrote his last will and testament.

I don't care about the fucking money or his assets. However, if we decide not to follow the stipulations, he pretty much ruins the town and all of his employees.

He scrubs his face down with both hands.

"Think about the implications," he states. "My son will be three by the time we leave. He might get attached to a bunch of losers who can't pick up the phone to say happy birthday every year. He's had enough disappointment in his life, and he's not even two."

I pat his back. There's nothing I can say because I've been there on the receiving end of getting attached and then disregarded. We could talk for hours about the pros and cons of the stupid will. There are no pros; the list of cons is lengthy.

I switch gears and propose, "Grace and I want you to come to live with us in Seattle."

"You two are finally together?"

"I'm the one with the jokes, not you." I head to his fridge, looking for something to drink. "Anyway, we can help you with Arden while you concentrate on getting that knee…I don't know, fixed? Is that the term?"

"Home is here, in Vancouver," he states.

"You want us to move here so we can help you?" I offer.

He smiles. "The other fuckers could learn a lesson or two about how to be a brother from you."

"I know I'm awesome as fuck, but I'm serious, man. You and Arden are alone most of the time. Wouldn't it be nice to have someone close by to give you a hand?"

He looks at his watch, then at me. "Why don't I get through this meeting and then we can talk about the future?"

"Sounds like a plan," I answer instead of arguing with him.

I don't want to think that he's in denial, but maybe he needs to reassess his goals. If I had an injury like his, I'd accept all the help I could get so I can get back on my feet. As they say, everyone feels and reacts differently. That reminds me of Hayes and his impromptu visit.

"Did Hayes come to visit you?"

He shakes his head. "Should I be expecting a visit from him?"

I shrug one shoulder. "Probably."

"What did he want?"

"He apologized for being an asshole," I respond and wave a hand. "It's mostly a shitty campaign where he promises to do better but asks to please join him in Baker's Creek."

He snorts. "I don't believe anything he says."

"Grace says he was being honest."

"Grace was there?"

"We were hanging out when he came to visit. I wasn't going to answer the door, but you know her…"

"She's the sensible one of the two of you," he remarks.

I scoff. "In any case, he swore to be a good brother from now on, but he asked me to go with him—for the town."

He snorts. "What if you don't go? It's over?"

I shake my head. "Surprisingly, he said something like, if I don't, he hopes we can stay in touch."

He sighs.

"As I told Grace, if Blaire forgives him, I'll do it."

Mills laughs. "She's never going to forgive him. Not in a million years."

"So, we agree. If she does, we go." I extend my hand, and he shakes it.

His phone chimes. When he looks at it, he grumbles. "The car service is here." He points at the fridge. "The emergency numbers are there. I should be back soon. Wish me luck."

"Good luck."

"HOW'S BABYSITTING GOING?"

I smile at the screen. There's nothing better in the world than staring at Grace's beautiful face. "It's been a long-ass day. Arden is on his second nap of the day."

"It sounds like you should take a nap too," Grace jokes.

"I might stay for the night," I state. "It all depends on how Mills is doing after the meeting. We were talking about going to Baker's Creek."

She sighs. "That inner battle is killing you, Beac. Just do what's right for everyone."

As I'm about to answer, the doorbell rings. I look through the peephole and grumble. It's Henry and Hayes. "Let me call you in five, okay?"

"Great. We have not just one but two assholes visiting this humble home." I move aside so they can enter.

"I see that you and Mills are close."

"Very close," I answer, and the bitterness in my words pushes me to continue. "So close that when you learn that your brother knocked up a puck bunny, you fly to check on him and visit him often to help him with his son. And when you learn that your brother's grandparents died, you go to their funeral."

Hayes sighs. "I had no idea that your grandparents died."

"I'm sorry, Beacon," Henry says. "You were not the only who lost a grandparent or had a shitty life. We all did. It is our role as older brothers to keep an eye on you, but don't think that you're the only one who needed that brother to stick with you. At least you had Mills."

"You're no different than William." I pause and glace at them. "Both of you."

"A few weeks back, I would have agreed, but after these few weeks, I discovered that I am nothing like William. By trying to avoid messy feelings and becoming him, I failed myself. We missed a lot of years. Fuck, I lost twelve years with my girlfriend," Hayes says.

I feel those words deep within my soul. I haven't lost eleven years of Grace, but how I wish we were *together*. I have a good reason; he's just a fucking asshole.

"That was pretty fucked up," I state. "I hope she doesn't forgive you. She deserves better than you."

"I agree. She deserves the best, but she forgave me."

My gut clenches because this is what I told Grace and Mills, didn't I? If Blaire stays, if she believes in him, then I'll stay in Baker's Creek. He has to be bluffing. "You two are back together?"

He gives me a sharp nod, then asks, "Where is Mills?"

"He should be back soon. He had a meeting with his people."

Hayes glances around the house. "Why are you here?"

"He needed a babysitter, and I volunteered. Again, that's what you do for your family."

He bobs his head. This is so fucking awkward. Things don't get any better when he says, "As a family, can you move to Baker's Creek with us?"

"Are you sure Skittles forgave you?" I use Blaire's old nickname.

"You can call her to confirm."

I don't want to believe him. Without losing any time, I call her right away. "Did you forgive his fucking ass?"

"Finally, Beacon! I need to find Mills, Hayes, or someone." Her panicked tone is making me nervous. *Where is the fire?* "The lawyer came today, and we need to be here tomorrow by midnight."

"What do you mean we need to be there by tomorrow?" I frown, check the calendar, and then say, "No, he said next Friday. I was there."

"It's a long story. I need you in Baker's Creek now, kid. We're all trying to do this for the town. I know Hayes screwed up, and you don't want to forgive your brothers, but be the bigger man. I did forgive Hayes, and we've been patching things along the way. We all can give him a second chance. Now, let me keep looking for them. I need everyone in town tomorrow."

I give Hayes my phone. "She needs to talk to whoever is in charge. I assume that's you."

The conversation between them doesn't last long. He assures her we'll be there on time and not to worry about anything. He reminds me of the sap he used to be back when they were in college and he was dating her. I was young, but I wanted Grace and I to have what they had.

At least it's working for one of us.

"I love you," he says before they hang up.

"She really forgave you." I sigh. "So, we have to be there tomorrow then?"

"Yes."

"What happened?" Henry asks.

Hayes explains to us that the lawyer's timeline was off. They had to count from the moment all of us received the news, not from the day the lawyer read the will. Tomorrow marks thirty days from the day they reached out to Blaire. Jerome Parrish, our father's lawyer and the executor of the estate, let it slide and added a note that he couldn't find Blaire until four weeks ago.

According to the lawyer, our legal team at Bryant, LLP was informed of the issue. Pierce's family owns the law firm. He's in charge of contesting the will or finding a way to change the fucking stipulations. We don't want the money, but if he can't find any loopholes, we have to stay for the town.

When he finishes recounting the story, he calls Pierce who answers annoyed as fuck. "I'm on my way."

"Did your family try to fuck us over?" Hayes questions. There's a lingering rage in his voice, but he's calm on the outside.

Pierce sighs. "Mom insists it was a mistake because they're all busy."

"And you believe her?"

"She doesn't win anything if I stay or go. Why should I believe Mr. Parrish?"

I tune out the conversation. Instead, I text Grace and the guys. They can pack some of my clothes and ship them over.

After the conversation with Pierce is over, I ask, "What's the plan? I could fly back to Oregon with you. I'm not sure about Mills though. Is Vance in?"

Hayes shakes his head.

Vance is not coming. Well, we're fucked. I haven't even looked into plan B on how to save the people and the employees if we fail. That's my task for next week. I bet these assholes don't even have a backup plan.

Should I tell them that we need to spend the night researching our options because if Vance isn't coming, we're fucked, and what's even the point of moving to Baker's Creek?

Mills enters the house in that moment. That gives me at least a few moments to text Seth and ask him to move our Monday meeting to tonight. We have a lot of shit to do before tomorrow—when Vance doesn't show up.

"Why are you all here?" Mills looks around the house.

"We need to be there tomorrow," Hayes answers without even saying where the fuck *there* is.

"No, I'm not going." Mills grunts.

Uh-oh, that sounds like the meeting was a clusterfuck. "What happened during the meeting?"

He closes his eyes and sighs. "They're releasing me from my contract. The doctor isn't sure if I can skate again."

"You can," Hayes assures him.

I want to punch him in the face and tell him, *you're a few months too late, fucker!*

"I can make that happen," Hayes insists.

"Only if I move in with you?" Mills groans.

"No, you don't have to move to Baker's Creek. We're setting up a practice, and you can visit us often. We'll treat you until you're ready to go back," Hayes promises, and his conviction is contagious.

I want to say, *yes, let's do this. We will make that knee better as a family.*

Which is why I vomit some words I never thought I would say in my entire life, "Just give the guy a chance and pack your things. Arden could use a break from the hockey life. Hayes needs us. Skittles already forgave him."

Mills arches an eyebrow. He knows what I mean with that. We made a deal. If she forgives him, we go with him. I guess pigs can fly and Hayes can change enough to make that woman give him a second chance. "She did?"

I nod.

"It's not just me. Henry and Pierce need you, too," Hayes says in a big brotherly voice. "We've been working our asses off to ensure that everything runs smoothly. There's a lot we have to figure out, but we have plenty of time, and hopefully, you two will help."

Mills rubs the back of his neck. "Fine. You're going to have to help me pack because I can't leave Arden's stuff behind."

"Let's take the essentials," Henry suggests. "We'll have Sophia come back for the rest next week. She's the only one of us who can travel around."

Hayes looks at me. "How about you, Beac?"

"Don't worry about my shit. I can borrow clothes from all of you, and my bandmates can move my stuff when the studio is ready."

I guess this is it. I'm going on an all-paid vacation to hell with my brothers. I grin. Let the fun begin.

Chapter Six

Grace

"THE MOST BORING man on the planet broke up with me." I tap my chest a couple of times, outraged at what just happened earlier. "He dumped me."

My cousin, Harper, introduced me to Hardy Roberts during her birthday party. She thought we'd be a match made in heaven. *Stick to what you know—plants. Matchmaking isn't your thing, Harp.*

"This is the last time I let anyone introduce me to the 'perfect guy,'" I complain.

"Stay single," Dad suggests. I give him an unamused glare.

Mom's jaw drops. "But you were breaking up with him. How is it that he turned things around on you?" I love how she humors me. "What happened?"

"He said, 'This has run its course, Grace.' I mean, it's not like we've gone out for a long time or we've had s—"

I'm interrupted by my father's sudden cough. This is precisely why my brothers are so immature. Dad might be able to take down criminals, but he behaves like a teenager sometimes.

"Sex is normal, Dad."

Mom rolls her eyes. "Mason, you either let her tell the story without the gagging noises and the immature remarks or leave the kitchen."

"My princess shouldn't have…" He pauses and shivers. "She's just a kid."

"I'm almost twenty-eight," I remind him, and I want to add that maybe I'm too old to be called princess.

He gives me a once-over and says, "Too young."

This man is exasperating. He doesn't have a problem while I'm on the clock working for his organization. But when it's about dating, I suddenly turn into a two-year-old toddler who should move back home because I'm a baby.

"And just so you know, this didn't go beyond four dates. I still can't believe I was dating him—and he's the one who broke it off!"

"Gather some data, analyze it, and maybe run a background check before you even give out your phone number."

I roll my eyes. Only my father could come up with something as ridiculous as treating my dating life as a project. But maybe he's not that off. It makes me wonder how he dated when he was my age. Maybe he's like Seth and had the occasional one-night stand when he had time. I know he wasn't like Nathan, who's been with his girlfriend forever.

"No, I think I should give up men."

"You have my vote." Dad smirks.

I groan.

"You know what they say." Mom, who always has some wise advice and tries to look at the bright side, says, "You have to learn how to weed your garden, and the only way is by knowing what plants are good for it and which ones are…useless."

She doesn't always make sense, though.

"That doesn't make sense. Maybe you were trying to say, kiss a few toads to find a prince?" Dad looks at her unamused. "Stick to what you know, Ainse."

"Be nice, and I might remind you what I do best later tonight," she teases him, and Dad takes her into his arms and kisses her.

My parents are one of the most adorable couples I know. I want to find the kind of love they share. Pure and eternal. It's impossible when I keep kissing orangutans. I can't even find a decent toad.

I make gag noises to stop them. They might be cute, but seeing my parents making out is a hard limit.

Dad looks at me and grins. "It's normal…you know." He changes his pitch pretending to sound like me.

He's about to walk out of the kitchen when he halts, looks over his shoulder, and says, "The meeting starts in five minutes, Gracie. Text your friend so he can connect with us. I think he should take a break while he's dealing with his family. But what do I know?"

When Dad leaves, Mom looks at me. "Are you okay about the breakup?"

I shrug. "Yeah. It's just so frustrating. I asked him why he thought it wasn't working."

She frowns. "You knew it was over."

"Yes, because he's boring and dumb. I can't have a mature conversation with him. I want to know what is wrong with me." She is about to speak, and I shake my head. "No, don't give me your usual, 'there's nothing wrong with you.' I am twenty-seven, and I haven't had a steady boyfriend. At this point, I think I'm a virgin—again."

She sighs. "Well, what did he say?"

"He got upset because I'm over-analytical. Then, he went ahead with the list of flaws. I'm always texting or on the phone in the middle of my dates." I pause, drink from the lavender tea she prepared for me when I arrived. "He's jealous of Beacon. He doesn't even know him. He's been living in Baker's Creek for a month."

I swear this is like a bad joke that never ends. What's the problem with me? Your best friend interrupts our dates. If I keep going out with a guy, Beacon points out all his faults, and it leaves me not wanting to date the poor guy.

When Beacon is not around, my brothers are the ones making it hard on my dates. They're younger, but they can be scary looking, like my father. Six foot five, dark hair, and their pale gray eyes are so freaking devoid. Sometimes guys swear they're possessed.

Seth and Nathan are a couple of kittens.

"How did you do it?" I ask Mom. "Uncle Jacob and Uncle Mattie can be scary too."

She grins. "My brothers were scared of your dad. Plus, your father is a friend of the family. It makes all the difference."

So, I need to date a friend of the family?

No thank you, Mom. I've been there, done that, and—*you told me to end it.* Well, he ended it first. I don't think about the subject or I'm going to start sulking.

"Let me call, Beacon," I say, pulling out my phone.

"Yo, G?" he answers right away.

"We have a meeting. Are you ready?"

"Always. Just give me a minute," he answers, and I hear the roar of a car engine.

"Did you steal one of your brother's cars again?"

He laughs, and there's some clicking over the phone—the call drops. Well, I hope he arrives at his house in time so he can video chat. Dad hates to wait.

I kiss Mom. "I'm heading back home after this."

"Don't stay up too late," she warns me.

"I love you, Mom."

I wave at her, walking toward Dad's office. I feel someone watching me. When I look up, I find Beacon leaning against the wall.

"You're here," I whisper.

His smirk widens as we run toward each other like a couple of kids who haven't seen their best friend in years, which is partially true. He's been busy dealing with the family that has never acknowledged him until now.

"Hey, G!" he says, lifting me from the floor and twirling me around.

I hold his face, looking into his deep dark green eyes. He seems happy.

"It's good to see you," I say, but the reminder of why he shouldn't be here makes me gasp, jump out of his embrace, and strike him on the chest. "You idiot!"

The passing of his father leaving a ridiculous will behind changed his life drastically. He and his brothers have to live together in Baker's Creek for the next eighteen months. He's not allowed to leave the town during the first six months.

There are so many ridiculous stipulations, and all of them are just so they can claim the inheritance, which none of the brothers want. It'd be easy to walk away, except William Aldridge will destroy—from the grave—the livelihoods of many if they don't do as he says.

Chapter Seven

Grace

"OUCH!" He flinches. "This is your new way to welcome your best friend?"

"What the hell are you doing in Seattle, Beacon Kirk Aldridge?"

"Technically, it's Mercer Island. We have a meeting," he reminds me, tilting his head toward Dad's office.

"You are supposed to be in Baker's Creek!"

"I am," he assures me with a grin. "Didn't you hear? The guys came to practice. We are in my studio."

"God, you're impossible!"

"You keep saying that, but am I?"

No, but if his brothers knew where he was, they'd kill him.

I glare at him.

"You're mad at me?" That sheepish, innocent look erases my anger.

"I wish I could be upset." I poke him in the chest. "You're jeopardizing the lives of a lot of people."

"You know that if I fuck everything up, I'll fix it."

It's on the tip of my tongue to ask how. It'd be impossible to fix anything if they sell the properties and tear down the buildings, wouldn't it? But I don't say a word because if I challenge him, he might do something stupid to prove that he's right. Then he'll be complaining that I don't have enough faith in him.

"So, how's Howie?"

"Hardy," I correct him.

"Whatever," he says with disregard. "He's a loser, and you should break up with him."

I cross my arms. "Let me guess. He's not good enough for me?"

Beacon grins. "You know that, but you like to keep dating guys who don't deserve you."

We open Dad's office, and my brothers are already with him. Nathan and Beacon do their weird hugging, hand shaking ritual that's just stupid.

Seth glares at the screen and says, "Let's get this over with. We have to be back in a few hours before anyone notices Beacon is missing."

I roll my eyes. Of course, Seth helped him. These two are each other's accomplices.

Dad leans back, grabs the remote, and turns on the big screen where everyone in The Organization is ready for the video chat.

Dad created a high intelligence secret agency in his early twenties. He never thought it'd grow to be one of the most important companies in the world, or that it'd be a family business.

He tried to keep us away from it, but we all showed potential and the talent to work with him. One day he and his partners will retire, and we'll be in charge.

"First order of business is Bryant, LLP," Dad says and focuses his attention on Beacon. The law firm is based in Colorado. His brother, Pierce Aldridge, used to work there. He's also the founder's grandson. "We just started the investigation. It's supposed to be simple. You said there was some discrepancy with one adoption, but there's a lot more to it than losing some application. My gut tells me there's a lot more happening there. I want to remind you that our company isn't a cheap PI service. We're highly trained to take down criminals. This law firm seems to have some of those. You want us to stop?"

Beacon arches an eyebrow and shrugs one shoulder. "Keep going. If there's more than what we bargain for, I'll talk to my brother."

"Talk to your brother," Dad orders.

"At least, give me something to show him. I'm not disclosing anything about this company, but I want him to see why he has to either stop us or live with the consequences."

Dad looks at Seth. "Give him what you've gathered. This is yours. Assemble your team, wait for Beacon to give you the green light, and…don't underestimate them."

"The second item circles back to our absent musician." He grunts. "We need to speak to your former Delta Force brother in person. I understand he's highly trained. He could be a great asset, but I need to interview him and test his skills."

"Vance can't leave Baker's Creek," he pleads his case. "Can you just take my word and videoconference him?"

I don't know much about Vance Aldridge. Beacon keeps the little he knows to himself. Not because he doesn't trust me, but because he keeps Vance's privacy just like he does ours. Beacon believes he'd be a good fit for our company.

Dad gives him an outraged glare. "Yet, you're here, Aldridge. Make it happen, or we won't consider him."

"You're considering him, or you wouldn't bring up the subject," Beacon challenges him. "We can meet halfway. We need him as much as he needs us."

"We're not thrilled about bringing a mercenary into our organization, Aldridge. We both know there's a huge difference between what we do and…them." He waves his hand toward the door. "You can always join them instead."

Beacon glares at him and then looks at me. He takes a deep breath. "I'll figure it out."

Dad nods and sighs. "Third item belongs to our golden boy again," he mocks Beacon. "Has your brother figured out a way to let you out of the will's stipulation while you're on tour? We're done waiting."

Beacon shakes his head. "No, he's working on it."

Dad grunts and looks at me. "It's easy to find someone to replace—"

"No," Beacon snaps. "Either we do it as a team, or you assign that project to another crew."

"You can't take that away from me," I complain.

Beacon's hands become fists. "That's not how we work, G."

Dad runs a hand through his hair. "Figure that out soon."

I am frustrated because I know what's going to happen. Dad's going to reassign this case to another team, and I'll be poking my eye for the next eighteen months. Stupid William Aldridge. It's because of him that the team is grounded. But our unit can run without Beacon in it. I sigh because who am I kidding. It'd be irresponsible to replace him with an outsider.

"It's not like I made up this shit to avoid my responsibilities." They stare at each other, and I swear Beacon is usually chill, but there are times that he'll go head-to-head with Dad for things that seem so stupid. "You know what's at stake, Bradley."

Dad turns his attention to the screen, and Uncle Harrison, Tiago, and Anderson shrug.

"We'll come up with a backup plan just in case," Harrison concludes.

The meeting continues without bringing more attention to Beacon, who hates his new assignments—doing research, paperwork, and surveillance from Baker's Creek. I can do some work for Seth or just take a break. Dad dismisses us and stays on the secure call with his partners.

Beacon shuts the door closed and looks at Seth. "Give me a few minutes."

"Don't take long." My brother gives a courteous nod and walks away, dragging Nathan with him.

Beacon takes my hand and pulls me toward the main entrance of the house. "Tell me about your Howie while I walk you to your car."

"You need to promise this is the last time you leave Baker's Creek," I say, following right behind him.

"Come to visit often, and I'll think about it."

"I'm running the summer camp you volunteered to organize."

"You insisted I stayed in Baker's. If it was up to me—"

"This is me you're talking to, Beac. Don't pretend you don't care about it, because I know you better than you know yourself," I warn him.

He smiles and pulls me into an embrace. "Fine, I might give a few fucks. Because I do, I'm doing my best to behave. You should come and visit me more often, though." His voice sounds like a plea. "There's a room with your name on it."

"There is not."

"Come and see it for yourself." He kisses my temple and looks at me. "What happened to the latest loser? Did you break up with him?"

I give him the SparkNotes. The asshole dumped me before I had the chance.

"You need a few lessons on how to date," he claims.

"Because you're an expert."

"You know what your problem is?"

"Beacon, I'm not in the mood," I grumble as we arrive at my car.

"I'm trying to save you time and energy," he replies.

"As much as I'd like to listen to your wise words, you have to go." I tilt my head toward my brother's car.

"I'm wise." He laughs. "G, you just need to stop dating losers and maybe…I don't know. I'd have to see your dating techniques and figure out what you're doing wrong."

"So, you agree there's something wrong with me?"

"No, you're perfect. There's a difference between being smart, talented, and gorgeous and knowing how to date."

I snort, "You're going to give me dating advice?"

This guy has never dated in his entire life.

"Mr. Casanova doesn't have any moves," I mock him. "You just snap your fingers, and women flock around you. What's today's flavor?"

"My, G, that's inaccurate," he says. "That was back when I was a stupid kid. Plus, you know my brothers and I have rules. We don't date the townies."

"You still act like a kid," I remind him.

"You like me that way."

"Not always."

"Well, the offer is on the table. Come to Baker's Creek so I can tame the shrew. I can give you a few tips. Maybe teach you how to avoid losers."

I burst into laughter. "Go home, Beac."

He gives me a weird look. "Come with me."

"Maybe another day, okay?"

He cups my face and says, "Swear, you're not going to start working with another team just because I'm not there."

"I'll try."

"Damn it, G!"

"How about just scouting work with Seth?"

"You're such a maddening, stubborn woman." He shakes his head, kisses my forehead, and leaves.

And maybe that's my problem. I don't let anyone dictate my life. I'm quiet, but I make sure people hear me. I'm shy, but I impose what I feel is right. I'm not some weak mademoiselle in distress. I save men who are in trouble.

Chapter Eight

Beacon

"HELL, DAY ONE THOUSAND AND TWENTY-SEVEN," I complain while preparing dinner.

I like to pretend I'm upset about the chores assigned to me or our situation when my family is around. It creates a fun atmosphere.

Henry gets irritated. Pierce pokes him. Hayes lectures them. Henry cusses in response because we're always judging him. Mills chides them for swearing in front of his kid. I toss a few more words to work them up and add Vance into the mix. That dude needs anger management. It's so much fun to stir them and watch them fight about some nonsense.

"We all have to cook," our oldest brother, Henry, argues.

He doesn't cook shit. The guy orders food from the chef of the restaurant and voilà, we have a fancy dinner for eight and a kid's meal. It really doesn't bother me to help. I'm used to looking after myself—and cooking large meals for my people. My brothers and their wives don't know it. I use everything they never cared to learn about me to my advantage.

See, that's the difference between my brothers and me. They don't use the weaknesses of their enemies to their benefit. Not that they are my enemies, but we're not on the same team either.

They are still unsure if they want to stay, and unhappy because we have to live together. Coexisting with each other is more challenging than any of us thought. We're older. Each one of us has some baggage. There's also resentment among us. We're mad because the other never called. If we were mature enough, we could be discussing everything as adults. We don't. I resent that neither one of them cared much after our brother Carter died.

Seriously, what was my father thinking when he decided to draw up a will where he shoved us all in this town for eighteen months?

Some days I want to dig into Dad's past to see if I can find something significant that will clue me in. Others, I just think he was fucking with us.

"You could've been a professional chef," Blaire says, grabbing a tortilla chip and dipping it into the guacamole. "Was your grandma the one who taught you how to cook?"

I nod. It wasn't, but I let them think that. It was actually G's mom. My grandmother was adorable—a saint—but she didn't have the patience to teach anything.

"I wish someone had taught Henry how to cook," Sophia complains about her husband. "Dad is trying, but he's a slow learner."

We all laugh at him.

Henry is used to having maids, nannies, and every service at his disposal. My grandparents worked hard to teach me that I had to clean after myself, among other things.

While in college, G, the guys, and I took turns cooking, cleaning, and shopping.

I still do everything for myself. Well, unless I'm on tour. During concerts we have roadies carrying our instruments, bringing the food, and sometimes driving me around.

If I could avoid it, I would. According to my manager, I have to have a crew. They are necessary. Lang just likes to have everything done for him. Since he has the support of our PR, I just let it happen.

"It's only September," Henry reminds me. "With that attitude, I doubt you'll last the next twelve months around here."

"In two months, I'm getting the fuck out of here," I say, baiting him.

There's a part in Dad's will where he allows us to leave town after we've been here for six months. In order to do that, we have to contact Jerome Parrish, the one who handles our father's estate, and ask for permission to leave. We have thirty days that can be used all at once or however we want. I don't plan to use them unless it is necessary. If I want to get out—I just do it.

"I might take the thirty days and keep you guessing if I'll return."

"You do that, fucker, and I'll hunt you down," Vance threatens me. "I swear if any of you bail, I'll kill you."

"See, he speaks," I say to no one in particular.

Everyone complains that Vance is always quiet and brooding. Obviously, they don't take the time to have a conversation with him. He and I aren't tight, but we get along. I still like to taunt him as I do with everyone else. I'm judicious that way.

"You just need to piss him off."

"Which is why he's always talking to you, isn't it?" Blaire, Hayes's wife, rolls her eyes. "Just when I think you guys have matured, you prove me wrong."

I grin at her while searching for the salt. "I like to keep the excitement around this house."

Vance's glare should scare me. It scares everyone—but me. If necessary, I could take him. Yes, he has some kick-ass training, but I do too. I wish he had accepted to join The Organization. When I indirectly offered him an opportunity to work with us, he declined.

I'm not sure if it's because he's hoping to go back to his friends. I hope not. If he does, we'll have a problem.

Of my five brothers, my favorite is still Mills. We've been hanging out for a long time, so it makes sense that we're the closest. After him, it comes to Hayes, the doctor who isn't that bad. He's just clueless, but fun to hang out with.

Pierce might be the next one. I'm still trying to understand him. He's more fucked up than I thought. His marriage is the weirdest thing I've ever witnessed in my life. I think we all just want to shove him and Leyla in a room and say, "Don't come out until you fuck away your issues."

Henry is another clusterfuck. He's getting better since he has a wife who keeps him in line.

Everyone in this house treats me like I'm still the baby of the family. They are also afraid that I'm going to leave town because I can't be contained.

News flash. I leave whenever the fuck I want.

"I mean it, Beacon," Vance repeats. "You better not do something stupid."

I lift the spatula and my free hand in surrender. "I wouldn't dare to piss you off."

Henry snorts. "You're such a fucking liar."

Oh, yes, Henry. I'm one of the best liars in the world. I trained for that. If only you knew.

I check the time. "I'm meeting the guys in Happy Springs. We're going down to Portland. I'll be back around one, maybe two in the morning."

"No!" Vance's voice booms throughout the kitchen.

Everyone jumps. I give him a lazy glance. "Come on, Dad. I promise not to break curfew."

"He's right, kid," Pierce, who always has to follow the fucking rules, sides with him.

These assholes are so fucking predictable. I'm getting bored. I need a challenge.

"Fine," I groan. "If you can't trust me, it's all the same. The music store opens at nine. Maybe I can leave for Portland at seven tomorrow morning if Vance allows it."

"You're a fucking pain in the ass!"

I take the warm tortillas out of the oven, plate the meat on a platter, and put everything on the table.

"Ready. Make sure to go easy on the tomatillo salsa. It's hot. The red one is mild. The guacamole doesn't have any jalapeno. We don't want Blaire to have acid reflux."

"Have I ever told you that you're my favorite, kid?" She kisses my cheek.

I grin and wave at them. When I reach the door, Hayes asks, "Aren't you going to have dinner with us?"

I shake my head. "Nope, I'm going to have dinner with the guys. I'll be back within an hour or so."

It doesn't take me long to drive to the cabin I own. It's between Happy Springs and Baker's Creek, near the river. The guys are already there waiting for me. I exchange cars. One of the rookies from The Organization is with them—the decoy we use so no one notices my absence. He's about my height. Slightly skinnier, but he can pass as me. No one has noticed my absence while I'm in Seattle. We have a routine that's worked so far.

The timing on when to leave the mansion tomorrow morning is key. Pierce and Leyla wake up early to feed the animals. Aren't I lucky that the guys are trained to be invisible?

Tomorrow, one of my brothers will be pissed that I didn't sleep in the house. They'll bitch that I'm putting everyone in jeopardy. I'll argue that they are wrong. They have no proof. It's my word against theirs.

See, Dad. You can't dictate my life. You lost the right when you abandoned me.

Chapter Nine

Grace

MY PHONE RINGS just as I'm about to leave the house. It's Beacon.

"Yeah?" I answer, closing my eyes and waiting for him to psych me about tonight.

I'm still unsure what's happening. Either I have a blind date, surveillance, or…God knows what my brother planned.

Seth said, "Dress nicely. Imagine the most romantic date of your life. Just make sure to leave your knives behind."

He didn't let me ask for any more information. It's not a surprise party because there's a family reunion at my parents' tomorrow. Everyone I know is going to be there.

"Ready for tonight?"

"Yep." That word doesn't even make sense. I could say yes or no. Something more specific, but I don't want to say anything out loud. I am tired of the nonsense. I should get a break since tomorrow is my birthday.

"You don't sound excited."

"I'm skeptical," I respond. "Seth was too cagey about it. He might just be playing some stupid prank—or giving me *the blind date from hell*."

Beac snorts.

"Do you know what's happening?"

"I have an idea," he responds. "Are you ready?"

Before I have time to answer, there's a knock coming from the backyard's glass door. When I turn around, I see Beacon on the other side with a big grin. When I slide the door open, I jump into his arms.

"It's you."

"Happy Birthday!"

"You're here." I hug him tight because I was already dreading my birthday without him.

Plus, it's been a couple of weeks since the last time I saw him. I'm helping Seth with the Bryant case in Denver. I don't have much time to fly to Seattle—much less to go to Baker's Creek to visit Beacon.

"I wouldn't miss your big day," he assures me. Before I can remind him that my birthday is tomorrow, he says, "You have me up until tomorrow at three when Seth has to fly me back to Portland."

When I look toward his backyard, I realize the deck is illuminated. The patio table is set too. There are streamers, a banner that says Happy Birthday, and balloons.

"How did you manage all that?"

"Your brothers," he answers. "I'm cashing in all the favors they owe me. See, I told you it was a good investment."

I roll my eyes because only Beacon can think that spoiling my brothers and driving them to places when they were young was a long-term investment. An investment that is finally paying off. If this man ever has children, he's going to do the same with them and then say that mowing the lawn is payback for changing their diapers.

"You promised you wouldn't skip town again," I remind him as we walk toward his house.

"No, I said I would only do it if it's necessary. It's your birthday. I never miss it."

He never does. Even when either one of us is out of the country, he comes to me. He should give a lesson or two on how to be swoony to the guys I date. If it weren't because he doesn't believe in relationships, he'd make an amazing boyfriend and husband.

Also, an amazing dad.

He's great with Arden, his nephew. When I get to babysit Mae, my niece, he treats her like a princess.

Perhaps, during this period where he has to interact with his brothers, he can open up to the possibilities of having his own family. He's always wanted one. Here's his chance.

"I don't want to sound ungrateful," I say. "But you broke your promise."

"Nope. You said, 'Promise me you won't be escaping just to fuck with your brothers,'" he responds as we walk toward his backyard. "First of all, I didn't escape. I left. Second, I didn't do it to fuck with them. It's your birthday. The most important day of the year. Third, I never agreed to it."

Instead of getting upset at him, I hug him because he came on my birthday. Ever since I can remember, he's made it special. I feel selfish because if he gets caught, things will end up ugly for so many people. I also trust him that he's careful.

"You should visit me this weekend," he mumbles. "I fucking miss you."

I release him and give him a sad smile. "Sorry, I have to be at work on Monday. Pierce's mom hated that I had to take a couple of days off because my family needed me."

This is the first time I've done undercover work that has lasted more than a weekend. I'm the assistant for Sarah Bryant, one of the senior partners at the law firm and Pierce Aldridge's mother.

The investigation is easy to deal with. It's my boss who I can't stand. I want to tie her to a chair and teach her how to be a kind human being. It's not hard. She should give it a try.

"I hate that woman," he complains, pulling out a chair so I'll take a seat.

"Join the club."

"I wish you had been in town with us. I made a taco bar for the fam."

"You made me tacos?" He's a great cook. Mom taught us well, but this man has some special gift that makes everything he prepares delicious.

"No, I went for tuna steaks," he says, heading to the grill. "Easier, faster, and leaves room for dessert."

"You spoil me." I don't sound grateful, though, more like bitter.

I should be elated that I have the most wonderful friend in the world. I am thankful for him. Seriously, some days I wonder how my life would look without him, and it is dull. We could say I'm the music. He's the rhythm of how the melody is played. We complement each other so well.

When I date other men, my expectations are set too high. If a friend can do all this fantastic stuff for me, why can't they?

"I could stop," he suggests while setting the plates on the table. "Rare like the lady loves them. The salad is just arugula, cucumber, tomato, and a drizzle of olive oil with lemon."

"Would you stop?"

He shakes his head and smirks. "Tell me about your day."

I grimace. "It could've been better. I don't want to talk about work. This case is making me confirm that I was never going to be able to work a nine-to-five job. If I decide to retire, I'll go back to school and get a teaching degree so I can work for Mom."

Mom owns an arts academy and a private school. Sometimes, I substitute for the preschool and kindergarten teachers. I'd give anything to be doing that instead of having to play assistant for one of Beelzebub's mistresses.

"By the way, did your mom call?"

He rubs his earlobe and sighs. "How did you know she's looking for me?"

"My uncle phoned to give me a heads-up," I answer. Uncle Jacob is his agent. His office gets a lot of calls and mail from Too Far from Grace's fans. Other times, he receives calls from Beac's mother.

He rolls his eyes. "There's nothing the Deckers can't keep to themselves, is there?" He shakes his head. "I didn't want to tell you because it's stupid, and you're going to worry."

"I am worried." *And angry,* I don't say.

Beacon sets his jaw. "She's planning on writing a tell-all and wants to include me. I assume it's to get some attention. I think she's trying to use William's death. I wonder if Pierce can figure out if there's an NDA or something that would've stopped her from talking before."

It's crossed my mind to pay her a visit and demand that she leave Beacon alone. Before his father died, it was all about singing together to revive her career. I didn't like that, but an autobiography, that's extra fucked up.

"You can stop her, can't you?"

"It's your birthday, G," he changes the conversation. "We're supposed to party. Twenty-eight. Isn't it scary that we're close to thirty?"

"You would know," I taunt him. I still have two years to go. His birthday isn't until March of next year, though. And I love to give him a hard time. "You're becoming an old man. Time to settle down."

"Talking about settling, how's the search for *the one* going?"

"Since I was visiting you often during the summer, I stopped. Maybe I'll try to date during my assignment. Which will be weird because I'd have to use my fake identity."

As we eat, I tell him about the place where I'm staying in Denver. It belongs to my cousin Tucker. He lived there for a few years and kept the place. I don't tell him that I miss this—being able to fly wherever he's at or having him drop by wherever I am at and hang out with him for a few days. If I do, he might just leave Baker's Creek and say fuck it all.

When he brings the special cheesecake he made for me, he lights a candle.

"Make a wish," he says.

"You make it for me."

"It's your birthday," he reminds me.

"You gave me your wish on your birthday. This one is yours," I insist.

The light of the candle illuminates his eyes. The effect makes them look strange. There seems to be a hunger inside—a fire burning. I shiver, imagining that maybe it's for me, but shake the desire away. We're friends. The best kind. This is our future together, and I'm happy with it.

I am, right?

Chapter Ten

Grace

"TONIGHT IT'S JUST you and me, buddy," I tell Mozart.

I should be at my grandparents' house. The annual New Year's Eve party started about an hour ago. All my family is there—including Mom and Dad. Being part of the Decker family has benefits. It also has obligations, like being at every family reunion. Today, I'm going to have to skip the festivities.

My grandparents aren't going to be thrilled. Sorry, but I'm not in a mood to be chiming in the New Year when this one sucked so much.

It's going to be a lot of work to stamp a smile on my face while everyone else is genuinely happy. I wish I could be, but Beacon isn't here. Richardson, the guy I dated up until yesterday, isn't coming. There's no one I can kiss or hug while ringing in the New Year.

This is one of those days where I wish Beacon wasn't in Baker's Creek. We have a routine. We spend the evening at my grandparents, leaving before midnight to receive the New Year at home. He gives me a *lucky hug* and leaves so he can be alone for an entire day in his house.

I hoped Richardson would be a good replacement, but no. He chose Stella instead of me.

Who is Stella? It seems as if he has not one, but five friends like me. Not exactly like me. According to him (please add a drum roll sound for effect), they aren't uptight. The one time I don't ask the guy what is wrong with me, he gives me a complete summary of why we're not right for each other.

His explanation included the fact that he doesn't believe in monogamy. A woman like me wouldn't accept him. He didn't even ask if I'd be okay with it. He just assumed. The rest, well, it's all me. I'm frigid, afraid of intimacy, and I don't even understand the point of dirty talk.

I ran out of spoons to deal with the outside world. If Beacon wasn't about to go into his annual "I don't care about the world" retreat, I'd be calling him. He'd skip his twenty-four hours of wallowing for me. He'd also skip town.

Beacon finds anything as a good excuse to show his brothers that he can break rules and never get caught. Not that they know about it.

"We'll have to do it without him, Mozzy," I tell my cat, who is licking his paws.

While cooking my dinner, I receive a text from Seth.

Seth: *You coming over? The 'rents are worried.*
Big Sis: *No, I'm tired. I'm staying home to rest.*

"Are you okay?" Mom calls me right away.

"Yes." I grunt, chastising myself for saying, "I'm tired."

Unlike many, I can't use that as an excuse because it means something different to my family. For them, it means my insulin levels are out of whack and I need to go to the hospital.

"Seth mentioned you're not feeling well."

"Mom, I'm fine," I assure her. "If I weren't feeling well, I'd call. Plus, my insulin pump has an alarm that alerts Dad."

Dad is a computer geek who likes to invent gadgets. Mom has had type 1 diabetes since she was eleven. Unlucky me, it can be hereditary, and I got it too. Needless to say, Dad, along with a company that manufactures insulin pumps, developed one that has GPS and sends a glucose report to an app every five minutes. Well, not that often, but I always tell that to Dad when he complains that I don't keep him updated about my health.

I get it. He worries because I live alone and if something happens to me, no one could reach me in time, which is why I allow him to monitor my glucose levels. The data is available to him at all times.

"But you're tired?" Mom insists.

"Yes. I'm tired of seeing everyone happy in Coupletown while I reside in Singlehell."

"Oh." She sighs.

Earlier I told her about Richardson, so there's no point in reminding her about it.

"Finn is going to propose to his girlfriend," I remind her.

My cousin Harper got engaged at the beginning of the year. She's getting married next August. My cousin Tucker is coming with baby Mae and his wife, Sage, for a couple of hours before heading back to his house where he'll be celebrating with his friends. Piper, who is younger than me, is bringing her boyfriend. I…I can't even get me one of those because apparently, I'm uptight and don't put out easily.

"Until I can replenish my spoons, I'm not going to be attending any events where I'm going to be introduced to 'a great catch' or reminded that I need to be a part of a couple. I don't need anyone."

"Do you want us to come and celebrate at your house?" she asks. "It'd be only your brothers, your dad, and me."

This is why Mom is the best. She knows what to say. I'm thankful that she doesn't say that being single is perfectly fine. Listen, when you feel like something is missing and your heart is incomplete, you can't just let it go. You have to find the misplaced piece. I don't depend on a man to be happy. I also want some company. There's nothing wrong with wanting someone to love me. I deserve love, too.

"You're the best Mom ever."

"But you don't want us with you?"

"I'll be fine, Mom," I reassure her. "Maybe I'll use this time to figure out my dating life."

Dad might've been right when he said I need to analyze the data, go through every relationship I've had, and determine the cause of every issue I've encountered since the first guy who dumped me. At this point, I'll try anything.

"Call at midnight, okay," she says.

"I will. Love you."

"Love you too, sweetie."

I SPEND my evening watching romantic comedies and downloading a few books and magazines onto my e-reader for research. I'm not one to make New Year's resolutions, but this upcoming year I'm going to rock someone's world in bed.

Goodbye, shy Grace. Hello, Vixen Bradley.

I need to work on those names. I doubt Vixen Bradley sounds sexy. Maybe that's what Richardson was talking about. I don't understand dirty talk, or words. When I'm kissing a guy, I concentrate too much on making it good or on not gagging if the guy can't control his saliva.

The art of seduction is a mysterious craft—at least to me. Flirting is a foreign language, along with the dirty talk. Since I can't stay up late, I head to bed before midnight. As I'm about to set my phone on the cradle so it can charge, I text Beacon.

G: *Happy New Year, Beac!*

Beac: *Same, G.*

I stare at the phone, waiting for more. He usually sends me a picture, a gif, or an emoji. This time nothing follows. He might be the other reason why I'm lost. Not having him around since last June has been strange. We don't go more than a week or two without seeing each other. It's been almost eight months of sporadic encounters.

Usually, he finds a way to visit me wherever I'm at, or I'm the one following the band like a groupie. It hasn't been easy to find time to visit him in Baker's Creek. His father screwed my father's company in many ways. Dad and his partners had to rework the entire plan to infiltrate a human trafficking cell in Europe because my team is grounded.

Also, I had to work undercover for Seth. It took a lot of self-control not to kill the people who work at Bryant, LLP. Selfish pricks. They take children away from their parents so they can fulfill the dreams of wealthy couples who'll pay a lot of money to have a family. Denver wasn't a great place to try to date, either.

Sighing, I open the notes app on my phone and start making a list. New Year, New Guy, Better Sex, Zero Inhibitions—New Grace. Hmm...that's a terrible name. Okay, I'll work on that later.

1. *Learn to flirt.*
2. *Learn to kiss well.*
3. *Learn to talk dirty.*
4. *Push away your inhibitions and stop being an introvert.*
5. *Find your G-spot (I mean, how can I expect a guy to know where it is if I don't even know it myself.)*
6. *Find good sex toys. According to* Today's Beauty *magazine, I should masturbate at least four times a week.*
7. *Take fish oil. It helps the small vessels in the clit.*
8. *Read erotica.*
9. *Figure out what you want in a man.*

When I get to number nine, it becomes clear that I need help. I hate to accept it, but Beacon was right. He's the best candidate to walk me through at least the first eight points. Once I know more about myself and who I'd like to date, I can make a new list.

Finding the guy.

Since Beacon is taking the day off from life, I just send him a text. Hopefully, once he's back in the living world, we can discuss my plan.

Am I irrational?

No, this is the best way to deal with my problem. If I don't do it now, then when?

Now or never, right?

Chapter Eleven

Beacon

WELL, here it is. The new year.

We're supposed to celebrate new beginnings. People around the world party, make resolutions, and feel like their lives are going to get better.

Personally, January is the crappiest month of the year. I am drowning in fucking sorrow. I usually don't drink. When I do, I don't go overboard. Except on New Year's Day.

That's when I take the day off from being responsible and, as Grace puts it, drink myself stupid.

At the beginning of each year, instead of feeling inspired, I feel raw. Everything inside of me hurts. My soul bleeds.

My grandfather died on New Year's Day when I was nineteen. A year and ten days later, my grandmother joined him. Many people see that as romantic. There are a few articles about one following the other right behind. One article read, "Mrs. Fitzpatrick couldn't live without her soul mate and joined him in the afterlife."

It's not fucking romantic. My grandfather had fucking cancer. Grandma didn't join him because they're soul mates. She died of heart failure. Media outlets and the entertainment industry romanticize the pain of others in order to sell.

Every year, the reminder that I'm alone constricts my lungs and I'm unable to breathe.

This year is no different, or maybe it is worse. I'm surrounded by my brothers. The ones who ignored me for years. None of them cared to come to my grandfather's funeral.

Those are the same ones who next November will send me packing back to Seattle and won't speak to me until one of us dies—if I'm lucky.

They can say all the shit they want, but I know the end result. Each one has their own life. I'm not a part of theirs, and I'll never be.

"Kid." Pierce, one of my older brothers, leans against the door frame and stares at me. "What's happening?"

I glare at him because no one is allowed to enter my home. In fact, last night before I left the main house, I made sure to lock it and set the alarms. There's no way in hell that they can open it until I unlock this place.

"This is my private residence," I say, or maybe I think about it.

He shakes his head and starts picking up the bottles and placing them in the trash can. "Let's go back home."

"I'm celebrating the New Year."

He shows me one of the empty bottles of Macallan. "By killing your liver?"

"You're not a doctor," I argue.

"No, the doctor went to his office to pick up some bags of saline solution to hydrate you."

I glare at him, clench my jaw, and warn him. "Leave me the fuck alone or you'll regret it."

He narrows his gaze and grins. "Kid, I'm not afraid of you. We let this isolation go for three days too long. Time to come home."

"I dare you to move me."

These assholes have no idea who I really am, and today I feel like inflicting some pain.

Before I can say more, Grace saunters into the living room, giving me a glare.

Pierce chuckles and points to G. "I am afraid of this one, though."

"Three days, Beacon?" Her voice feels like cats scratching metal. "I've been texting and calling you, and you've been ignoring me."

"Go home, G."

She glares at me and whistles. I hold my head, squeezing my eyes. "Are you trying to kill me?"

"No, you'd be dead if those were my intentions."

"Come on, boys, you know what to do," she says, and that's when I realize she brought the band with her.

Lang, Sanford, Manelik and Fisher pick me up from the couch and throw me into the bathtub—clothed. Grace turns on the cold water.

"I swear, you're going to pay for this," I threaten them.

They stare at me, amused. When the fog begins to clear, I'm finally able to stand up and switch the water to a warmer setting.

Grace and the guys leave as I begin to strip from the soaking wet clothes. I stay under the stream of water for a while. I'm trying to recall why I stayed longer than usual. It must have been that there wasn't enough alcohol to numb the pain. It wasn't just about my grandparents, but also about Grace. I'm losing her. I can't fathom life without her.

Once I feel like myself, I turn off the water, pull a towel, and wrap it around my waist. When I walk into my room, Hayes waits for me with an IV fluid bag in one hand.

"I'm fine," I claim, pulling out a shirt from my drawer and a pair of jeans from the other.

I won't lie, it's hard to get dressed, but I do it. If he realizes I'm still drunk, he's going to take me to his practice, and who the fuck knows what he's going to do to sober me up.

"Leave me alone," I order

"Humor me," Hayes insists.

"No. Look, I can stand up on one foot," I argue, and when I try to do it, I fall to the ground.

Okay, maybe I'm not sober yet. As a matter of fact, I'm so fucking drunk that I'm seeing double—possibly triple. There are too many Aldridges in my room. Well, just the older ones: Henry, Hayes, and Pierce.

"I hope you enjoyed this one time," Henry begins. "It's the one and only that we let you brood on your own."

"If you ask me, we shouldn't have let him go for so long," Hayes says, as he pinches me with a needle and starts the IV. "This is to hydrate you. Blaire added B12 to it."

Pierce squats and gives me that fatherly look he's been perfecting since…well, since he became a father a month ago. "We understand. You don't trust us. Seven months can't erase all the years we neglected you. But give us a chance. I had to call Grace to figure out how to get into this bunker. Not even Vance could break into this place, and he's some secret elite force."

I snort because I won a bet. I told Vance he'd never be able to get into my lair if I ever set up the locks.

"It's not funny," Henry chides me.

"Depends on how you see it," I answer.

"We're worried sick, Beacon. I can't lose another brother." Hayes sighs, running a hand through his hair.

"I needed to be by myself."

"But you're not alone," Henry cuts in my explanation. "Whatever you need to deal with, you come to us. I get it. Sometimes there's shit that weighs you down. Let us be there to carry it for you."

"This. Is. My. Day. Off."

"What do you mean by, *your day off?*" Pierce asks.

"The day when I like to do whatever the fuck I want. Like drink my weight in alcohol."

"You took three," I hear Grace's voice and look up, finding her standing by the door, hugging her midriff, and glaring at me.

She's pissed. Fuck. Why did they call her? I was going to come out eventually.

I frown, looking at her in disbelief.

She nods twice. "I ignored your family's calls on New Year's Day because…I know. But—it's never three days."

"Come here." I pat my side.

She gives me a dirty glare. "The guys and I will be at Tucker's place. Call when you're sober and you have fixed your shit with your family."

"G."

She turns around and leaves. Okay, I pissed her off, and it's going to take more than a miracle to get her to forgive me.

"Somehow I feel like the extra two days have to do with her." Henry stares at the space Grace occupied only a few seconds ago.

"Can I go now?" I stare at the needle pumping the solution through my veins. "This is unnecessary."

Hayes shows me a second bag. "We have time to kill, kid. Tell us what's happening. The way I see it, you're a danger to yourself."

"I'm fine," I protest. "So, what if I took a day off?" I ask again.

"Three," Pierce corrects me.

"I lost track of time," I excuse myself.

Henry snorts. "Try again."

"Grace mentioned this isn't typical of you," Hayes starts. "I'm ashamed to confess that I have no idea how you behave. You're a rock star, and we know that many of them like to overindulge."

"I agree, there are a lot of people in the business who like to party. Not me." I rub the back of my neck and sigh. "Listen, I lost my family when I was twenty. Well, my grandfather died a year before my grandmother. Both of them left in the same month, January. I'm mourning and celebrating them just for today."

"We can't be here for you if you close yourself off." Henry takes his role of big brother pretty seriously. "I'm sorry I wasn't there when it happened, but I'd like to be here when it gets rough. Everyone is worried about you. We're trying hard, kid, but you just don't want to believe us."

"That's one day," Pierce says. "Why were you fucked up the other two?"

"I lost track of time," I repeat.

"Grace," he answers. "The only reason I was shit-faced a few times last year was because I was losing my wife."

Because you were being an asshole. I'm not.

"Just know that we're here if you ever want to talk about it," he concludes.

"There's nothing to discuss."

What can I tell them?

Well, she went out on a date with some asshole for New Year's Eve. She's been with him for a month. She never lasts with anyone for that long. There's nothing I can do to stop it because I can't leave this fucking town. Daddy dearest lets us go out for thirty days, but we need to request that in advance—unless it's an emergency.

Her brothers won't intervene anymore because if I'm not going to make a move, I should just let her go. It's not that simple—I need her. She's my music.

I could fly out without my brothers or Dad's lawyer noticing, but I promised Grace I wouldn't do it unless it was a fucking emergency. Interrupting her in the middle of a date is important to me. And yet, I can't make a fucking move.

Grace is off-limits.

Do I love her?

Denying it is the only way to continue this sham.

Every time I see her, my entire world brightens. It sounds like the beginning of a romantic song. It's not; it's my life. It's happened ever since I can remember. Things aren't as bad when she's around. Everything works out when I'm with her.

Grace is loving, bright, and quirky. I am the one who understands her the most. We make sense, but we can't be together.

My brothers wouldn't understand why I'm brooding for her, and I can't explain it to them. Things aren't simple. I might look like a rule breaker, but I'm actually pretty good at following the ones that matter.

One of the rules of the organization I work for is that I can only tell what I do to those I trust and will keep my secret.

If I told them, I'd really need to kill them because I don't trust them.

Pierce is right. It takes more than seven months to get over my past. More so when I've no fucking idea what the future will bring.

"Take it from us," Henry says. "Tell her how you feel now. Tomorrow isn't guaranteed."

"I thought you weren't afraid to speak about your feelings," Pierce cuts in.

Talk about things biting you back in the fucking ass. "You're just assuming that I love her. I'm attracted to her. She's hot."

"Denial," Hayes intervenes.

Before they can continue giving me some words of wisdom, the rest of the Aldridge family make their way into my sanctuary. Not only my house, but my room. I want to kick them all out, but when my sister-in-law, Leyla, hands me over baby Carter, my nephew, I can't help but smile.

He came to us last month. They named him Carter after our brother who lived for the moment. Maybe I should take a page from his book. I'm done doing the right thing for everyone. Maybe I should take the fucking year off and do whatever the fuck I want.

Chapter Twelve

Beacon

MY BROTHERS and their wives are easy to deal with when I'm sober. I either make them uncomfortable, or I act like their latest lecture has been life-altering. It's hard to do either one when I'm drunk.

It's easier to let them fuss around me. It's a whole troop against me, and I have to let them "take care of me." Let them be a part of my world. They are cute, but let's see if they do this next year when we don't have to play happy family to save the town.

While the IV's saline solution flows through my veins, I hear Henry complain about my poor behavior and Blaire blaming my brothers for ignoring me for years. They understand I'm a loner, but I should let them into my life.

No. I'm not a fucking loner. I just don't like to be with people who don't stick around. A fight for another day. Something I'll bring up around next November when we all have to leave. They are just not part of my tribe. Disagreeing with them will start a discussion I'm not planning on having with them tonight.

For the time being, I listen to everything they have to say. My only response is a few grunts and plenty of nods. During this "we're here for you" campaign, everyone is fussing around me. I try to limit how much I talk, making them believe I'm too tired and ashamed to contribute to their conversation.

Once Hayes and Blaire decide I'm not dehydrated or drunk, we move to the main house where they feed me.

It's dark outside when I'm free to go, but as I make my way toward the door, Henry says, "You're not alone, kid."

"We are here for you," Pierce agrees.

Someone should remind them that I am not a kid anymore. Also, they have to stop saying that we're in this together. They can say all the shit they want, but I'm not sold on their newfound family.

I'll decide when this whole "we're all in this together" is real and not some bullshit they keep saying.

Listen, I'm not a cold asshole.

My brothers tend to be a lot like my father. They seem like they give a shit, but they are always looking after number one. Don't believe me? I can give you the best example. Our brother, Carter, was diagnosed with melanoma stage four during his senior year of college. No one was there for him. Only his best friend, Blaire, and I were with him.

Hayes was in London, too busy to pay attention to his younger brother. Henry and Pierce didn't learn about it until Carter was almost dead. Vance was busy with school and training with the general (his grandfather). Mills was in college and training to become a hockey superstar.

They can say shit, but I know that when things get rough, those guys walk away.

It's a short walk from our place to where Grace is waiting for me.

"Good evening, Beacon," Mrs. Heywood, the owner of the bookstore on Main Street, greets me. She's also Tucker's grandmother-in-law. (That's a real thing among the Deckers. It makes them family.) By the logic Grace's family lives by, the Heywoods are like my grandparents.

I wave at her. When I spot her husband, I decide to get closer. A few years back, he had a stroke, and even though he's doing well, he needs assistance more often than he wants to admit.

"Isn't it a little too cold and late for you to be outside?" I ask, wondering if I should come more often to check on them.

"We were next door, visiting Sage and her family," Mrs. Heywood answers.

Great. Tucker and family are in town. If they are here, maybe his bandmates came along.

I sigh. "There's a full house, huh?"

I don't even know what a full house means when it comes to Tucker's house. Before my father died, we used his place as our vacation home. Those were simpler times when the townies knew me as Beacon the rock star and not one of William Aldridge's children. Believe it or not, I had more freedom back then than now. Baker's Creek hates to love the Aldridge family—or is it loves to hate?

She nods with a smile. "They plan on staying all week. They are good kids. Stay out of trouble."

I salute them and wait until they enter their house before I head next door. Usually, I'd enter without knocking, but I don't know who is inside.

Seth is the one who opens the door.

"The prodigal child is alive," he jokes, lifting the bottle of beer he carries and taking a couple of gulps. "Are you here to grovel?"

"How upset is she?"

"I wouldn't want to be you," he answers.

"What are you doing here?"

"Someone had to fly your crew," he responds. "You know what would be a good idea? Building a landing strip on your property. It'd save me a lot of time."

"What's next? Telling my brothers I sneak out of the house when they aren't looking?"

He smirks. "There's that. I'd have to kill them in their sleep, and they seem nice."

"Where's your sister?"

Seth opens the door wide. "Probably in the music room, geeking. I don't get why she has to be attached to an instrument all the time."

I stare at him and shake my head. "Are you sure you're not adopted?"

"Fucker." He flips me the finger.

"Hey, everyone in your family has some musical talent, and you —" I whistle. "I can teach you how to play the tambourine. It's not that hard."

He shrugs. "What can I say? I'm my father's son."

He can keep up with us when he wants, but unlike Grace or Nathan, he doesn't care much about music.

When I walk into the house, I notice there are more people than I expected. Tucker, who is the oldest of the cousins, likes to gather his family often. I wasn't expecting to see everyone.

I wave as I march toward the music room, and it's not hard to find Grace. She sits by the piano. Eyes closed, hands almost touching the keys. She's dressed in a pair of yoga pants tucked into a pair of long knee-high fuzzy socks. Her hair is pulled up into a messy knot. Several streaks of pink, teal, and indigo are loose around her neck.

She's without a doubt the most beautiful woman in the world. Though, my Grace is more than a pretty face. She's fucking smart, brave, and talented. I not only admire her but adore her. The ultimate answer to life, the universe, and everything is a number, according to *The Hitchhiker's Guide to the Galaxy* by Douglas Adams.

For me, it's Grace.

"Finally," she mutters, her eyes remain closed. "I hope you have a good explanation for your poor behavior, Beacon Aldridge."

"What are you playing?"

She grins, and her beautiful soft gray eyes open and stare at her delicate hands. "Something new. I just don't want anyone to listen to it, yet."

If I'm lucky, I might be the first one, though.

"It's a work in progress," she mumbles and smiles. That smile makes my heart skip a few beats.

Everything about her is astonishing. Her ethereal beauty comes from the inside. She has a depth to her that no one cares to reach. I do. And how I wish I could say she's mine. But Grace is off-limits.

Except, you're taking the year off and can do whatever the fuck you want—including Ms. G. You just need to figure out how to convince her to say yes.

"Are you going to explain yourself?" she asks.

"No," I answer. "I'll do whatever you want to make it up to you, though."

Grace and I are honest with each other, and when we're not ready to speak about something, we say it, and the other respects it. It's better than giving her some bullshit explanation.

"I might have a thing or two in mind." That mischievous grin tells me she's going to make me work hard for it. If only it was in sexual favors.

"How was your New Year's Eve celebration?" I ask.

This might qualify me as a masochist. I guess, after all these years, I'm used to listening to her dating life. I don't like it, but if I am not going to step up to the plate, I have to just be there for her, right?

The answer might kill me. At the least, I might want to go back to my bunker, change the locks, and not allow anyone to come inside ever. This might be the part where she reaches for my heart, rips it from my chest, and stomps on top of it until it stops beating.

The grand moment when she says, "It was perfect. We finally took that step, and I think this is it."

So much for taking a year off and doing whatever the fuck I want while I live in Baker's Creek without The Organization's watchful eye.

She sighs. "I spent it at home with Mozart."

That, of course, doesn't sound right, so I dare to ask, "What happened with Richards?"

"Richardson," she corrects me with an annoyed voice.

I look over my shoulder, trying to see who's around. "Did you bring him?"

Please say no, because that means you're on your way to being with Mr. Right and leaving me behind.

It feels like the air is sucked out of my lungs when she smiles. This is it. She found the guy, and one of these days she's going to show me some fucking ring and invite me to her wedding. She'll even ask me to be a bridesmaid or some shit like that.

Her gray eyes finally focus on me. "That would mean we're still together."

My pulse goes back to normal. "Another one bit the dust?" I ask, trying not to show relief, but if I'm honest, I'm fucking glad that's over.

She opens her mouth, taking a deliberate sip of air. After she exhales, she says, "Apparently, we weren't together, together. He had several more friends like me, who were less uptight."

"Ouch?" Okay, not the right word to say when I'm supposed to be sympathetic, but at least I'm not doing some air fist pump while celebrating a somehow victorious outcome.

Do I want to find the asshole and kick his ass on her behalf? Yes, but I wouldn't do it. She'd get upset with me for fighting her battles.

"My dating luck is shitty, but I think"—she twirls one of her loose strands between her fingers—"I know what I'm going to do. Also, don't fake sadness. You hated him. No one is good enough for me, according to you."

My eyes drift to the floor momentarily.

"I'm not gloating, and as I keep telling you, you choose losers. You're a prize." Shoving my hands inside the pockets of my jeans, I ask, "What's the plan, Bradley?"

This is the part where I have to think fast and act faster. She's probably preparing to open an account on some dating app. She might accept Nathan's offer to test his love-algorithm app. I don't even know if he has it or if he's just teasing her. With him, it is hard to know what's real and what's not.

Maybe she'll be applying to one of those companies where they find your match according to their database and charge you a gazillion dollars to find your happiness.

"You're right. Since the beginning, I've been with losers who say,

'Thank you, but I'm going to the next best thing,'" she explains. "Instead of tracking all those men, I'm going to start with the first one. The one who said it was great, but we should stay friends."

"What?" I choke on my own saliva.

Can you not say that out loud?

At least five of her cousins and Seth are in this house. They'll kill me if they hear her say that I took her virginity. I can defend myself, but not against those guys who know how to fight just like me.

"Plus, you offered to help me figure out what's wrong with my dating techniques."

This is the part where I should say, "Thank you, Jesus."

She's making this easier than I thought.

I can't be fooled by what appears to be dessert served on a silver platter. Nothing that involves Grace is easy. Even when she's knocking on my door, I have a hell of a road to walk before I can make a real move. Why? Because as she said, I was the first loser who said this isn't working for me.

"Technically, we never dated," I whisper, getting closer to her and praying that no one is around to listen to our conversation.

She gives me the look. The one where she says, "Don't be fucking obtuse." It annoys the fuck out of me.

Lifting her index finger, she points at me. "You were my first kiss."

"You were mine too," I remind her.

"We kissed, we—"

"You don't need to list what we did, Grace. I remember everything."

Her saying, *"Have you ever kissed anyone?"*

"No," I answered, staring at her lips. *"Have you?"*

She shook her head. *"I've never been kissed. If I ask you to be my first…?"*

I had wanted to kiss her for a long time.

"Would you want me to kiss you, G?"

She's the only person I've given my heart to. She still has it. She just doesn't acknowledge it.

"So, you agree that we were each other's firsts," she continues. "But then you told me you didn't think we should be a couple."

"Your point?"

"What was so wrong with me that you called it off?"

I gulp. Eleven years and I still can't articulate more than, "This isn't a good idea."

There's a long story behind it. I doubt I'll ever tell her. The consequences can be catastrophic.

But she has to know if you're going to try to date her.

For now, I answer the first thing that comes to my mind. "I panicked?"

Can you sound lamer?

Probably.

"What scared you?"

"I was seventeen. You are my best friend. If I fucked up, I would lose you. It seemed like the best way to proceed. I recall you saying that I was right."

She chews her bottom lip and nods. I frown because maybe there's more to her response, "You're right. We're better as friends," than she never told me.

Okay, so maybe we harbor a secret or two from each other.

"If I was wrong, you could've told me," I explain.

"Why haven't you dated?" she suddenly asks. "Like ever?"

"There's a lot to the art of dating," I respond. "I'm too busy to pay attention to anyone else. It wouldn't be fair, would it?"

Is this bullshit? Somehow, it's the truth. I just cut a few words to make it Grace acceptable. I don't have time for anyone but my Grace. Dating would require me to notice someone else. It wouldn't be fair to string along a woman who I'll never love. It'd be so much easier if I can say, "How can you expect me to love anyone else when I belong to you?"

Okay, I omitted a few sentences.

"Well, you offered to help me, and to the best of my knowledge, you've never gone out with a woman. Fucking a groupie doesn't count."

I flinch. Hey, I never said I was a saint.

"It's been a long time since I slept with a groupie." Or anyone, for that matter.

She rolls her eyes. Of course, she doesn't believe me because I built my reputation when I was younger. I've never been a manwhore, nor a playboy. However, that's how I painted myself. When I stopped sleeping with other women, I never took the time to clear my name. Not even with Grace.

When did I stop sleeping around?

I was named the Sexiest Man Alive. Grace's reaction was, "Great. He's going to be sleeping around more than he already does."

She had it all wrong. I had a fling here and there, but they weren't often.

So, she dared me to stop sleeping around until I found the woman who would make me fall in love with her. It's been almost five years since it happened. I've been faithful to the woman I love. We go out on friend dates; she just doesn't know it.

"I know the theory. We could apply it so you can learn. Give me a few months, and you'll be ready to find a non-loser who deserves you."

Listen, I'm aware that there's a glitch in my plan. After eleven months, it's going to be hell to let her go, but what's the other option? I made my choice, didn't I?

"You sound like a late-night infomercial offering the perfect solution to a problem."

"And it's all yours after five easy payments of nineteen-ninety-nine," I try to imitate the tone they use on television and wiggle my eyebrows. "Plus, shipping and handling."

"Ha, I wouldn't pay for your services."

I wink at her. "I can make it good for you—and it'd be free." I tap the surface of the piano.

"I just need to figure out a way to keep a guy interested," she explains. "At this rate, I'm going to end up being the cat lady—and I don't even own Mozart. I share him with you."

For fuck's sake, she's kept me interested since…it's been so long.

"You're just twenty-eight," I remind her.

"God, you sound like my father," she protests, exasperated. "If things continue like this, you're going to find love before me. Look at your brothers. They're all getting married. Mills is next, then Vance, and you—"

"I doubt I'll get there," I stop her.

"You say that now, but one day someone is going to come, knock you down, and take you away."

How do I explain to this woman that she owns me?

She's owned me ever since I met her, I just didn't know it. I'd walk through the storm, climb mountains, fight death only to be beside her. She's insane if she thinks that someone can come and tear me from her.

"Away?" I try to sound cool.

"From me." She sighs. "We know how that goes. Friendships don't withstand relationships."

"We're forever, Grace," I remind her. "No matter what happens in life, you're my person. Is this why you're in such a hurry? Because you think I'm going to fall in love and forget about you?"

"No…"

I glare at her.

"That's partially true." She slumps her shoulders. "Ever since your father died and you moved here, I realized that I'm alone. It's made me wonder about our future. What's going to happen once you grow up and have a life?"

I live for you. You're my entire world.

We can't happen. I made my choice all those years ago.

You break rules all the time. How different is this from the rest?

I have to think about this long and thoroughly.

"Are you sure I'm going to grow up?" I smirk, gently pulling some of the loose hair strands, like a small child bugging his first crush.

She bursts into laughter. "We both know there's a lot more to the Beacon you show to everyone else. He wants a family. You might not want it right now, but later you'll find the woman that'll be perfect for you. She's going to fill that emptiness in your heart. I can see it already, a full house filled with little Beacon Aldridges."

I could tell her that she's wrong. There's no emptiness in my heart because she lives in it. Though, she's right. I want a family. Kids were never part of my fifty-year plan, but that changed a month ago. Carter stole my heart when I met him. Wanting and being able to have something are two totally different things.

I want Grace. I can't have her.

I want kids. I don't know if Grace and I have a future.

But will I ever deserve her heart?

Would it be amazing to have a little version of her? It'd be life altering. I don't even know if that's possible since she's reluctant to have children who might end up with diabetes just like it happened to her.

Then there's our undercover gig.

"Are you quitting The Organization, G?"

She shakes her head. "It has nothing to do with…" She closes her mouth and sighs.

Her father might've made things work for him. However, he didn't marry until he was in his thirties, I think. By then, he started slowing down.

Grace and I have a double life. We each have our music careers, and when The Organization needs us, we do some undercover jobs that no one else can do. Most of them aren't too dangerous because we're public figures and have to keep a low profile.

That is also why they use us. It's impressive how much information people provide to celebrities without even noticing.

"Would you quit?" she asks after a long pause.

"G, this is too deep of a conversation when all you want is to learn how to date, don't you think?"

"Why did you stay in the bunker for three days?"

"Let it go," I request.

"That's not you."

"Maybe I felt alone?"

"How can you feel alone when you live in a house filled with people who love you?" she asks, exasperated.

"Do I?"

"Do you even understand what you're doing?"

I'm sure something so stupid is driving her insane, and she's finally going to chide me about it. "No, but I'm sure you're going to explain it to me."

She growls because she hates when I'm obtuse.

"You can't accept my family as yours, and you can't trust your family either. Nothing can make you happy."

"You make me happy."

See, right here, I don't lie to her. She just chooses to ignore me when I tell her how important she is to me. Maybe she doesn't believe anything I say because I take life lightly and joke about almost everything.

She gives me a sad smile. "I"—she sighs—"I'll let it go for now."

"So…" I wiggle my eyebrows. "When do we start this dating crash course?"

"Don't try to flirt with me. That doesn't work!"

I toss my hands up in the air. "Right there is your problem. You overthink everything. Go with the flow. Let things happen…flirt back."

She blinks twice. "But this is you."

I sigh. "You haven't thought this through, have you?"

"I have a list."

"Of course, there's a list." I groan, exasperated.

She's never going to finish one of those lists, not because she doesn't work on them, but because she keeps adding to them.

I tilt my head toward the main entrance. "Let's go to my place. Where are the guys?"

"They went to the diner," she answers. "I'll text them that we're on our way to your place."

"Did you have to bring them?"

She shrugs. "Your brothers made it sound like you needed an intervention."

"I needed time."

"Why?"

"No matter how many times you ask, I won't answer."

"You're impossible, Aldridge," she states as I pull her into my arms and say, "You forgot to give me a good luck hug for the New Year."

She hugs me back, and the scent of her floral shampoo calms me. Let's hope that list includes staying with Beacon for the next eternity to learn how to date. Wouldn't that be amazing?

Chapter Thirteen

Grace

DURING THE WALK toward Beacon's studio, I focus on what I'm going to tell him and ignore the cold air cutting through my bare cheeks. This might be a bad idea. A lot can happen between us. One kiss might lead to another; and what if I end up falling in love?

The pros are that he knows me better than anyone. After all, we're best friends.

Maybe it's because of our friendship that I shouldn't do this. What if things end up weird between us?

Of course, it's right when I'm about to ask for his help when I realize the plan has an infinite number of holes.

That's what happens when you base your future on romantic comedy films and ask for your cat's advice.

I won't complain about my night. I loved receiving the New Year while eating popcorn in pajamas and fuzzy socks. I was on my second movie, *Holiday*. Please don't confuse it with *The Holiday*, the cute movie with Jude Law, Cameron Diaz, Kate Winslet, and Jack Black. Nope. This one is totally different.

I'm talking about the old movie with Cary Grant and Katherine Hepburn. He's playing Johnny and dating a character named Julia.

It's evident that they aren't meant for each other. It's Linda, the character played by Katherine Hepburn, who is his perfect match. She's not only fun and outspoken but also has a lot in common with Johnny.

By the end of the movie, it was established that I need someone with whom I can share everything and can understand my personality. I'm not hard to get along with, but sometimes I can get lost in my music room for hours at a time. Whoever I'm with has to understand it. Then there's Beacon. No matter what, we will always be friends. They have to accept our friendship.

Of course, I followed *Holiday* with *An Affair to Remember*.

The kiss Cary Grant shares with Deborah Kerr on New Year's Eve is one of the most epic, in my opinion, though the entire plot made me think about my life. What if I already shared that perfect kiss with someone, and I missed my chance?

My brain went into a rabbit hole, searching for answers from the past. Remembering every guy I've kissed, dated, or slept with. I've kissed many toads, dated not as many because, apparently, I'm undatable.

Sleeping with them?

Just a few—fine, two guys—not counting Beacon.

Yes, an unbelievable number when I'm single, twenty-eight, and actively dating. It's not about being a prude or having intimacy issues. It's about believing in love. Have I fallen in love with every guy I had sex with?

I side glance at Beacon. He might be the closest to being in love than any other guy I've gone out with. Was I in love with him?

Maybe I'm in denial. It's by choice though. I rather say that I just did it because it's best to get your first experiences over with the one person who understands you the most. Your best friend.

When he said we should cool it off, I agreed because…well, it was for the best.

We're better as friends, right?

Bridget Jones's Diary made me decide to take charge of my life and figure out where things went sideways in my love life.

The best way to begin my quest is to figure out why Beacon said, "Let's keep this simple."

Why did he do it? I thought there was something growing between us. Instead of answering my question, he responded with one of his own. I hate when he does that.

Well, if you didn't think I was right, you should've spoken. *Seriously, Beacon? I should've told you, "Please don't leave me."*

First of all, I refuse to acknowledge to him or anyone that I was in love with him at some point in our lives. My heart beats erratically remembering those days. We were about to leave for New York. College awaited us. It was going to be easier to date him away from my father's overbearing watch.

Yeah, I was definitely in love. It was that young, innocent, first love. I think young me believed we'd be together forever. Now, I just love him as a friend.

But it'd be nice if he could tell me what is so wrong with me that he had to say, "Let's stay friends."

We will be together—always—but just as friends.

It's right there where the flaws of this ingenious project begin to crack the perfect plan. He plans on flirting with me. The guy is irresistible.

What if I fall for him?

He's going to break my heart. Back when I was sixteen, I got over it because nothing changed between us. Now, things could get ugly, and I can't lose my best friend.

As I take a seat in my favorite oversized bean bag, I say, "On second thought—"

"No!"

"You haven't even heard what I'm going to say."

Beacon rolls his eyes. "You're second-guessing your amazing idea. I think we just need to polish it."

"It won't work," I assure him, but my voice comes out so weak he exhales exasperated.

"Are you doubting my skills, woman?" He touches his chest and lowers his chin. "If you lose faith in me, I have nothing left."

"Now you're being dramatic."

He smirks. "Are we renting you a house in the area?" He doesn't wait for me to explain why this is a bad idea. The man has made up his mind. "I don't think living at Tucker's place is wise. You can always stay here, in my house."

"As lovely as this place is and looks a lot like your home in Seattle, I can't stay underground. It gives me the creeps."

"You don't care about sleeping in a cave, but you can't live here?"

"Don't you remember that movie where the couple stayed underground for thirty years? At least, they had enough food to live long enough, but you don't have much."

"If I get enough provisions for thirty-five years?" he jokes.

I glare at him. "Don't even joke about it."

"You can stay at Leyla's house." He mentions the place she bought when she divorced Pierce.

She never moved there because they reconciled and remarried. That circles back to the theory of once you love an Aldridge you can't fall out of love. In my case, it's either a myth—or I never fell in love with Beacon. I'm in denial.

"That's your brother's office."

"And people think you're simple and low maintenance," he teases me. "I can buy you a house."

"No." I wave a hand. "Let's forget about my ridiculous idea."

"Why the sudden change? At least tell me a few of those flaws so I can work them out for you."

"Let's say we do it, but there's at least a glitch or two," I say, thinking fast. "For example, there aren't many men I can date in this town. How am I supposed to practice?"

"You are going to be dating *me*."

"That's not what my list says." I wave my cell phone.

He pulls out his own phone. "Send me the list."

"Nope."

"You want me to get it?" He smirks.

I frown. This was a terrible idea. "Stop it. This is serious. I'm not playing."

"Me neither. I don't have much to do this year, and I think we should focus on you." He's sauntering like a wild cat about to attack his prey.

His gaze holds mine. I swear if I didn't know better, I'd say he's hungry. Starving. He's looking at me as if I were a feast, and he's planning on devouring me. My heart beats fast as I imagine him pouncing on me and kissing me hard.

Not that I have any fantasies about my best friend. I never dream about him or his taut body. I don't care much about his muscular, tattooed arms. Well, maybe just a little.

I clear my throat and my thoughts. This is a bad idea. I need to figure out another way to accomplish what I want. A plan where my best friend isn't involved.

"Give me the phone, G," he orders with that low, sweet, commanding voice that makes everyone think he's sensitive. They are wrong. The guy is actually demanding. He wants everyone to do as he says. The guy is bossy as fuck. Also, he's a big subscriber of the saying, you catch more flies with honey than vinegar. Beacon always gets his way.

It works with everyone—but me.

"What's the big idea, Beacon?" I keep my voice steady and don't make any sudden movements.

This guy will take anything as a challenge and fight the phone off me. "I'm not one of your minions ready to do whatever you want. I can do this on my own. Thank you for going along with it though."

He leans closer, caressing my cheek with the back of his knuckles.

My skin prickles, and I don't understand the reaction my body is having to him. Maybe it's that gaze that's making me shiver.

"Back off," I order.

He takes a step back, and I jump out of the chair. We need distance. I need to shake off the stupid tingly feelings.

This isn't me.

I don't swoon after him. He's a player. Guys like Beacon aren't my type, not since I was sixteen.

"What are you doing?" I cross my arms, glaring at him. Fighting a series of feelings that don't belong inside me.

Those are exclusively for Beacon's groupies.

"Well, I plan on giving you the courting-boyfriend-swoony experience. After that, you'll know how to be less…awkward. You'll also know what you like."

I huff. He doesn't have any of that in him. Does he?

"So, if I don't like any of the stuff you do?"

"I switch it around until we find what makes you happy." He uses a bass-like voice that reverberates all over my body.

If I didn't know any better, I'd think he made up his mind, and he's already in character.

"What's your ulterior motive, Aldridge?"

"There's no motive, G. You know I'd do anything for you," he says, and the honesty in his eyes alters everything inside me.

He will do anything, just as I would for him, but dating is…It's a bad idea. Isn't it?

"If we do this, we should set some limits."

He rolls his eyes. "There aren't any limits in dating."

Extending his hand and wiggling his fingers, he requests, "The list. I need to see it."

Instead of giving him my phone, I text him the list.

"We can have fun with number one." He wiggles his eyebrows. "Lots of fun. I can't wait to fluster the fuck out of you."

"Limits," I repeat.

"There're no limits, and when you flirt, you have to dish it back," he counteracts. "Imagine we're playing a melody, and I start a solo riff with my guitar. You join with the cello and play just as hard. Can you listen to the beautiful music we're making together?"

I close my eyes and I do. That's exactly how we always play the best melodies.

Have we been flirting all this time? I open my eyes, confused. "Flirting is like music?"

He nods. "I play hard. You sweeten it with your melodic voice and some delightful charm."

"Sounds easy."

"And fun," he adds. "Just go with the flow."

I take a long breath before saying, "I can do that."

"Number two is a good one. I think it'll need a lot of practice though. Learn to kiss well…" He winks at me. "You're in for a treat."

"Cocky much?"

"No, just being honest. You want a demonstration?" He takes a step and closes the short distance between us. "I'd love to give you a free sample."

I stare at his lips. It's been so long since the first time we kissed. It feels like decades.

Fourteen years, but who's counting. Wow, it's been more than a decade since the day I told him, *"I've never been kissed. If I ask you to be my first…?"*

I wanted my first kiss to be unique. From someone I cared about and who cared about me in return. It wasn't perfect, but it was addictive. So addictive that we found time to do more and more until two years later, we made love.

When he said we should stop, it felt like a sign.

Mom warned me that we could break each other. I shared her fear that I would end up hurt pretty bad. Would he have broken me, though?

What if he breaks me this time?

"You're overthinking, G," he says with that easy voice that makes me feel like everything is possible.

"What if this ruins our friendship?"

"Nothing can ruin it," he assures me. "I'm yours forever, remember?"

My heart stops because he's always told me that before, but the way he says it now, it feels more than I'm your friend forever.

Maybe he's right. I'm overthinking everything.

"Learn to talk dirty." He laughs, moving on to the next point. "It's right next to push away your inhibitions and stop being an introvert."

"What is so funny about them?"

He starts coughing. "I volunteer to figure out number five. Actually, we should dedicate an entire week to do that."

I frown and check my phone because I can't remember what number five is, and when I see it, I gasp. Finding my G-spot.

My heart is about to jump out of my chest, and I'm not even sure if it's panic or lust.

"We're not kissing or having sex," I make everything clear.

"Kissing is necessary." He taps his phone. "As a musician, you know that the difference between ordinary and extraordinary is practice."

"Stop involving music in this conversation, Aldridge."

He smirks. "That's our language. It's the best way we can communicate."

I stare at him for a couple of beats. There's a lot involved in that sentence. So much I don't want to think about because then I'll have to analyze every note, lyric, and melody we've played separately and together.

To stop myself from evaluating this any further, I warn him, "I might say yes to the kisses, but there won't be sex involved."

"Unless"—he licks his lips—"you ask nicely."

"Beacon Kirk Aldridge, we're not having sex," I insist.

"We're not half-assing this, Grace," he answers. "You know I'm all in or nothing."

He takes my hands, lifting them to his mouth and kissing my fingers gently, softly. It feels like a feather caressing my skin.

His green eyes look at me, pointedly. "How's it going to be, Gracie?"

He takes my face in his hands. Slowly, leaning down his mouth, almost touching mine. I'm holding my breath, staring at his lips.

Wishing he'd kiss me. This is a bad idea. But the irrepressible desire to be devoured by his mouth is bigger than the reluctance.

"Are we going to compose this sonata? I promise it'll be like Beethoven's 'Moonlight.'" His words are playing in my head, just like Beethoven's Sonata. No. 14, my favorite.

"You promise nothing will happen to our friendship?"

"Do you trust me, G?"

"Always," I answer. The desire coursing through my veins blinds my judgment.

His lips brush mine lightly. Mine part with the friction, expectant. He teases me a couple more times before his tongue licks my bottom lip.

His big hand rests on the back of my neck, the other tilts my chin, and he finally lowers his mouth to mine. He kisses me slow. Very quietly. It's as if he's playing a romantic sonata. Not precisely 'Moonlight,' but we're following the rhythm. Beacon is the one dictating the pace. Slow, possessive, hungry.

It's nothing like our first sloppy kiss, but it has just the same feel. A deep, sweet caress in my heart. A song that hasn't been played in forever, but I knew it existed. I just didn't want to remember it.

But I remember us.

Chapter Fourteen

Beacon

I DON'T KNOW if it was the alarm announcing someone entered, or that I couldn't help myself and changed the kiss's rhythm from slow to a fast tune. Something along the lines makes Grace jet off with the excuse of having to visit Arden and baby Carter.

Lang, Sanford, Manelik, and Fisher stare at the door for a couple of seconds before San gives me a weird look. "Did we miss something?"

I shake my head.

Mane, who is the most perceptive of the group, arches an eyebrow. "Seeing as she didn't kill you, I'm guessing that you guys *kissed* and made up."

Lang shakes his head. "How long did it take, twelve years?"

"About." Fisher shrugs. "Maybe in twenty, he'll ask us to help him pick out a ring."

"We're not discussing Grace," I warn them.

"You never discuss her, but you're always moping," San complains. "Did you hear that she's registering for a *How to Date Bootcamp*? If you don't wise up, she's going to be dating a real man and forgetting about you."

So, Grace told them about her plan, huh? It doesn't surprise me. They are her best friends too.

These guys know my deal with Grace. They're my family. My brothers. There's nothing I don't tell them.

"She wants me to mentor her." When I say it out loud, it sounds somehow ridiculous, because why would I want to teach her something she plans to use with someone else?

Am I capable of letting her go?

Do I want to let her go?

My bandmates burst into loud laughter that lasts for several minutes.

"Come here, Little Red Riding Hood. I'll teach you the ways. Sincerely, the Big Bad Wolf," San jokes.

I flip him the finger.

"He's no wolf. He's just a fucking pup," Lang says. "Grace snaps her fingers, and he sits like a good little boy."

"Stop it!"

The four of them ignore me.

"I bet he's forgotten how to fuck," Sanford continues. "Not that he's going to be able to do it. Mr. B will have him killed when he learns Beacon has made a move."

"He can try whatever he wants. I can take him," I say, partially bluffing. If he sends the entire organization to hunt me, then I have no way to defend myself.

Mason Bradley adores his daughter. He's so protective of her that even though he lets her be a part of The Organization, he has someone watching her all the time—me.

"See, he went silent. He's worried because he's going to need a sex-ed refresher." San pulls out a condom from his wallet and throws it at me. "Lesson one, always use one of these before you fuck."

"You shouldn't worry, man. It's like riding a bike, Beac," Lang says, smirking. "I can buy you some porn in case you forgot what to do with it, other than jerking."

"Fuck you," I mumble.

Mane clears his throat. "How long has it been?"

I shrug in response. It's not his damn business. People swear that men can't keep it zipped.

We can.

Though it's fucking hard when the star of all my fantasies is always around me, and all I want to do is take her into my arms and make love to her. I can't act upon it. Well, that ends today. Bradley wants me to take some time off. I will do so and enjoy the perks.

"You have it bad." San pats my back. "Are you planning on giving up everything and getting the girl?"

"We don't discuss that part of my life," I remind them.

"Beacon, you're losing your shit," Mane gives me that serious stare. "This is the first time I have to interrupt my annual trip with the family because you're MIA. Honestly, I thought you went rogue and did something stupid until Grace said your brothers couldn't open the bunker."

"It's designed to keep undesirable people away," I remind them. "I wanted some time alone. My brothers blew everything out of proportion."

Let's hope Jerome Parrish didn't hear about it.

"I wish I had five fuckers giving a shit about me the way your brothers do," Lang complains. "If I die, my parents and siblings wouldn't give a shit—unless they have to pay someone off to keep any scandals away from them."

That's how Lang and I bonded when we were young. Our shitty

families. His family doesn't care about him or each other. It's pretty depressing.

"Just because they seem to care today, that doesn't mean they'll care in a year. May I remind you how they've never given a shit before."

"That's fair. I wouldn't believe it if my family had a sudden change of heart either."

The rest of the guys nod in agreement. We've been through a lot. How can they forget everything just because my brothers seem nice?

"I'm not doing this just to fuck with them," I assure them. "I lost my grandfather, then grandma. I know I have you guys, but I needed to take a day off."

"You disappeared for three days without warning us." San shows me three fingers.

"I know how to count."

"It's okay to go off the grid. Next time, call us, idiot," Lang remarks.

"What the fuck happened?" Fisher crosses his arms.

"I was being stupid," I say, because there's no other explanation.

"Tell us something we don't know," Mane argues, then says, "I'm not joking. You owe us at least that. I need to know why it is that you shut everyone down for so long."

"It was the thought of Grace and the new guy," I mumble.

Mane rolls his eyes and says, "There'll never be a new guy. You two are this weird couple that can't accept they are meant for each other. I can't say that she's in love with you because if she is, she hides it pretty well, but we know you adore her."

I tell them about my decision and Grace's proposition.

"What's going to happen when you have to go back to your life?"

"I…"

I need to figure that out because it can get messy. I stare at the wall, thinking of a solution when Fish says, "We support whatever you choose to do. Just don't fuck it up because she's our friend too. You know we're in this together."

By this, he means life, and she's a big part of it.

"He's going to move in here permanently, marry Grace, and become a farmer like his big brothers," San jokes.

"We still need to figure out Grace's housing if she's staying for this experiment," I say, moving the conversation along. We can make fun of my brothers another day.

"Why can't she stay in your room?" Lang reminds me.

So many reasons. Let me count a few. If Parrish suspects that we're dating and serious about it, he's going to try to impose my father's sanctions onto her. If she stays in my room, but she's not ready to go all the way with me, I'll have to sleep in the studio—or on the sofa. I can only fake that I'm sleeping in my bedroom for so long.

"It's too complicated."

"Tucker's place?" Mane suggests.

Grace loves her cousin, and the family is really close, but I doubt she'll want to live there for a year.

"Nope," I answer. "You know he'll take that as a big brother project, and we might end up fighting."

"I'll pay to see who wins. My money is on Tucker." Lang laughs.

"Fuck you," I growl.

Tucker worked for The Organization after his band broke up. He only lasted a couple of years. He retired after he got shot and almost died. His family begged him to quit. I think I would win because I have more practice, but I have no desire to find out if I'm right.

"We can buy a house," Lang suggests.

Why am I not surprised? Buying shit is his answer for everything. He's better than his family, but he still has some traits from their shitty attitude. Not everything is for sale. Money won't buy you happiness.

"We can use it for the band," he continues. "The next time we want to visit, lay a few tracks or just play at the bar, we don't have to stay underground. The place is cool but creepy."

Though it sounds like a great idea, it worries me that if I have to fly out without permission, my brothers—or worse, the lawyer—will catch me. Then again, The Organization isn't giving the team any new cases until next year.

I don't argue with them that it's up to Grace where she wants to stay. The woman hates when others make decisions for her.

Lang scratches his temple. "So now that your life is somehow solved, let's talk about the band. Can we set up some shows this year? We promise to bring you back before curfew, Cinderella."

I ignore the last comment. In theory, I am allowed to leave the town and the state for concerts. The catch is being back on time.

"Why would we want to do it?"

"I'm bored to tears, and I need something more than just coming to this town to do absolutely-fucking nothing," Lang complains. "Watching you guys play in the studio isn't the highlight of my life."

Instead of Julliard, Lang went to Columbia for business and Yale for law school. His family thought he'd be joining their business. It wasn't pretty when he told them he was becoming a music manager.

"You manage other bands," I remind him.

"It's not the same," he growls. "I have to be fucking professional with them."

San laughs. "Just give this poor man something to do. He spent the holidays like a good Mr. Scrooge planning some gigs."

"I don't know, guys," I say concerned, because I really don't want to be the one who fucks the town—even if I can save it later. "What do you have in mind?"

"We were thinking about the stipulations, and if we recall, you can play as long as you're back on time," Lang begins. He explains a couple of scenarios and names a few cities. "We'd have to talk with Jacob and Pria, but we think it's doable."

"You haven't run it through our label and our PR?" I huff. "They might say no, it's last minute or something like that."

"Please, Jacob doesn't sell your souls because he can't find a buyer," Lang jokes. "We can work out something this week."

"Okay, but you have to work the schedule and be precise. The concert is over by eleven, and I'm back no later than two in the morning," I remind them.

"It's feasible. As I explained, we stick to the West Coast," Lang assures me, and the guys nod.

"Vegas is also a possibility, yes?" Fish asks, hopeful.

"Let me sit down with my brothers and talk about it before you get on the phone with Jacob." I stop them before they announce the

Northwestern tour, or however they might want to call it. "Just like I don't trust them, they don't trust me either."

Okay, so maybe if I want them to trust me, I need to confide in them too. This better be fucking worth it. I'm not sure what exactly I'm talking about. My brothers, Grace, the band, or this year. I just hope it doesn't fuck me.

Chapter Fifteen

Grace

FIREWORKS GO off when Beacon begins to kiss me. My knees weaken. I want this to last longer—for an eternity. The sound of the alarm announcing someone is entering the house makes me stop. I push away from his embrace. I touch my lips and stare at him. There's a wildfire happening in his eyes.

I have a hard time recovering my breath.

"G," he whispers.

The steps in the hallway remind me that someone is coming. I say, "I need baby hugs from Arden and Carter." And I leave.

On my way to the exit, I happen upon Mane, Fish, Lang, and San.

"What's the rush, little fawn?" Mane asks. His dark brown eyes examine me. "You okay?"

"Yep, just need to leave."

"Okay, then. We're in a hurry," one of them jokes. I'm pretty sure it is Lang, but I don't engage. "Do you need anything, princess?"

Definitely Lang. He's the only one who still calls me princess. I owe that to my dear family.

Do I need anything? Another kiss, Beacon's arms, a plane to fly away.

All I know is that I have to get out of the house. Maybe leave the property all at once.

Or Baker's Creek…

Maybe the country.

That kiss wasn't what I expected. I don't remember him kissing in that way. I could feel him all the way down to my soul, branding his name. Flares of desire began to spread in my skin. I'm still burning, and if I don't extinguish the flames, they might consume me.

As I walk outside Beacon's place, I shiver. It's not the cold air. It's the lust that's giving me Beacon withdrawal—yes, it's real.

God, what did he do to me?

I need to cool down.

Instead of going to the main house to visit his family, I jog to Tucker's place. It seems like the best way to put out the fire. I'm burning, and not even the steady fall of snowflakes can extinguish it.

I haven't walked two blocks from the Aldridge mansion when I stumble upon my brother.

"Good, I was coming to find you," Seth mumbles, pulls the sleeve of his coat, and checks the time. "Gotta go, princess. Are you staying?"

"Nope, I need to go home…" *But I can't just yet.*

There are things Beacon and I have to discuss before I do so. We have to clear the air. I need to make sure that things between us won't get awkward.

I mean, that kiss was…How do I describe it without adding feelings to it?

You don't kiss your best friend like that and say, "Hey, go and find your forever man." Do you?

That kiss felt like an "I want you to be mine forever. I want to be your guy."

Okay, so it was incredible and so, so good that I'm making up stuff in my head.

How can I not when the kiss just keeps replaying in my head and makes my lips and everything inside me tingle?

I'm so confused.

This is one of those times where I'd call Beacon or Mom to ask for advice, and I don't think that's a good idea at the moment.

Beacon is the source of all this mess.

Mom…I can hear her saying, "He's a celebrity. Those relationships never last. You're better as friends."

She'll then add the laundry list of stories she knows about celebrity romances going bad—including her own. The one she had when she was sixteen. She dated this famous guy who had been her friend for a long time, and it ended up in tragedy.

The same one she used as a cautionary tale when I told her I kissed Beacon. I might've lied because the first kiss happened two years before. We had done a lot more since then. I felt like it was time to come clean and tell her about us. I stopped myself from telling her more. As of today, we've never discussed what I had with Beac.

I can hear her already, "It won't work. You know his reputation. Men don't just change because they claim they've found the right woman. That's just fantasy."

I know his reputation. The same way I know he fabricates all that publicity. I'll never understand why he makes up so many stories. He's not a saint, but he's neither the playboy he personifies when he's not at home.

Seth stares at me and bobs his head a couple of times. "So, we're not forgiving him for scaring the shit out of us, huh?"

I look intently at him, puzzled by his comment, and I immediately understand. I've been too quiet, overthinking the kiss. Should I tell him about it? Nope, he'll probably try to kick Beacon's ass. Or laugh at me because I can't get laid and have to approach my hot, sexy, smart-ass best friend.

I redirect my thoughts and say, "Are you upset at him?"

They are pretty close, and I'm sure if something happened to Beacon, he'd be pretty messed up, just like me.

"Nah, I knew he was fine." He rolls his eyes. "That guy is like a cockroach. Nothing can kill him—not even his stupidities."

"He can be reckless," I agree with a sigh.

Beacon is impulsive. The guy is a genius, and he's always a few steps ahead of us. When we're scouting, he's already tracing a plan on how we're going to proceed. Sometimes, he just says follow my lead without waiting for Dad's approval to continue.

"I guess that's why he's one of Dad's best men." Seth looks at his watch. "Can we leave? We could borrow his truck or one of his brothers can fly us to Portland."

Vance is the one who picked us up from the airport and flew us here. He said he'd take us back whenever we wanted. The guy was angry that he couldn't open the locks. Maybe it was a way to hide the worry. He doesn't know Beacon as well as we do, or they would have just waited for him to come out from his hiding place.

"Why don't we go to Beac's house? I'll introduce you to his family."

He smirks. "I know them well enough. I could even tell you what brand of toothpaste they buy."

"Maybe— and this is just my opinion—it might be different if you introduce yourself. Because they don't know you," I remind him. "They have no idea you've been watching them since their father died, just to check if they are worth being close to your friend."

He grins. "It wasn't like that. Beac asked me to do it."

I roll my eyes. "You two are ridiculous."

"By the way, the lawyer is in town." He suddenly changes the subject.

If there's one thing I'd like to do, it's kidnap Jerome Parrish and interrogate him until he tells us what his deal is. He drops by every so often to make sure "the boys" are complying with the will. He throws in a few unrequited life lessons. There are some letters William Aldridge left that he didn't just hand over. He's giving them one by one. As if those were golden stars they only deserve when he feels like it.

What is his game?

"Are you going to tell them?" I look around, wondering if the asshole is nearby.

"Beacon already knows, if he checked his text messages."

"Where is Parrish staying?" When the guys moved into town, they kicked him out of The Lodge. That's the only hotel in Baker's Creek. Since they own the place, they decided to not allow him to stay there.

"He's been renting a house in Happy Springs since late September when one of the brothers bought the bed-and-breakfast."

"Interesting."

"We should run a thorough background check on him. He should be in New York running his law firm," I say, pulling out my phone and taking off one of my mittens. "Why would he spend his time in Baker's Creek babysitting six grown men?"

"Money?" Seth asks, then shakes his head. "His firm does well enough."

"He's getting something out of this deal," I insist. Beacon doesn't believe me. He thinks his father paid him to fuck with them, and there's nothing more to it.

Beacon loves to fuck with people, so he put a detail on him just for fun.

"Let me finish my caseload, and I'll start digging into his life," Seth assures me.

Maybe I should help him. What if we discover something useful that can end these stupid stipulations sooner? Now, that's something I can get on board with.

Chapter Sixteen

Grace

SETH and I go to Tucker's home to say goodbye, just in case we don't have time later. Our cousin isn't thrilled that we're leaving. He thought we'd be sticking around like everyone else.

"It was unplanned," I say, apologetically. "I left Mozzy alone and there's no one who can check on him."

That is true. My family usually goes on vacations right after the New Year. Not to the same place, but everyone takes off the first day of the year. Our cousins are here.

"I have work to do," Seth informs him.

"It's cool," Tucker says. "We can get together some other time."

We say goodbye to everyone and leave. As we approach the Aldridge mansion, we spot Beacon walking toward us.

"Just the person I was looking for," Beac says, then greets Seth. "Please, tell me they didn't pull you out of a mission just to come and *rescue me*."

"You owe me," Seth responds.

"He doesn't owe you anything. You volunteered to come," I protest, look around, and ask, "Where are the guys?"

"With my brothers in the game room. They're staying for the rest of the week. I was coming to check on you." He points toward me, looking at Seth. "If you don't mind, I need to have a word with the lady. Why don't you join the guys downstairs? It's about time you meet my family."

"Fine, but *now* you owe me," Seth, who doesn't like to deal with strangers, sighs and walks away.

"Where do you want to go?" Beacon asks. "My room or the studio?"

"If I say I want to go home?"

He shakes his head. "We're talking first, Grace. You can't throw something like your list, the request, and that kiss on my lap and then run away. I read your texts. You wanted *to proposition me*."

"I didn't phrase it like that."

He pulls out his phone, slides his finger, taps it, and clears his throat. "I found a solution to my problems. Based on your suggestion, *I have a proposition for you*," he reads one of the texts out loud. "Correct me if I'm wrong, but you did use the word."

"Not what I meant."

He crosses his arms. "Grace, bedroom or studio?"

"Why those?"

"They are both soundproofed, and no one will hear our conversation."

"Your room?" I'm not sure if that's the right answer. Honestly, I don't know if I want to be in a closed space with him. What if I just strip him down and jump him?

It's been a long time since I've had sex. So long, I might need a few pointers before we do it. He takes my hand the way he usually does, but even though I'm wearing mittens, I can feel the heat of his skin. God, I made this all weird.

We enter the house. Blaire, Leyla, and Sophia are in the living room with Arden and Carter. I could use them as an excuse.

"Hi," I greet them.

"See you later," Beacon says, waving at them and pulling me toward the stairs. Okay, he's not going to let me delay the conversation.

He shuts the door, locks it, and leans his hip against the handle while he looks at me. "Why did you run away?"

To anyone else, I can lie. I could argue that he's wrong. He knows me too well to even try. I'd lose the argument.

"The kiss was too much," I answer.

He gives me a satisfied grin. He met his goal. He wanted to fluster me.

"Do you understand what this can do to our friendship?" I ask, confused at his laid-back posture.

Beacon is truly relaxed. Nothing about this worries him, and here I am, almost chewing my nails down and trying to keep my breathing even.

"You can't think it's okay to kiss me like I'm your first meal in ages. Leaving me breathless," I argue. "It's too much, and for what? So you can send me packing after this experiment is over. Do you think it'll be easy to search for someone else after you let me go?"

"Who told you I'm letting you go, G?"

His possessive voice makes my stomach flutter. I stare at him, dumbfounded.

"We..." I sigh. Is that a real question?

He's kidding, right?

"There are many reasons why we couldn't work out in the long run, Beacon. I don't know about you, but I need you in my life."

He rubs his hands, probably warming them up. It's so cold outside, and he's only wearing a sweater.

He watches me intently for several beats. I need to know what's on his mind. Something is bugging him. Either he's afraid to share it or—

no, afraid isn't the right word. God, I hate when he closes himself up and doesn't let me into his mind.

"It's obvious that you're out of my league, Beacon." I change strategies. There are many ways to break his walls. Two can play this mind game. "You are billions of years ahead of me when it comes to the relationship world—even when you don't date. Other women might be fine with those kinds of kisses, but to me…"

I can't finish the sentence because I don't even understand what I'm trying to say. Kiss me again because I need more? Give me a kiss that lasts—and lasts forever. That thought, those words surprise me because I shouldn't want more of him, and yet, I feel like I have denied myself an essential necessity.

Him.

No, you're just lusting because he's a good kisser and nothing more.

"This was supposed to be helpful and educational. What if I fall in love with you? I can't just move on and try to find another guy."

He arches an eyebrow. "Have you noticed you're talking in circles?"

"You flustered me, and if you grin again, I'll wipe it from your face."

"Anger," he says, pressing his lips together. "You are confused as fuck."

I could ask why he's so chill, but I know the answer. This isn't affecting him at all.

"The guys and I think it'll be best if they buy or rent a property where you can stay while you're around," he says, not even acknowledging what I tried to tell him. "Maybe you can give Mills a hand with Arden during the day. Pierce is trying to amend the part where we can't hire anyone to help us, unless you're still working on the Bryant case."

He's already moving on to the planning stage. We haven't agreed on my plan, which is a bad idea to begin with.

"Did you hear me?"

"Loud and clear," he responds, shoving his hands inside his pockets and balancing his weight from one foot to the other. "You have a list. There's a plan. We need to proceed."

"It was a mistake. I'll figure this out with—"

"Don't say someone else," he says, his eyes flaring with anger. "You made that list for a reason. You thought about me because you trust me. I will take care of you. I always put you before anyone else—even myself."

"When this ends, it won't affect you, will it?"

He saunters toward me, cradles my face, and I'm starting to love the way he does it. So delicate and loving. The adoring way his eyes look at me makes my heart skip. "Maybe this is our chance to write something new. This is our chance to create something so imperfect, messy, colorful, and fulfilling that will be ours. If it only lasts a few songs, that'll be enough to fulfill me for a lifetime."

"Those are serious words, Beac," I mumble, unable to look away. "Lyrics of a love song that might end in a heartbreak."

He sweeps my lips with his and kisses the tip of my nose. "Hearts are made to beat, to love, and sometimes they break. But they mend and love again. If you break my heart, I'll survive."

Beacon kisses my temple, then my jaw, finally my bottom lip. He nips it lightly with his teeth. Then his arms wrap me into an embrace where it is just us. Everything that I swore to erase and forget about us finally comes out floating to the surface.

He might survive a heartbreak, but can I?

Chapter Seventeen

Beacon

THERE ARE times when talking to Grace needs a particular skill. She needs logic. I don't want to lie to her, but I don't want to come out too strong.

I'm not sure how she'll react when I say, "I love you. I've loved you for years."

She's going to want an explanation about my behavior for the past eleven years. I'm not ready for that. When she says she can't have a relationship, she's not kidding. Grace only opens up to the people she knows, which makes it impossible to get past the second date because she's a closed book. I feel for the fuckers that've tried and failed.

Here's the thing; they aren't patient with her.

She might go out on a date every other week, but she doesn't like to deal with feelings. Because of that, she's not well-versed in intimacy. She needs to warm up to people, and as I always say, those assholes she's dated are impatient as fuck. They seek immediate gratification. That's never going to happen with Grace. She needs to be emotionally invested to let anyone in.

Has anyone realized that she fears three things?

Emotional entanglements, people, and failure.

Hence her dating life sucks. My Grace needs someone who is patient and willing to learn how her mind, soul, and heart work.

Or…she can stay with me forever. I have ample knowledge on all things Grace related.

I don't know how I'm going to handle the end when our time is over. It's going to be hard as fuck to let her go. For now, I'll focus on the present. I'm going to give her everything I have.

No holding back.

No reservations.

No restrictions.

And rules be damned.

That's how I kiss her. Surrendering myself and my feelings. When the intensity of the kiss is about to break my self-control, I stop.

Though I'd love to do more than kiss the fuck out of her, I stop devouring her and work on evening my breathing.

"Please?" I add to the speech I gave her before I tried to suck her soul and steal her heart.

"How is this supposed to work?"

"Trust me, G," I plead.

"Maybe I don't trust myself," she whispers in a low, raspy, sexy voice that sends logic flying out of the room.

I slant my mouth to hers and kiss the fuck out of her. I tease, taste, and claim her with my mouth. Her tongue meets mine, matching stroke for stroke. I lower my hands to her body and unzip her parka, pushing it out of the way. Something overtakes me. Desire surpasses reasoning. I have to have her. I need her.

Desperately, we begin to peel each other's clothes. Fuck, she's so beautiful. I run a finger along the soft skin of her throat, my lips follow right behind. I trace the outline of her breast.

"Beac," she whispers.

"Do you want me to stop, G?"

"No. Yes." She exhales harshly. "I don't know. This is happening too fast."

I pull her into a hug, pressing her bare skin against mine. I had no idea how much I had missed her until now.

"This isn't what I came for," she mumbles. "I just needed to know that you were okay."

"There's also the list," I remind her, sliding my hand down her spine.

"It's a bad idea?"

"The list or what we could be doing right now?"

I love that instead of pushing me away, she rests her head on my shoulder. Her arms are wrapped around my body and her hands rest on the elastic of my boxer briefs. I could persuade her and continue kissing her. Get reacquainted with her beautiful body.

Today isn't the day to make love to her. She's not even ready to proceed with her idea. If I make a mistake, this is over before it begins. I don't have the luxury of losing her when she's so close I can taste her.

"Go home, pack your stuff, and I should have everything ready when you come back, okay?" I say, making the decision for both of us. It's not only her. I'm not in the right place to take this step. There's a lot of stuff we have to clear before we can be like this again. "I'll take you on a date when you're back."

"Should I remind you that I need more than just *a* date," she states. "Today doesn't count."

I chuckle. She's sobering up from the kiss. "Of course, you do. We'll tackle that list while we date."

"Are you serious about it? We're dating?" She lifts her chin. Her gray eyes, filled with desire, stare at me confused.

"We are going steady." I wink at her, picking up her long sleeve shirt. "We are doing this old school. I might even serenade you."

"Okay?" I hate the hesitation and fear in her voice.

"Do you trust me, G?"

"Stop asking me that question," she says with annoyance while we're getting dressed. "You know that I do."

"Then stop doubting me," I state, trying to keep myself from arguing that she's the one who came to me and opened the doors to having some sort of relationship.

Now, she doubts that this will work. She doubts me.

I should be hurt. I could tell her how I feel. How I've felt for years. I don't. It has to come organically—when she's ready. At some point during this exercise, she's going to learn that I never joke when I tell her I'm hers. That I'll be by her side forever.

She'll understand that every time I say, "I'm yours, you make me happy, you're all I need," it's the gospel truth.

This year I'm taking time off to finally have what I need.

Who I need.

"Operation, *Get G Out of the Loser Slump* starts now."

"That's a ridiculous name," she complains.

I kiss the top of her head and hug her tight one last time before letting her go.

"Come on, let's go downstairs. I assume Seth wants to leave right about now."

"You know him. He can only be social for so long."

Seth is not an introvert, but like his sister, he avoids social gatherings with strangers. The youngest one of the Bradleys is the social butterfly.

Chapter Eighteen

Beacon

VANCE TAKES Grace and Seth back to Portland, but not before Seth suggests a landing strip near The Lodge. He spends about an hour discussing the pros and cons. So much for wanting to leave right away.

In the end, Henry decides to build a better helipad and a hangar that can fit two or three helicopters.

My brothers have no idea what they've done, giving Seth the green light to come and go and use this as a base for The Organization. Will my brothers get pissed when they realize what we've been doing since we arrived in Baker's Creek? I might never tell them.

I plan on speaking to the five of them tomorrow. Not about The Organization but the tour and Grace moving to Baker's Creek. As I'm heading up to my room, Mills intercepts me.

"So, what happened?"

"With what?"

"You locked yourself away for three fucking days. I'm here if you need me," he offers. "I'm not Grace or your bandmates, but I thought you trusted me."

I slump slightly because I can only keep so much shit from him. We go into my room, which is the only place in this house where I can have some privacy. I had the contractor soundproof it.

"It's too fucking complicated." I sigh.

"As complicated as when you get the fuck out of town whenever it pleases you?"

I arch an eyebrow and press my lips together.

"You think I don't know when you leave town?"

"What are you talking about?"

"I know you have a cabin in the woods," he states. "That you exchange cars and head to Portland, leaving some scrawny asshole to play the part of Beacon."

"Can we keep that between us?"

"I have to because if I don't, we are all screwed," he chides me. "What the fuck are you thinking?"

"Listen, it's best if you don't know. I promise it's not for selfish reasons—unless you count the times I've gone to see Grace because I fucking miss her. Most of the times it's to help a cause."

He shakes his head. "What kind of cause?"

"It's a good cause, I swear."

Maybe I should tell Mills what I do, but what if it puts him in danger? I wouldn't forgive myself if something happens to him or Arden…or to my family.

"Listen, I know you have your reasons not to be with Grace." He rubs the back of his neck. "You should do something with that. Move on or be with her. I wish I could have someone that understands me the way she understands you—and loves you."

"I'm actually planning on making my move," I confess and smile. "It's time to see where this will take us."

He nods.

"You okay?" I ask.

"Living here makes me feel lonely. Does that make sense?"

"It does," I agree, because that's how I've been feeling.

"When I decided to have Arden, I thought how hard can it be to do it on my own?" He pauses. "It's not hard, but it feels incomplete. Like someone is missing."

"Do you ever regret telling his mom to keep him?"

He shakes his head and smiles. "He's the best thing that's happened to me. It'll be fucking hard to tell him why his mom isn't part of his life though."

It's fucking hard to learn that your mom didn't want you. She wanted to become Mrs. Mills Aldridge, and since Mills didn't want to marry her, she almost got rid of our boy. Mills paid her to have him and took charge of him since day one.

I pat his shoulder. "Your soul mate is somewhere. She's not here yet because maybe you two aren't ready to meet."

"Have I ever told you that you're fucking corny?"

"I'm a little of everything."

I WAIT until the next evening to talk to my brothers. Since I'm trying to work things out with them—they're still worried and angry about my disappearance—I let them come to the game room on a weekday.

They are only allowed to be in here Fridays or Saturdays. I don't joke when I say I need my space.

"Where are your bandmates?" Pierce asks, walking to the cue rack.

"At Bar None, hopefully not hooking up," I state.

"Are you ready to talk about what happened to you?" Henry asks and points his cue toward Vance. "This brooding shit is something I expect from him. Not you. Drinking yourself stupid was irresponsible. Should I be concerned about alcohol or drug abuse?"

"Can we stop the lecture?" I ask. "It's something I don't often do. I. Am. Clean. In fact, I need to stay drug and alcohol-free or I get fired."

I almost flinch as I say the last words. I hope they don't look too closely into that statement. Musicians and celebrities do whatever the fuck they want, and they don't get fired. They might lose their fans, contracts, or sponsorships.

Pierce stares at me intently. He wants to say something, but he just shrugs it off and sets the balls on the pool table. Since The Organization began to look into his family's firm, he's been asking too many questions. He swears I'm part of the people who are investigating his mother. I work for them, but I haven't done any work for that case.

"We just want to understand you," Hayes explains. "Personally, I feel like I have less than a year left to prove myself to all of you or I'll lose you permanently."

Henry clears his throat. "I'm staying in this forsaken town with you."

"Well, Henry and Pierce are a different story." He points at Mills, Vance, and me. "You three are closed up to us. I'm still wondering why you and Mills stayed in touch. You could reach out to him but not to us too."

"I read in the paper that his grandfather died and called him. You didn't give a fuck," Mills answers, but it's more like a growl. "It was all over the news. No one reached out to him. Not even William—but I expected that from him."

Everyone nods in agreement.

"It's like with his injury," I snarl as I point to Mills. "Everyone knew he was hurt. It's the second time it happened, and you couldn't reach out. You didn't even care to accept him as your patient after the team's doctor reached out to you."

Hayes scowls. "What the fuck are you talking about?"

Mills shakes his head. "Let it go, dude."

"His doctor tried to get an appointment with you," I explain, puffing my chest and ignoring Mills. I've been wanting to punch him since Mills told me about this. "Your excuse was your long-ass waitlist. He's your fucking brother."

He looks at Mills and shakes his head. "I had no idea. My assistant never mentioned it to me. I'm sorry about that. I wish I had followed your career closer. I can't fix what happened before our father died."

Pierce glances at me and shakes his head. "No matter what I say or do, I can't make you trust me. I'm not giving up on you, Beacon, but maybe you want to give in a little?"

"We take responsibility for what we did wrong," Henry says. "But it's time for you to stop using it as an excuse to keep us at arm's length."

Vance huffs. "Typical Henry, just trying to close a deal. This time it's getting his younger brothers to trust him. Your wife needs to teach you to keep your family out of your goal board. We're not some weird five-year plan."

"Year five, organize the annual Aldridge family summer trip," Mills jokes. I high five him.

I'm impressed that instead of trying to punch one of us or yell at us, Henry asks, "How else can I prove to you that I'm here for the long run?"

I take this as the perfect moment to bring up the tour. "Well, the guys and I want to organize some gigs for this upcoming year. A small tour. Most of them will happen only on the West Coast. We might go to Vegas if we think the times line up with my curfew."

"We agreed you wouldn't go on tour until this is over." Henry is the first one to protest.

He can't trust me. According to him, I'm a loose canyon which is precisely what I want him to think. He doesn't know I'm methodical. I can be ten times more demanding than him. Unlike him, I'm not fastidious as fuck.

"Which means you don't think I'll be back on time because you can't trust *the kid*," I taunt him.

"You were drunk at your *secret* house for days. If Parrish learns about it, we're fucked," he growls.

"I had that covered," I growl. "You just think I'm a stupid kid. News flash, I'm not."

"Stop!" Pierce orders, pointing at him, then looking at me. "Why the sudden need to add some gigs?"

"The guys proposed it. I personally think that if we work within those parameters, it can happen. Also, we can try to keep everything within an hour's flight," I explain. "As I told them when they suggested this idea, it's up to you."

Pierce nods. He looks at Hayes, who shrugs.

"Twenty dates," Pierce offers. "Set twenty dates throughout the year and the rest here or in Happy Springs."

"Don't encourage him." Henry's eyes narrow to crinkled slits.

"If we want him to trust us, we have to trust him too," Pierce explains.

"It goes two ways, Henry," Hayes agrees. "We need a few rules, though."

"I think it'll be smart if we request those dates as your free days—in case you are late," Pierce suggests. "That gives you ten days to do whatever the fuck you want."

"Isn't it against the rules to use them for work?" I ask.

"Let me worry about the details. I can bend the rules slightly." He looks around the room. "You want to vote on it?"

"I'm cool with it," Mills says.

"Same," Vance agrees.

"I trust you to do the right thing. So far, you've managed to stay in town," Hayes says. "Honestly, I thought that you'd be flying out of here within the first week."

I did.

"Give me some credit. I know how to be careful and not just do something stupid," I say with a straight face.

It's not a lie. I wouldn't do anything stupid. That's different from I've been out and about. I just know how to cover my tracks.

Henry looks at me. "Get Sophia, Blaire, and Leyla on board, and you got yourself a deal. I trust you, but if you fuck this up…"

I cross my arms, smirk, and give him a challenging look. "You're going to ground me?"

"No, I'm going to make you fix it."

Fix it is the wrong word. I could save the people affected. The properties will be sold, and the Lodge demolished. However, I am ready to step in and manage to save the town and the livelihood of those fucked by our father. He doesn't need to know that, though.

"Don't challenge him," Mills warns Henry. "Or underestimate him. Maybe if you stop calling him *kid* and start giving him more credit, he wouldn't have the need to leave the main house and come to this place every day because he can't deal with your attitude."

"I'm trying to make sure he doesn't fuck up anything," Henry defends himself. "He almost died."

"I didn't." I snort. "You need to chill. When I'm on my death bed, you'll know."

"Enough, Beacon," Hayes orders with a low, commanding voice. "He's not handling this well."

Pierce looks at me and says, "Look, we're trying our best, but as the doc said yesterday, we can't lose another brother. You scared us shitless by disappearing, and it wasn't because we thought you were gone but because something could've happened to you, and there was no way to reach you in time. Henry is concerned. You have to remember that sometimes his emotional constipation only allows him to yell like a wounded animal. We're a work in progress."

"You have fewer hang-ups than we do because your grandparents did a great job raising you," Hayes says reassuringly.

What he's really saying is that Henry's behavior has a lot to do with his fucked-up life and nothing with what I'm doing. Fine. I'll give him a pass.

Neither one says what we all know; their mothers' bitterness made them the way they are. I understand. If my grandparents were alive, they'd chide me for being an asshole to my brothers. Maybe I should ask for a day and drive to Seattle. I should hang out with Grace's family. They keep me grounded.

Grace is my anchor, though.

"By the way, the guys are buying a place, and Grace might be moving into town."

"Are you finally going to tell her how you feel?" Henry asks with a smug grin.

"I always do. She just doesn't believe me."

"Clearly, you don't know how to do it well," Hayes says mockingly. "Maybe compose a cheesy song."

I could list all the songs I've written for her. Instead, I change the subject. "Well, just so you know, she'll be around for the remainder of the sentence." I hope.

Pierce's eyes brighten. "Do you think she can give us a hand with the little ones?"

"You still haven't found a way to get us a nanny?" Mills groans.

"No, I haven't. We can't pay anyone for their services. I'll find a way. I promise."

"You should definitely ask Grace," I encourage him. "I'm pretty sure she'll be able to do it."

And with that, I've just made them think that getting Grace to help is their idea. They also agree to the concerts since I agree to have up to twenty dates outside the state. My brothers are so easy.

Chapter Nineteen

Grace

I'M A GEEK.

I like to research and know everything there is about a subject or a product before I try it. I'm one of those people who reads the instruction manual right after I open the box. Unlike Beacon, who will open the box and touch everything before he even asks, "What the fuck is this for?"

My tablet's memory reached its limit a couple of days ago. I had no idea it was possible until I filled it with books about flirting, sexology, and finding love.

The book I'm currently reading mentions that learning the language of love is as easy as learning how to speak. Language comes effortlessly for some. It does for me. I speak four languages—five if I count music. Still, love isn't something that's happened to me, unless it slapped me in the face and I didn't notice.

Does having a crush on Beacon when I was sixteen count?

Stop lying to yourself. It wasn't just a crush.

I keep thinking about the kisses he gave me the last time I saw him.

Do I regret not going all the way with him?

A little. I can still feel his hands running along my back, burning every inch of my body. The touch of his lips grazing my skin. I haven't been able to get him out of my head. The next time I might beg him to take me.

Why did he stop us?

I shake my head, fighting the memories of the most exquisite kisses I've ever had in my entire life. My focus should be on these books, not that I can pay much attention to them. It's hard. They make no sense to me. It's either the brain fog or the ridiculous analogies.

Saying that learning to flirt and fall in love is like a child learning how to talk sounds a bit weird. They need to reword everything.

Maybe I'm taking things too literally.

If I could fall in love as easily as I can speak other languages, my life would be different.

I spoke and understood Japanese and English by the age of three. Since I can remember, Dad spoke to me in Japanese while Mom and the rest of the family talked to me in English. My paternal grandmother is second generation Japanese-American.

I also know French, Spanish, and music. The latter is a universal language.

Should I have started flirting with guys at twelve like most of my peers? No, I was a freshman in high school, and everyone thought I was weird. Thankfully, I was in the same grade as Beacon, Lang, San, Mane, and Fish. They made that stage of my life a lot easier.

Is Beacon right? Should we start dating and everything else will come easily?

Then what can I get from all the books, magazines, and articles I've been reading, not that I can follow them. I can't see myself wearing a provocative outfit to allure my "desirable objective"—that's how one of the books I'm reading refers to the person we're trying to charm.

It's winter. I need thick jackets, baggy sweaters, and leggings to keep me warm. And most of all, I'll never give up my knee-high socks and combat boots, unless I'm undercover or at a concert. I dress to express myself and feel comfortable, not to attract the opposite sex, as described in the book, *How to Flirt your Way into the World of Love.*

That's a long title fitting for a book filled with nonsense. At least, it's nonsense to me.

If this was a class, I'd fail. My first F. Unbelievable. I just don't understand how else to do this. Beacon said flirting is like music. I don't see any similarities. There's no rhythm or rhyme to the nonsense I'm reading.

This is a lost cause. I turn off my tablet and move my attention to my computer. I have to check on the house I rented in Baker's Creek. It's close to the Aldridge mansion and far enough from Tucker's place. I adore my cousin, but he can get too overprotective. Cue on the *too overprotective.* He's just like Dad. I feel for Mae, his daughter. She will have trouble getting places when she is older because her dear dad will say, "You're too young."

In just a couple of days, I'll become a temporary citizen of Baker's Creek. The moving company should be here on Friday morning to take my bed and some of my furniture. Once they leave, I'll drive to Oregon.

I stare at the cardboard boxes leaning against the wall. I still have to pack. Maybe I should do it while taking a break from doing more research.

That sounds better than wondering if I should practice kissing with someone other than Beacon.

Mmm…Beacon, I sigh.

Who knew he gives the best kisses in the world? Toe-curling-brand-your-heart. The last kiss he gave me before I left Baker's Creek still plays in my head. I don't think I'll ever be able to find someone who kisses that good.

Where did he learn how to kiss like that?

What was I thinking when I said he should help me?

I wasn't thinking.

It's just our nature.

We are each other's person.

He can call me at any time with any request, and I'm there for him. That goes both ways.

The bigger question is, what was he thinking when he agreed to go along with my request? Or when he kissed me? Or when we almost...I swear that felt as if he was about to claim me. There are nights when I wish he had done just that. Other times, I hear a little voice saying, "This is a bad idea. You're going to lose him."

Still, I can't help but think about the what ifs. I even imagined what he will do to me as things progress between us. We had sex twice when we were young. Both times were sweet. He was so careful. I don't have any complaints about it. But now, I don't think I want that gentle, delicate love making guy. I want things to feel real.

Is it because of my reading material?

I've been reading some erotica as part of accomplishing my list. When I was reading *Never Kissed by a Duke*—my first erotic literature—I couldn't help but imagine Beacon as the Duke. During that scene when Antoine was taking Lady Beth in his arms and fusing his lips with hers, the emotions I felt when he kissed me came back in full force, crashing against my chest. They made my pulse accelerate. My core ached with need, just like the narrator described.

I was agonizing, wanting for Beacon to be close. Oh, how I wished he was sucking on my ample bosom just like the book described. Confession time. I touched myself and came really hard while reading how Antoine drove his hardness inside Lady Beth's sweet heaven.

It's funny how they refer to the privates, but the scenes are so intense I don't have time to fixate on that. All I want is to reach a high and release some of the pent-up frustration I've accumulated since the last time I saw Beacon.

Now, that's when a nagging voice comes to play. The one that says, "But Beacon is your best friend. He's like your brother."

But is he really?

I say it because he is as obnoxious as my brothers. Though my brothers aren't as caring as he is. Beacon always watches over me, even when I can take care of myself.

We've never lived in the same household as brother and sister. We did as roommates during college. One of Dad's friends leased us a brownstone in Brooklyn. We treated each other the same way we treated the rest of the guys. That's not being sibling like, right?

Am I just finding excuses to justify the lust and forget that we grew up together?

He nags me like a big brother, but he's never confirmed my statement that we're like brother and sister. I should discuss that with him. I would never in a gazillion years flirt with a family member. I flinch in horror.

I text him. He needs to clarify our non-familial status.

Grace: *Do you ever think of me as your sister?*
Beacon: *Never. Why would I do that?*
Grace: *I always say you're like the big brother I never wanted.*
Beacon: *And I always have to remind you that I am not related to you.*

I read his text twice. He is right. He always remarks that we're in no way related. If anyone asks about me, he gives a vague explanation of why I'm with the band. I am a lot of things. His best friend. A family friend. I'm related to his agent. I'm his college roommate.

I'm the one saying that nonsense since he said, "We're better as friends."

Beacon: *I always make that clear. You and I don't have any familial ties. There's a huge difference between growing up close and being siblings.*
Grace: *Yes, I remember you always denied my statement. Why?*
Beacon: *If I had a sister, I would never imagine her naked as I do with you.*

I gasp, staring at the phone. Well, at least I'm not alone in the *wanting to do a lot more than kissing* department. Again, why did he call it off?

Grace: *You imagine me naked?*

Beacon: *Often, and the things I do to you are sinful and hot. I could demonstrate—when we're ready.*

Grace: *Maybe that's a bad idea.*

Beacon: *Hey, I'll call you later tonight. I'm in the middle of a boring meeting with the fam. Apparently, we're about to launch a new line of chocolate, and I am the spokesperson.*

Grace: *You shouldn't be texting.*

Beacon: *:eye roll emoji: You contacted me.*

Grace: *Since when do you answer my texts right away?*

Beacon: *Always, unless I'm too busy. Miss you, G.*

I stare at the phone and try to remember the times he ignored my messages. I scroll up and there are barely any unanswered texts.

Chapter Twenty

Grace

THE REST of the day goes by quickly. I spend all my afternoon practicing cello. At five, I drive to my parents. Mom invited me to dinner since I'm leaving soon. I've yet to tell Dad about my plans. I can see him wanting to move in with me. That'd be the worst idea in the history of the world because he'd be cockblocking me, the same way that Beacon does with almost any guy I date.

Ugh, the men in my life are infuriating.

Around eight, I arrive home. I'm about to go to the music room when Leyla, Pierce's wife, calls.

"Hey," I answer. "Are you calling because baby Carter needs to listen to my voice?"

Her son is the most loving little boy in the world. He's only eight weeks old, but I would do anything for him. I can spend hours rocking him and singing lullabies.

She laughs. "He's too concerned about naps and his formula to think about you. I'm actually calling because Beacon mentioned you're moving in with us."

"Ha, he wishes," I say, wondering what he told them. "I'm renting a house nearby. Moving is such a broad term, but yes, I'll be living in Baker's Creek for a few months."

Beacon and I didn't discuss the length, but I can't see myself leaving home for an entire year.

"We are in desperate need of someone to help us with Arden and Carter," she says. "I was wondering if you could do it for us. In case you're wondering, Pierce already checked with Jerome Parrish, and he said that family friends are acceptable."

"As long as he knows that I am just a family friend."

"Afraid to be stuck in Baker's Creek because you're the heart-throb's significant other?"

"Not again," I complain, because she, Blaire, and Sophia insist that something is going on between Beacon and me, but we're in denial. "We're just friends."

Friends who are about to start dating. Friends who kissed with the passion of a thousand suns. Friends who got naked and almost fucked. Should I tell her?

"That's not what we heard," she states.

I groan. "What do you mean?"

"Beacon mentioned something about you two finally dating."

"Ugh." I deflate and plop myself on the couch.

Mozzy leaps onto my lap and rubs his head against my hand so I'll pet him.

"He's helping me with my disastrous dating life," I clarify.

She laughs. "Sure, let's call it that. I've never heard about your so-called *dating* life. Is that even a thing? You two are always together. If not, you're on the phone texting each other or on a video call."

Clearing her throat, she says, "You know, like couples do."

The way she says it sounds weird. She's wrong. We're not.

"I thought you wanted me to help you with your baby?"

Leyla clears her throat. "Yes, I do. Fine. If you want me to lie and pretend that I don't find that plan ridiculous, I will. You two refuse to face the facts."

"There aren't any facts to analyze," I argue, but my voice doesn't come out as strong as usual.

Should I look more into my friendship with Beac?

"Ah, to be young and in denial."

"No comment." I huff.

"I want to believe you. Tell me what you are going to accomplish with this nonsense?"

I ignore the word *nonsense* and I tell her all about my brilliant plan. At least it was great when I thought about it. But now it seems like maybe the second worst idea I've come up with. The first is asking Beacon to help me.

"I know a place close to Portland where we can find your *toys*," she says. "When are you moving in?"

"This Friday."

"We can go out on Saturday."

"But it'll be in the middle of the crochet festival?" I gasp. "What will the town say if one of you is missing?"

Baker's Creek is famous for its ridiculous and outrageous festivals that happen almost every weekend. Don't get me wrong, I enjoy them. Before Beacon's dad died, we used to visit the town often just to go around to the vendors. The things they sell are amazing.

"Well, I need a break after the Yodeling Festival. You should've been here to control Beacon. He was singing and trying the instruments in every booth. I don't think Henry has been that embarrassed in his entire life."

I can't control the laughter as I imagine Beacon being, well, Beacon. He likes to have fun. Sometimes, he seeks attention. Others, it's just for the laughter. A couple of years ago, we were in Germany during Oktoberfest. It was entertaining to see the man singing, playing, and just becoming part of the festival. However, his brothers don't understand him. It actually makes them uncomfortable, and that's something Beacon likes to exploit.

"Not even after the anal beads incident?"

Last year, during the Beads and Handmade Jewelry Festival, he made an entire production about using them without lube. Beacon said it was hilarious to see his brothers flustered. The best part was the murderous glares because he was discussing their sex lives in front of the entire town.

She laughs. "No. It was worse because Beacon carried a microphone and a small portable speaker with him. He made Henry sing."

"Please tell me you guys recorded it."

"Of course, we did. You know we always find the time to record Henry's best and most embarrassing moments."

"I can't wait to be there. I feel like I'm missing half of the fun."

Sophia keeps telling me that this is better than a reality show. She's right. I'm tempted to tell Uncle Matt about everything that happens. I bet he'll be interested in writing and producing a show based on the Aldridge brothers.

"So, is that a yes, you'll help us with the kids, and we're going to an adult store on Saturday?"

"Yes, to both."

"Just don't bring Beacon along because even though I love that kid, he can be pretty embarrassing."

"It's just when his brothers are around,"—or my father—"But yes, let's make this a girl's trip."

"And just a piece of unsolicited advice, go and kiss a few more toads before you come to Baker's Creek," she suggests. "Or at least go and get yourself a couple of hunk guys to buy your next cup of tea."

"I'll try," I answer, without disclosing why I wouldn't do it.

Leyla is fun. I like her a lot, but we're not at the point of telling each other our most embarrassing moments. Telling her my plan is more than enough. Heading out to a coffee shop, a bar, or any place where I can meet a guy will bring the same results. A couple of bad dates and one of those men will be saying, "I'm just not that into you."

I'm done with the humiliation.

"Text me when you're on your way to Baker's Creek. Sophia and Blaire are excited about this."

"I hope you don't regret it," I say in a singsong voice. "Say hi to Carter and Arden."

After hanging up, I notice Beacon sent me a text.

Beac: *I can't wait until Friday. I'll call you before bedtime. Thinking of you.*

We always text, but he's never told me he's thinking of me. My heart can't help but flutter at his words.

Chapter Twenty-One

Grace

"I DON'T UNDERSTAND why you're moving to Baker's Creek," Dad says, staring at the boxes sitting in the trunk. I'm quite sure he's thinking about driving my SUV to his house.

"It's temporary, Dad," I remind him.

I'm outside of the house, packing my car and listening to my father's latest lecture. He's not happy with my relocation. Dad's very protective, but he's gone from "I'm looking after my child" to "I should build a crystal case and keep her there forever."

My grandfathers—Mom's dads—say it's karma, and they're enjoying the show.

"You need your family with you," he insists.

Mom presses her lips together and shakes her head. She's about to burst into laughter at Dad's show. This is worse than when I went to college—at sixteen. The only reason he let me go without a bodyguard is because Beacon was going to be there too. Back then, Beac and the guys weren't famous at all, and they had trained with Dad for a few years.

"It's going to be okay, Dad," I assure him.

I should remind him that I live on my own. I have traveled around the world without the need of anyone watching over me. Most importantly, I can fend for myself. He's been teaching me martial arts since I was four.

"What I don't understand is why you are doing this." He looks at the pet carrier Mom's carrying. "Mozart is not going to like it."

Is he for real? He's using my cat as an excuse. Dad wouldn't like my answer to his questions. He won't love it if I say, "Beacon is teaching me to date, and I might even get a few pointers on my sex life."

To avoid giving him a stroke, I say, "Mozart travels with me, always. If he had a passport, it'd be filled with stamps from all over the world. Since I don't have anything to do at least until August, I will help the Aldridges. The stipulations in the will prevent them from hiring a nanny. As a family friend, I can help them with Arden and Carter."

"You know, I never liked William Aldridge, but now..." Dad pauses. "So, it's the kids, and it has nothing to do with Beacon taking a sabbatical effective last week."

I arch an eyebrow. "Beac requested a sabbatical?"

He gives me a sharp nod. "You didn't know about it?"

"No. He mentioned taking a break," I mumble, trying to recall exactly what he said he planned on doing this year. He definitely said he would do whatever he wanted. What he said included a lot of cussing and nonsense that I ignored. "A sabbatical is—he doesn't plan on doing anything for The Organization?"

"Exactly, which is why I think it'd be best if you stay with us."

"If he wasn't taking a sabbatical, you'd be okay with this?"

His lips press together in a slight grimace as he stares at me for several seconds before exhaling harshly and saying, "You need medical attention."

My mouth opens, agape. *Is he freaking kidding me?* I don't have an argument because he's absurd. I glance at Mom, who shrugs. Clearly, she's having too much fun watching her husband be ridiculous. She doesn't plan to intervene because that will cut the entertainment too soon.

"Seriously, Dad?"

"I don't like this."

"It's just until I find something to do."

"I have plenty of stuff in the office," he offers.

"If it's not in the field, I don't want anything, thank you," I retort. "You don't let me work without my team." I toss my hands up in the air, exasperated. "You are impossible, Father."

"Where are you staying?"

I pull out my phone and show him the house I leased a couple of weeks ago. "It's close to Tucker's home and the Aldridge place," I explain.

"What happens if you need to go to the hospital."

"Just a reminder that Beacon's brother and sister-in-law are doctors," I continue and touch my pump. "This gadget is working perfectly fine. If not, you'd receive a message."

"Ainse, reason with your daughter," he says, exasperated.

I look at Mom and say, "Control your husband, please."

"We support you, but why do you have to do this?" Mom's question is somehow more reasonable than the third degree I've been enduring for the past couple of hours.

I sigh and look over my shoulder because a truck just parked in the driveway. Beacon steps out of it and smiles at me. "Mr. and Mrs. Bradley."

Why is he here?

Well, it doesn't matter. Since he's here and he doesn't care about taking heat from Dad, I throw him under the bus. "I'm also going to live there because Beac is teaching me how to date."

My parents look at each other, and their eyes open wide. I'm not sure if it's because they don't like the idea or if there's something more. Mom bursts into laughter.

"That's not going to work," Dad barks. "I forbid it."

Beacon snorts. "I'm not sure what's funnier, your face or Grace's line, *'He's going to teach me how to date.'*"

Dad sighs, relieved because, apparently, I'm wrong. I won't be getting any dating lessons.

"You promised to teach me how to date."

"No, you wanted me to teach you, and I said, 'We're dating.'" He turns to look at my father and says, "By the way, *I am dating Grace.*"

"No, you're not," Dad growls.

Beacon grins. "Sure, I am."

"We have rules," Dad argues, and I want to ask what rules he's talking about because now I'm so confused.

"I'm not working for you, so they don't apply to me."

I frown. Do we have a no fraternizing policy in place, or is there an unspoken rule within The Organization that says we can't date?

Maybe there is one that says, "Grace is off-limits."

"I can dismantle your team, then." Dad is provoking him, and I don't know why.

"Sure." Beacon calls his bluff. "Let me know how that works since my team is taking a sabbatical with me."

Dad's jaw tenses. "You know what that means."

"That you can't boss me around for a year." Beacon smiles at me, gives me a peck on the lips, and says, "Hi, stranger. I missed you."

I can't help but smile with him and sigh. "Hey."

"Ready to go?"

"You're not going anywhere with him." Dad glares at Beacon, and I swear the vein on his temple is throbbing. "Beacon, a word."

"I would love to, but I need to be back at home by tonight, and this lady and I have a few things to do before we arrive in Baker's Creek," he says nonchalantly. "You can always call me or visit us."

"I'll reassign your primary duty since you're on a *sabbatical*."

Beacon snorts. "There's no point, but you do whatever you think is best, Bradley. I can't wait to see what happens when you do that."

Dad huffs and slowly expels a couple of breaths before he speaks and points at him as if he's threatening him. "You do something stupid, and I will—"

"Mason," Mom says his name with a scolding voice.

"Define stupid," Beacon challenges Dad.

"Stop," I order Beac.

"I'm just—"

"Taunting him, and I want you to stop, please."

Why he likes to undermine my father's authority is beyond me. He never does it when there's a real threat, a mission, or he's assigning him a job. It's usually like today, outside of work.

"Anything for you, G." He takes the carrier from Mom, looks at Mozart, and says, "And you will be traveling with Uncle San who should be here soon."

"I was planning on driving myself," I protest.

"Yeah, but we're going to Portland first, and this guy won't like staying in the car for that long."

"I agree, but I need my car."

"Which is why San and the guys are meeting us here. San's driving your car to Baker's Creek," he assures me just as Lang's car parks right behind Beacon's. "This is a slight change of plans because last night, I had an epic idea."

"Fine, let's go," I concede.

"Call me," Mom says when I hug her. It's not, "Call me when you get there." Nope. She's telling me to call her because I didn't tell her about Beacon and I dating.

"Love you, Mom," I say and smile. Then I hug Dad and promise him, "I'll be fine, Dad."

"I'll be watching you, Aldridge," Dad warns Beacon.

I groan because these two are planning on making each other's lives miserable. I can just feel it.

Chapter Twenty-Two

Beacon

MASON BRADLEY and I have had a love-hate relationship since he learned I kissed his daughter. Back then, I was a skinny, stupid, short kid who was terrified of him. Thank fuck he never found out that we more than *just* kissed.

I'm no longer that kid, though. Now, I'm a highly trained asset who could give him a good fight. I care about and respect him. He's been there for me since I was young. Those father-son Boy Scouts camping trips were possible because he volunteered to take me.

He taught me how to catch and how to fish, and he helped shape the man I became.

When he began to teach martial arts to Grace, I asked him to teach me too. My grandparents agreed to it. I doubt they knew back then what Mason did for a living. They thought he was some geeky IT guy. Without meaning to, Mason trained all his children, nieces, and nephews. He just did it to give them a way to defend themselves. Some of them know martial arts, while others learned a lot more—becoming part of The Organization.

His original idea wasn't to recruit any of us. Yet, we showed potential, and here we are. I've been working for him for the past eleven years. Some of us have primary duties. Mine is to watch over Grace. Technically, I'm Grace's bodyguard.

Why would she need someone to look after her?

In my opinion, she doesn't. For Mason, there's a lot at stake. She's the granddaughter of Chris Decker—the musical legend. She's the granddaughter of Gabe Colt—producer, screenwriter, and award-winning actor. Her uncles are the famous Decker twins. Those might be important reasons. The most important one is that Mason, the owner of one of the best high intelligence secret agencies, has made a few enemies worldwide.

She's not in danger, but we are cautious.

When he was going to assign the duty to one of his men, I volunteered. Who better to watch over her than me?

I wouldn't trust her safety to anyone. Plus, I'm her friend. She's never felt like someone is watching her every step. It's always just me —fun, reliable, and silly Beacon Aldridge. If I'm not with her, I assign the people who watch over her during concerts.

He never felt the need to disclose my duty to Grace, nor the fact that she has a bodyguard. I don't know what she's going to do when she learns about it.

Good luck, Mason Bradley.

She's going to be pissed at me. I'm going to have to grovel and persuade her to forgive me.

This dating thing has a big obstacle. I could be worried if it wasn't for the fact that I'm counting on it to swoon the fuck out of her, so she'll forgive me. Chicks dig that groveling thing pretty well. I've seen it with my sisters-in-law.

My relationship with Mason and my job with The Organization might be in jeopardy. He's going to try to kick my ass—which isn't skinny anymore. I can take him. We'll just have to deal with it later. As always, my priority is Grace.

Before I warn him, because he is pissing me off, the guys arrive to pick up Grace's car.

I respect him. He's done a lot for me, but I'm tired of doing everything he says to avoid losing my primary duty.

Grace gives San her car keys and we wave goodbye.

"What was that?" Grace asks as we pull out of the driveway.

"I'm not trying to be dense, but what exactly are you talking about?" I ask, glancing at her briefly and then returning my attention back to the road.

It could be one of two things—the throwdown with her father or the fact that I picked her up without warning her. Either way, I'm going to play dumb until we get home. I'm not thrilled that she rented her own place. If she had agreed to live in the house the guys leased, I could switch places with one of them and stay overnight with her.

She huffs. "Never mind."

"No, really. Tell me," I insist.

"For starters, you never told me you had a primary duty."

Because why would she start with something as light as, "Why were you taunting my father?" Nope, she wants to know what will make her say, "Drive me back home. We're over."

"It's classified," I remind her.

There's sensitive information within The Organization that we can't share. Not even with our team. In our case, she's the only one in the team who doesn't know about it. Fuck, she's going to kill me.

"Oh God, don't give me that crap, Beacon Aldridge," she warns me. "I know about all your missions—even the ones where you go alone."

"Missions, yes," I clarify. "Not duties."

"Now you're obtuse," she complains. "What are you hiding?"

This is the part where I tell her the truth. She'll kick my ass and refuse to see me again. I will have to grovel and probably stay with her until she forgives me. Which will affect the entire town of Baker's Creek.

"Can we discuss it tonight?" I ask, requesting some time because I definitely need to warn Mason.

I might not be able to leave town, but his daughter can, and she's not going to be happy after she's done with me.

"Why wait?"

"Because the last thing I want to do is talk about work," I answer, and it's the truth.

"So, if I ask about the sabbatical?"

"It has to do with my primary duty," I respond. "Again, something we can discuss later when we arrive home."

I feel her glare. It's that intense. She's either upset or trying to figure out a way to just quit the operation and head back home. I wait for her next question. "Did the lawyer agree to let me babysit Arden and Carter?"

"Yeah," I answer, knowing that Leyla already told her it was cleared. "It wasn't even an issue. Apparently, *reaching out to our community* is allowed."

"What does that mean?"

"It means that we can ask for help from the town, as long as there's no financial exchange."

"Hmm."

"What are you thinking?"

"So monetary exchanges aren't allowed, but you could exchange services," she says. "Not that you need anyone to come and help, but we could figure out a way to get a nanny for Arden and Carter. Like, 'I give you a horse in exchange for your services.'"

"Just a reminder that the horses are family," I say, imagining what Leyla and Pierce will say if they hear this blasphemy. Poppy and Alistair are their children. "Also, you're in charge of Arden and Carter when their parents are busy."

She sighs. "The horse is just an example. I would imagine that you'd buy a new horse with the idea of exchanging him."

"We don't need another horse," I protest. Again, we bring an animal close to those two, and they'll just add the creature to their growing family. "We've plenty. I've no doubt that Pierce is going to buy a pony for Carter so he can learn to ride. By then, I'll be long gone. Now back to you. Where are you going?"

I'm not freaking the fuck out, but I am. She gave me a year.

Didn't she?

Technically, we didn't discuss the time frame. I assumed she understood that she'd stay until I'm allowed to leave Baker's Creek. News flash, I'm not staying.

My careers require me to travel often. Also, Grace is close to her family. When I say close, it means Sunday dinner at her grandparents', brunch at her mother's, and being at every celebration the Deckers might have happening. I wouldn't take her away from them —ever.

"I got a call from an old teacher. He's proposing a series of concerts in Carnegie Hall and wants me to be part of it. It's just a proposal that, if approved, will start in August. If all goes well, then he might want to organize a world tour."

This is the part where I wish I can tell her no, because the entire team is taking a sabbatical. I wouldn't trust her safety to just anyone. I don't care if Mason Bradley has capable agents who could take over my job. I doubt Seth is going to stop what he's doing just to babysit his sister.

We usually discuss her projects. It's a way to plan the logistics. Also, what the fuck? I need her with me.

Have I mentioned that I need at least until the end of the year to figure *us* out?

"It's just a proposal," she continues. "Unlike Lang, who can get any venue whenever he wants, he has to get *the hall*. We both know it's not that easy."

I breathe with relief when I realize she's right. This is something that most likely won't be approved for this year. Even if the teacher is trying to use Grace's name, they won't be able to set anything until next year—or the year after. We are going to be in a different place by then.

What's going to happen after Baker's Creek and her dating experiment?

Manelik asked me that stupid question last night.

The answer is even more stupid, *I have no fucking idea.*

"We have to have a plan for when I have to leave town," she continues.

"When would that be?"

"Any time I want," she concludes.

And I'm fucked. Luckily, the guys agreed to go with her.

"Of course, but it sounds like you're not staying for long—as we agreed."

"Not exactly, but think about the days I need to go home to visit my grandparents. Remember, they aren't as young as they used to be."

"You can work that out with Mills," I say, controlling my answers because there's a lot more I'd like to say.

Let's start with the four-hour drive from Baker's Creek to Seattle. Then add the road conditions during winter. Icy and dangerous. I feel for Mason Bradley because he's always trying to keep his daughter within his watchful eye, but Grace has a mind of her own. I've known her for a long time. You need to know what battles to fight, and I honestly try to always be on her side—by her side. It's easier to support her.

During the first hour of the drive from Seattle to Portland, we talk about her old professor's idea. She likes the concept. It's something she can do since she's free, at least until next March when we start touring. I need to figure out a way to find something exciting.

I'm excited and can make things a lot more fun for her. There's a nine-point list she needs to achieve, and knowing her, it'll be twice as long by the end of the month. The more things she adds to it, the longer she'll stay.

Let's just hope she understands me when I tell her about my primary duty.

Fuck, I'm doomed.

Chapter Twenty-Three

Grace

"WE'RE HERE, SLEEPYHEAD." Beacon's deep, breathy voice wakes me up.

The same voice that in my dream was whispering naughty things in my ear after a lengthy kiss. He had his long, strong, tattooed arms wrapped around my waist.

When I open my eyes, I meet his hot, heavy gaze. His eyes are lit with passion, just like in my dream. This time, when his lips crash down on mine, it's real. His tongue sweeps the bottom of my mouth, and I open it for him. Our tongues dance to a slow, tender waltz that becomes an intense samba. Sometimes I forget how this man can switch rhythms and loves to play with them.

He's like his art. Whimsical, chaotic, and temperamental. And sometimes his magic makes me feel a little too much. How I wish I could stay in his embrace forever, making beautiful music. This is the first time I realize that our kisses are on a different level. Even when they aren't long and deep, there's a desire lingering under that sucks me into a vortex of want.

I want him to touch me.

I want him to tear off my clothes.

I want so much more of him.

"Beacon," I moan, pleading him to, "Touch me."

"Not here."

"Please," I beg.

"You know I'd do anything for you—except that."

I pull away from him, but he holds me in place. His deep, penetrating gaze locks with mine. There's a fire in those green eyes—the flames threaten to burn me. I want him to sear me with the heat. So why is it that he won't touch me?

"Not here, in public," Beacon whispers, leaning closer to me and running his lips along the shell of my ear. "You have no fucking idea how much I want to do it."

I can hear it in his voice, the—"But?"

"We're going to have to wait."

"Until we arrive in Baker's Creek?"

"No." His lips travel along my neck. He places a gentle kiss on my collarbone. "It'll happen when we're ready."

I'm ready!

"Ready for what?" I ask, taking a long deep breath.

What is he waiting for? For me to melt into a puddle of need. I'm there. I've been waiting for this since he kissed me three weeks ago. I've been prepping myself and fantasizing about him every night. I want his long fingers touching every inch of my skin. Fucking me the way I've been doing it myself because he's not close.

And he wants to wait longer.

You've gotta be fucking kidding me, Aldridge!

He lifts his shoulder with an unapologetic shrug. "I want this to be perfect, G. Dates, flowers, and slow dances. I promised to make this unforgettable."

"What's going to happen in the end?"

He caresses my jaw with the back of his hand, those green eyes looking at me tenderly. How can they switch so fast from loving, to burning passion, to indifference? This version of Beacon is confusing.

"Maybe we can figure out a way to keep it going," he answers. "Melodies are everlasting. Maybe we can create one that will be timeless. Eternal. Or this is just a tune we play once during a concert that we'll always remember. I don't have an answer yet."

I don't understand why it is that my heart hurts when he hints that there's an end. I doubt I'll be able to go back to the way things were between us where kisses, caresses, and those loving gazes never existed.

But what if I fall so hard that I won't be able to breathe without him?

He kisses my forehead. "There you go, worrying about things that'll never happen."

"What are you talking about?"

"No matter what happens after this, I'll still be by your side." His assuring voice makes the weird dread that was overtaking me dissipate.

"You promise?"

"I swear," he states, and I can breathe with ease. "Now, let's go and have our first real date."

"Because we've had fake dates before?" I joke.

He looks at me and shrugs. "Many, many friend dates."

What are friend dates? Seriously, when did we go out on a friend date? As far as I'm concerned, we've never gone out. I am about to ask about this new development, but the sight of a tall building with the Merkel Hotels & Spas logo stops me. Henry's business.

"So, where are we going?" I ask as I climb down from the SUV.

Beacon takes my hand. We walk along toward the steel and glass building. I'm wondering if we're picking up Henry or Sophia. They come twice a week to check up on their corporation.

"We're picking up a new toy for you," he states as the doors slide open to the interior of the new and impressive building. The high ceilings, white and gray marble, and black and white decor throughout the floor are astonishing.

My heart pounds. It's fear.

What can he possibly give me that he's picking up at the corporate offices of Merkel Hotels & Spas?

Beacon's favorite sport is to embarrass people. Practical joking is a real activity in his dictionary.

Pranking is one of his guilty pleasures.

He teases me but never pranks me. I've never been on the receiving end of his practical jokes. I don't think I'm exempt from them either. There's no written law stating that he's not allowed to pull any of his antics on me.

It's his nature.

"Toy?" I sound too scared.

Oh God, what did he do?

I can see him buying a huge dildo, an inflatable man, or the Fifty Shades of Sex beginner set. The one Seth shared with us last week. The same day he found out about my list. Everyone who belongs to our group chat knows about this dating exercise. Since Beacon is in exile, they've been cracking a lot of jokes.

My two brothers and the guys know that I'm heading to Baker's Creek to…well, I said learn how to date. It doesn't look like that's the case anymore. We're really dating, aren't we?

I look at Beacon, wondering if we should discuss what's happening. I stop overthinking when I notice his grin. He looks so happy, I smile. This is how I like to see him—relaxed. From the outside, he looks chill. Everyone thinks he gives no fucks about anything, but it's obvious they don't know him at all. He's the most caring guy in the world. He's always watching over everyone.

Beacon's mission is to protect those around him. He never lets his guard down. Unfortunately, he's also cynical. He has a hard time trusting those who have hurt him. My mission is to see him like this: happy, calm, and trouble-free.

This might be the result of not working for Dad. Is it his primary duty that keeps him stressed all the time? I need to figure out what he does on the side.

"Mr. Aldridge," the receptionist greets him. "We have your package in the security room, as your brother requested."

"Thank you, Monica," he says, saluting her.

Though I stayed at some of the Merkel hotels worldwide, I've never been to their headquarters. I know they have a great security team in each location because Beacon makes sure he has access to them when either one of us is on tour. That's the problem with traveling with a world-renowned celebrity. We have to make sure his groupies can't get to him.

"There's a security room here?"

"It's actually more than just *a* room. You can monitor every hotel in the world from here," he explains.

"How do you know? Have you told any of them about The Organization?"

He shakes his head and sighs. He tried to convince Vance to join us, not that he told him he's part of The Organization. He said he's okay without working for now.

"Vance is in charge of their security," he explains. "He convinced Henry to centralize everything here."

"He did?" I ask when I see his grin expand.

"Sure. I just gave him the information about a *buddy* who has the best equipment. This friend happened to consult with him and gave him some suggestions."

"Indirectly, you sold him the equipment and set it the way you wanted."

He nods and smirks like a child who played his big brothers.

"Yep. We actually convinced Henry to replace all his equipment around the world." He gives me a mischievous look. "The Organization has access to everything. In theory, we just expanded our reach around the world. My brothers just don't know it."

"Not even Vance?"

He shakes his head. "They still think I'm just a stupid musician. I want it to stay that way."

When we get to the room, he tilts his head toward the handle. "Try it."

"It requires a code and fingerprint recognition."

"Just do it," he insists.

I humor him. The reader lights up after scanning my thumbprint. I enter my access code, and the locks open. I wiggle the handle and push the door wide open.

"How?"

"We set it so most of the agents in The Organization can use it," he states.

"And they pay for it?" I ask, impressed. "Dad agreed to this?"

"As long as we're in control, we can access the system. It's part of the package they purchased," he continues. "Seth's team did a great job selling the equipment and our consulting services. They can't access our system because they wouldn't know what they are looking for. Plus, your dad's security wouldn't allow them to enter."

I roll my eyes because this sounds like something Seth and Beacon would concoct together. When I pay attention to the room, my heart flutters. "Oh, my God!

It's not the panels or the room that look a lot like my father's security room at headquarters. Nope. It's the Joseph Grubaugh & Sigrun Seifert box standing only a few feet from me.

I might be wrong and he has a dead body in there, but what else can it be? If I'm right, that's a big, beautiful, and gorgeous cello.

"What is that?" I ask, with a giddy voice.

"Well, you don't like to drag Camilla out of the house—unless it is just next door to mine," he refers to the first full-size cello I've owned and still use for practice. Mom and Dad's gift when I turned twelve.

Most girls my age wanted a horse, a new phone, or a laptop. I wanted a full-size cello.

"Constanza is your traveling girl, but you only use her during concerts," he continues. "I decided to buy you a new cello so you can practice here."

Women might love flowers, jewelry, or candy. I adore musical instruments—new, old, collectibles, or souvenirs.

I want all of them.

"Beac." My voice comes out breathy, surprised.

His intense gaze sets on me. It casts an air of danger, boring through me. It's filled with so many unspoken emotions. He looks like sin. Like a fantasy that I want to fulfill right now. The tug he has over me is new, yet it feels like a part of me that I've repressed for years.

"I just know it's important for you. Renting one wasn't an option." I hate when he finds ways to make big gestures insignificant.

"Wait, I thought you were wooing me with this instead of flowers. Don't give me a lame excuse of why you did it."

He shoves his hands inside his pockets and balances his weight.

"It's harder than I thought."

"What? Dating me?"

"No." He gives me that boyish smile I adore. "I mean, stop pretending that everything I do is because we're friends."

"You're telling me that everything you do is because you…" I frown. Is there any other reason?

"The short answer is yes. You never see me buying shit for the guys or your brothers," he says. "Now, let's go to our next stop."

Instead of leaving, I take a couple of steps and wrap my arms around his neck. Pushing myself onto my tiptoes, I press my lips against his. He opens his mouth, and my tongue sweeps inside his. Beacon's palm clamps around my neck, deepening the kiss. The fingers of his other hand dig into my ass, and I want him so badly to press me against the wall and just take me.

"You're going to stop us, aren't you?" I ask as soon as he breaks our contact.

"This hurts me a lot more than you think." He sighs, releasing me from his embrace. "You're throwing a few curveballs. I'm having trouble dodging them."

He picks up the box. "Open the door for me, G. We have plenty of places to visit. My agenda doesn't include making out in the dashboard room."

"I was thinking about sex," I correct him right as we're on our way outside of the room.

"Later, Monica," he says.

I wave at the receptionist, who glares at me.

"PLEASE, DON'T GET ME WRONG," I start.

"Did I fuck up?"

"What?"

"You're about to tell me what I did wrong?"

"Not at all. I loved our day together," I correct him. "It's just that this felt like any other day with Beacon Aldridge."

After leaving the corporate offices of Merkel Hotels, we went downtown where we spent the day visiting stores and enjoying each other's company. He even prepared a picnic for me. We ate in the car since it's too cold to go to a park.

His attention remains on the road, but his smile widens. "I told you we've been on friend dates."

"Right," I quip. "That's a creative way to tell me that you don't know how to date."

He laughs, reaches for my hand, and kisses it. "Sure."

To no one's surprise, I fall asleep. It's already dark when we reach Baker's Creek.

"You're the worst traveling companion," he complains when I'm stretching.

"Why are we here?" I ask, noticing there are at least twenty cars parked in this huge garage. We're at his family's place. "I have a house."

"We're just leaving the car here," he explains. "It makes sense since later I have to unload the cello in the studio. The guys already dropped your stuff at the rental. We're walking there so you can get ready."

"Ready for what?"

"You think this is it?"

"It's not?"

"We have reservations "—he licks his lips—"at The Lodge. We got the private dining room."

"Upping up the game."

He gives me a peck on the lips. "Are you challenging me, Grace?"

"So far I haven't seen anything new."

He takes my hand, feathers kisses on the inside of my wrist, and we walk away. I don't understand what's happening between us yet. I'm loving it, and it's just day one.

Chapter Twenty-Four

Grace

WE WALK to my new place in silence. That's an unspoken rule among the Aldridges. Anything they say is tweeted before they reach their next destination. They are like the town's celebrities. It didn't use to be a problem before they came to live here. I guess it's because not many knew that Beacon was an Aldridge.

When I get to my place, Beac gives me a quick peck on the lips. "I'll be back in thirty minutes."

After I close the door, I check my phone. There are a few texts from Mom. The last one makes me laugh.

Mom: *Call. Your dad is having a conniption.*

Instead of reading the rest of her texts, I call her.

"Gracie," she starts. "I feel like you skipped a chunk of information when you told me you were temporarily relocating to Baker's Creek."

"Hey, Mom," I greet her, trying to sound cool.

It's hard to erase the guilt in my voice. I feel like I was trying to sneak into the house past curfew, and my parents caught me. Not that it ever happened. I was out of the house a couple of weeks before my sixteenth birthday.

Most of the college parties I attended were at our place, and alcohol was never a problem. The Organization has rules. Underage drinking would've gotten us fired immediately.

"You and Beacon are dating?" I'm not sure if she's upset, asking a question, or about to lecture me.

The silence on the other line makes me feel uneasy. "It's a trial," I continue. "More like a teaching moment."

Okay, now I sound desperate and foolish.

"Those can go wrong." Her motherly warning voice doesn't go unnoticed. "What are you planning on doing when this trial ends?"

She's already skipping the entire story and heading to the end. Her tone implies it will be tragic. She's such a positive person. Why does she have to be gloomy when I need her to be Mrs. Positive?

I love Mom. She's wise, but she has her faults too. Today, I won't deal with that flaw of hers that I hate so much—her catalog of useless experiences. Sorry, but just because it happened to someone she knows, it doesn't mean it will happen to me.

Some days it feels like she wants me to stay at home—forever in a safe haven where nothing and no one will hurt my feelings because she's watching over me.

"Please, don't tell me you have some cautionary tale about this situation, too," I say, and this time I am slightly upset. "I'm not you, Mom. When things end, Beacon and I will continue to be friends."

I think.

I hope.

I need to believe that this won't damage our friendship. Beacon promised me that. He's never broken any promises so far.

She chuckles. "I did have a stupid friend who was my friend with benefits for some time."

"Oh." My stomach drops because I wasn't expecting that. Nor the humor in her voice.

At least, she remembers him fondly. That means it's going to be okay with Beacon, right?

Listen, I'm really not my mother, but sometimes I do listen to her because she's lived longer than me. I still hate that she's always warning me.

Like seriously, let me experience life, woman.

Should I have continued with Beacon after her forewarning when I was sixteen?

I'll never know. She's never told us much about the first guy she dated. We learned that they were together for almost five years—without the knowledge of my grandparents. Things ended up bad because he was an addict and abused her.

I don't think she can compare that guy with Beacon. Maybe Beacon and I could've worked in the long run, but I won't go back to the should've, would've, could've word game. Nobody ever wins it.

"So, how did that turn out?" I ask curiously.

"It was good in the beginning. Then it turned messy for a couple of weeks until he pulled his head out from his ass."

"So, you dated him?"

"More like I married the man. We have three kids," she responds.

"Interesting." I try not to gloat, but what she's saying is that it worked out for her.

My parents have been together for a long time. I didn't know they were just fooling around. It adds a layer to the "we were friends first" tale they always tell us.

And if it worked for them, it might work out for me too.

"I'm concerned about what's going to happen after because I know you two are close, and he's not family material. Your dad is concerned because he thinks this might end up bad for other reasons. Either way, I want you to reconsider your plan."

"What reasons?" I ask, curious about his motives.

"Your safety for one. He's famous, and we know how his groupies react when there is some news of him dating."

"If you recall, he handles his private life." I pause and sigh. "Listen, he wouldn't let anything happen to me."

This is not a joke. Beacon has always been watching over me.

"Why are you doing this?"

"Because it feels right, Mom. It always felt right, but we never dared to take that leap."

After a long silence, she says, "Call me if you need me."

"Love you, Mom."

Chapter Twenty-Five

Grace

THIS IS the first time I set foot in this house. Beacon gave me a virtual tour over the phone so I could have an idea about the setting. The walls are a cream color. They remind me of beach sand. The flooring is dark wood. The furniture I bought is already here. It's just a sofa, an oversized couch, and a dining room table and chairs. According to the text Mane sent earlier, my bed is already in my bedroom.

I walk through the place and find boxes in each room. The guys put my luggage in the main room and the packages they brought inside the second room.

Mozart isn't in the house. When I text the guys to ask about him, Mane answers that he's in the studio with them. He's not familiar with the place. They didn't want to leave him alone. Since I don't have to worry about him until later, I shower and dress.

I choose a long black skirt, a halter top, and take out one of the thick parkas to protect me from the cold weather. I pick a pair of knee-high boots and add a little touch, a garter to hold my stockings.

Right as I wrap my purple scarf around my neck, Beacon rings the doorbell. When I open it, my heart skips a few beats. It's not that he looks handsome—he always does. He's holding a red rose and a small box.

"Hey, stranger," I greet him, taking the rose and the box.

"So, are you finally taking me seriously?" he asks, kissing my nose.

I arch an eyebrow, not understanding his question.

"Your dad called. He threatened to kill me in my sleep." He gives me that shrug that says, I just deduced. "Sounds like you told him I'm more than the string of guys you like to send to the hospital because they complimented your shoes."

I glare at him. "It was one time!"

He bursts into laughter. "Sorry, I couldn't help it."

Since he's talking about Dad. I ask, "What's that duty you never talked about?"

He sighs. "Can we have dinner first? I need to woo you, make you fall in love, and then afterward, I'll tell you. I have a feeling that you're going to decimate me."

That answer doesn't make sense for some. To me, it is the piece I need to solve the puzzle. Everything is so clear. Why my parents are so concerned about the outcome. Why Dad's so apprehensive and threatened to replace him. Why Beacon is always too protective.

"Are you kidding me, Beacon Aldridge," I say, glaring at him.

He's right about one thing. I might kick his ass for agreeing with my father. They know I can take care of myself.

Or they never trusted me.

"When did it start?"

He scratches his eyebrow and swallows hard.

"I have a wild guess that it happened when we moved to New

York," I state. "Because there's no other way my father would let me out of his sight if not by entrusting me to one of his security details."

I lift my arms, as in giving up, at not sure who or what. "I can't believe it. All these years, he…" I close my mouth and sigh harshly. I place my index finger on his chest and push him against the wall. "Have I been just a job for you?"

I don't want to sound like an irrational woman, but he knows better.

"You're more than a duty to me," he says, his voice wavering, and I don't think I've ever seen him this frightened. Not even when he's had a gun pointing at him. "It was just—"

"You lied to me." I press my finger against his chest.

"By omission because he requested it. If I told you, he'd fire me. I stepped into the role because I couldn't imagine anyone else watching over you."

That's his excuse?

"I don't know how to feel about this."

I want to punch him, to shake him because he knows better than to lie to me. Like a bucket of cold water, the truth of why he called it off all those years ago hits me.

"So, if you're in charge of my safety, we can't…" I'm so mad at him. How do I even finish that statement?

This strikes me as a betrayal. He knows how I feel about having a bodyguard. He's my best friend. Which means we understand each other. I know him better than anyone. That thought pushes me to analyze what he just said. He can't imagine anyone taking better care of me than him. I believe him.

This is what Beacon does best, taking care of those he loves. He also knows that I want to stand on my own. I am more than capable of protecting myself.

"Is this why you said we are better as friends?"

"I had to choose between you and the job, which sounds cold, but really, it wasn't. I love you too much to let just anyone else be in charge of your safety."

We stare at each other for several beats without saying a word. I'm not sure if either one of us is breathing. His familiar face is filled with worry. I want to run my hand down his cheek. Assure him that everything is going to be okay. But I also want to break his nose.

"I won't apologize or regret what I did," he says without hesitation.

If he's working for my father and he's my bodyguard, there's one rule he can't break, or he'll fire him. We can't be together. My throat clogs. I don't have any trouble understanding emotions. I have difficulty handling them.

"So, what is this?"

"We're dating."

"Until you're back on duty? Then what's going to happen?"

"I don't have all the answers. Don't you think I've been asking myself the same question over and over again?"

I'm not sure where the rage flooding through my veins comes from, but it's so much I can't bottle it up. I increase the volume of my voice when I tell him, "You chose the one thing I never wanted over me."

He's about to speak, but I cut him off. "I don't care what you say, Beacon. That's exactly what you did."

"Your options were to have a bigger, more intrusive team at your service," he offers. "Have your family move to New York with you. Or stay at home and go to the local college. Your dad thought about retiring just to keep an eye on you."

"So, you're blaming Mom and Dad?"

"No. I..." He exhales loudly. His shoulders slump. "I'm not going to get through to you. You're pissed at me because it's easier to take it out on me than your parents. I'll take the heat."

"You didn't let me choose," I yell.

Maybe he's right. I'm unloading everything on him. He's not the only one to blame.

"He wasn't going to give you a choice, Grace," he roars. "You know your father."

"Then what? You took on a job to become his favorite?"

"No. I. Chose. You," he insists.

"No. You can't say that everything was done because you loved me." I exhale, trying to push away the anger. It's impossible. I'm furious. "So, you left me, chose the job, and then slept your way around?"

"Did I sleep with all those women, Grace?" His voice is harsh. The hurt in his eyes pulls my heartstrings. "If you believe it, well, then I have to pat myself on the back because I've done a spectacular job letting people believe I'm a playboy."

"You're not a saint," I retort.

He crosses his arms. "Grace, I think you're trying to place your anger on the wrong person."

"I could take care of myself," I argue.

"I know."

"Then, why would you take on that job?"

"I already explained it to you. If someone was going to watch over you, that should be me. He was going to do it, G. It's his nature. Just like it's my mission to watch after you—always."

"This..." I trail my voice, not knowing how to finish my sentence.

"If you want to kick my ass, just do it."

"No!" I warn him. "Do not throw jokes to soften the blow. I'm so, so...I'm mad at you. At my father. I don't know what to think."

"Please don't leave."

"You'd rather have me here spewing venom and wanting to punch you?"

He nods. "I prepared for it."

"So, you were aware that I'd be upset, and you didn't care?"

"I care. This wasn't an easy choice. It was the best though," he counters. "I understand what I'm facing. It's going to take a lot to convince you that I love you. That you're not a job. To get you to forgive me. I'm prepared for all that."

"Well, then you know it's time to call it a night." I point toward the door.

"You need to eat. We don't have anything in your fridge or pantry."

"I'll figure it out."

He nods, steps closer to me, and I take a few steps back. "Come closer, and you'll end up with a black eye, Aldridge."

"A black eye in exchange for a kiss?" His eyebrow lifts, and he moves an inch toward me. "What do I get for two?"

"Beacon, I'm not kidding."

"I thought we're negotiating."

"Out!"

"I'm leaving only because I know you need space. You're not only upset at me but at *him*." He shows me his phone. "Call, okay. Remember that he tries his best. He's one of the best dads I've ever met."

He leaves, and I stare at the door before I pick up the phone and call my father.

Chapter Twenty-Six

Beacon

LEAVING GRACE SEEMS WRONG.

I have to respect her wishes and give her space. My mind is running at a hundred miles per hour, wondering how I'm going to grovel. I want to get the fuck out of town to burn some energy. I could use an outlet. Checking on the guys is my first option, but I'm not in the mood to be around anyone. Which is why going home to play mind-fuck games with my brothers isn't an option.

When I reach the mansion, I march toward my studio instead. It's better if I avoid everyone. Banging some drums could be the ticket to release the pent-up energy I accumulated since I spoke to Mason. This situation could've been prevented long ago.

I'm concerned about G. She's pretty levelheaded. She also hates when people lie to her. I send her a quick text before entering my place.

Beac: *I'm here if you need me.*

I put my phone away. Knowing Grace, she's already talking to her dad. Instead of going to the studio first, I go to the underground house. I need to change from the stuffy suit I wore—just for her—to a pair of jeans and a T-shirt.

When I hear a commotion, I cock my head toward the game room.

My jaw clenches when I notice my brothers and my band are talking on top of each other while playing pool.

Fuck. So much for being alone.

What the fuck happened to no one is allowed in this place without my authorization?

I need some time for myself.

Get the fuck out of here, people!

Ugh. When the guys learn what happened, they're not going to want to leave. It's not like I'm going to grab a case of scotch and drink myself stupid. I walk by, hoping they don't notice me. If they do, I'll just ignore them.

When I check my cell phone, there's nothing from Grace. Is she still on the phone with her Dad?

Probably. That's a long, overdue conversation. After she hangs up, she's going to have to process everything she learned today. Fuck. I knew this day was coming, but I wish she hadn't kicked me out. I blame *him*.

Who assigns a security team to his daughter without her knowledge?

Mason fucking Bradley, that's who. If he had tried reasoning with her…well, he never gave her a chance. Did he?

Grace likes to find the logic behind everything. They could've compromised. At eighteen, I just did what I believed was best for Grace. I was just a stupid kid in love who would've died for her. Well,

I'll still die for her. Four years ago, I told him he should discuss the subject with her. He responded that I didn't know shit about his daughter.

I fucking know her, asshole!

Because of him, my first date was a bust. I should be wooing my woman with a nice dinner. I'm not helping him get out of the hole he dug for himself. It's every man for himself.

"I thought you had a date," Henry says when he spots me.

"Yeah, well, her father forgot to mention something—eleven years ago."

Mane glances at me. It is Lang who says, "You came out unscathed. I thought she'd at least break a bone or two when she figured it out."

"What is it?" Pierce asks, his gaze narrows.

He's onto me. I shouldn't have offered to look into his family's business. They sell babies to wealthy couples, as in illegally taking them away from their mothers to make some couple happy. According to Seth, they've prevented at least three kidnappings from happening. Placing them in jail and shutting down the operation will stop them forever.

Okay, I don't regret stepping into that. I'm glad I did. Those people need to be stopped. I feel bad because Pierce's mom might end up in jail, but she's getting what she deserves. Seth is now working with the authorities. The Organization hopes to close this case by late March.

"It's a family thing. Unfortunately, he dragged me into it," I answer vaguely. "She's upset at me too. I'll have to grovel my way back into her good graces. It's a matter of just doing all the shit you, Henry, and Hayes had to do to convince your women that you're worth the hassle."

I glance at the three of them and chuckle. "If you could do it, I can."

"Eat something," Henry orders. "You must be starving."

"Fuck!" I mumble and look at the guys. "Would you mind picking up the food they were prepping for us at the restaurant and delivering it to G? If I do it, I might not come back alive."

"Not it," San raises his hand. Mane and Fish join him.

Lang groans. "Fine, I'll take the cat with me. Maybe she'll forgive me if I bring him along."

"Good, I was about to mention that Buster doesn't like felines."

"Well, teach him to like Mozart," I retort. Our cat is a friendly guy. He gets along with almost every dog he's met. The Bradleys have three dogs and two cats. Mozzy loves to hang out with them. "This is his place too."

"He's yours?"

I squat, and in two leaps, Mozart is on my lap. "'Sup, dude. Did you have a nice trip?"

"Meow!" he answers.

I straighten up, look at Pierce, and say, "Yes, he's mine. Let's get this straight. He has the same rights as your *children*. Therefore, let's train them to get along."

Pierce sighs. "This isn't going to be pretty."

"You want me to take him to Grace's house?" Lang asks.

I shake my head. "No, I'll do it when she's less…aggravated."

"Okay, kid, level up with us," Hayes says. "What could you have done so long ago that came back to bite you?"

"Leave it," I order, and usually, my voice comes out pretty chill, but this time I can't pretend that everything is cool.

I regret the tone when my brothers turn to look at me, surprised.

"What? If you tell us you'd have to kill us?" Henry jokes.

"No, that's Vance's line," I point at my brother, trying to redirect the attention. "Isn't it, Vancy?"

He glares at me. I shrug. "Always in a good mood."

"They know what I do," he says with a loud voice and chuckles. "I'm not a deceiving asshole making up shit."

"You sure about that? Maybe you forgot to disclose a thing or two," I say, giving him a fake smile. But what I want to tell him is that he's a fucking liar.

Nobody knows what he does. He's always vague about his military life. When it comes to his former crew, he always avoids discussing them.

His friends are a bunch of mercenaries. He used to work with them. They work for money and not for a cause. I wonder if he knows the dirty jobs his former *partners* do on any given day. Did he agree to work for cartels willingly, or does he believe in his friends blindly?

Unfortunately, Seth dug too deep and found too much crap about his former team. I want to believe that my brother isn't capable of shit like those guys. I'm just not sure if I'm right.

"You know something I don't know, Beacon?" He laughs. "Did your little friend find crap on me? Am I under investigation like Pierce's family?"

We know he's always on alert. He never lets his guard down. Right now, he's on high alert, ready to attack. A few months ago, I'd be happy to show him that I'm not afraid of him. All our brothers walk around him like fragile glass. I don't. But I don't want a throw down. I'm too upset. I might not be able to control myself.

He looks at Mozart. "Cat got your tongue? Little Beacon is afraid of me?"

Mane glances at me and moves his head so slightly. No one can see the movement or understand his gaze. He's telling me, *fucker, don't take the bait.*

He doesn't need to warn me. Vance might be all broody and shit, but he's pretty predictable. He wants a fight. Also, there's a reason he's onto me. I need to retrace all of my steps to figure out where I might've fucked up and given myself away.

"Obviously," I answer. "Not to the point of peeing my pants like Henry, but I'm fucking scared."

"I've never peed my pants," Henry protests.

"A time or two, but we won't tell anyone," Pierce jokes.

Hayes' cell phone buzzes. "The wife wants me back home. I'd love to stay and see how Vance kicks Beacon's ass, but we'll have to reschedule that for another day." He gives our brother a warning glare. "I mean it. Beacon doesn't have your training or your strength. I am not going to spend a day trying to put him back together. Do you understand?"

Fish snorts.

"What's so funny?" Vance is just looking for a fight. "You want to take his place?"

Fish winks at him. "Babe, you're so hot I'd let you walk all over me."

We all laugh because Vance turns white and leaves the game room immediately.

"I'll follow him," Mills says, hugging me. "Call me if you need me. I know you're saying that it doesn't matter, but I'm sure it does. You live for her."

"Thank you."

My brothers leave, except for Pierce.

"What do you know about him?" he asks.

"About whom?"

"Vance," he explains. "You know more, don't you? I'm not going to pressure you to disclose more than you want to, but is everything okay?"

Fish shakes his head.

I sigh. "That's a loaded question."

"Packed, awkward, and classified," Fish mumbles but is loud enough that Pierce can hear it.

"What do you mean? Is he in any trouble? Are we...?"

"Nah." I wave my hand. He has an elite team of secret agents living in town. Nothing could happen while we're here. "I assure you that no one is in danger."

"Because Vance is here?"

"Sure."

"I wish you would trust me," he says, disappointed.

"Maybe it's not a lack of trust, but to ensure your safety," I say. "*Trust me* when I say this place is secure. I don't mean my bunker. I mean the entire town."

"Who are you?" he asks, and I swear this time he's giving me almost the same scared look he gives Vance.

I look at the guys and then at him. "We're musicians."

After he leaves and we're sure that no one else is in the house, Mane says, "Why haven't you told them? Is it because you don't trust Vance or all of them?"

I shake my head vigorously. "I'm not sure."

"Dude, did you seriously almost lick his brother's balls?" San asks Fish, slapping the back of his head.

"He's not my type, and I have a girlfriend. I just deflected the attention," Fish answers looking all innocent. We stare at him because he and his girlfriend have an open relationship. That has never stopped him from fucking other people. "He'd at least have to buy me dinner to let him into my temple."

"Who is buying you dinner?" Lang asks, entering the room.

"No one," Fish answers a little too fast.

"He came onto Vance," San answers.

Lang's jaw sets, but he doesn't say shit. I could ask what that is about, but I don't want to hear that he'd let my brother do shit to him. My brothers are off-limits. He knows it.

"How is Grace?" I ask.

"Raging," he answers. "I'm surprised you're still alive."

"Do you think she's going to leave?"

"Doubtful," he replies. "Unlike you, G thinks before she acts. Is she planning how to kill you? Possibly. Make sure your windows are locked. She might smother you in your sleep."

I comb my fingers through my hair and sigh in relief. He's right. Unlike me, Grace thinks before she acts. She agreed to take care of my nephews. I can see her leaving for the weekend to confront her dad or avoid me though.

I'll just have to wait and see what her next move is before I make mine. Fuck. I hate not being able to do anything to fix what happened between us until she's ready.

Chapter Twenty-Seven

Grace

THE CONVERSATION with Dad leaves me fuming. He never trusted me. I hate that most of his arguments were valid. For a man who can build a computer within hours, hack into government servers, and run an entire operation to stop a trafficking cell, his fears can get the best of him.

My family looks typical from the outside. On the inside, we're all a little damaged. I was five when Mom almost died. She was pregnant with Nathan. It happened too fast. One moment we were all happily preparing for the arrival of my little brother, and the next an ambulance came to take her to the hospital.

While they were wheeling her in the ambulance, my grandparents were taking us into their house where we stayed for a long time. It was less than a month, but still, it felt like years. Seth and I never left each other's sights.

We love our grandfathers, but no matter what they said or did to keep us entertained, we were afraid to lose Mom. I still remember Grandpa Chris and Grandpa Gabe assuring us that they were fine. I also remember listening to the adult conversations where they said they had no idea if Mom would make it this time. I learned then that she was sick when I was born too.

My grandparents, uncles, aunts, and Beacon's family tried their best to care for us. We never complained. But everything was so strange. We went from having a house, a mom, and a dad to going from one home to another without understanding what was happening. We only knew that my parents were gone. I behaved because what if they got tired of taking care of Seth and me?

I cried every night because I thought I had lost my parents just like Beacon did—or worse, what if they were dead?

Mom came back with a tiny baby who I adored. I had my parents back, but it was hard to go to sleep. I would stay up all night watching them, making sure they wouldn't leave. They sent me to therapy to help with the trauma. I didn't lose them, but it felt like a loss.

When Dad said, "I can't just do nothing, Grace. I can't lose you. Do you know how many times I've been close to losing my family? Several. I lost one kid. Almost lost you and Nathan. I can't take any chances."

My parents lost their first child, James, before he was born. He'd be thirty-five this year.

I was nine when I ended up in the ICU at the local children's hospital due to diabetic ketoacidosis. You'd think that because Mom has type 1 diabetes too, they would've caught it in time. It wasn't their fault. I have a tendency to keep any pain or struggles to myself. I never told them I wasn't feeling well. It's part of not upsetting my parents, who already had dealt with a lot.

Needless to say, they figured out something was wrong with me when they found me lying on the floor, pale and unresponsive. It'll be unreasonable and maybe even selfish of me to invalidate his fears. It's true, it'd kill him, losing one of us. That doesn't make him right, either. He should've handled this situation differently.

"You'll understand when you have your own children," he said.

"Maybe you'll never find out," I answered and hung up the phone.

I stare at the food that Lang brought. I have to eat, but I'm not hungry. While I'm debating, my phone rings. It's Mom.

Instead of greeting her, I say, "You knew?" with an accusatory voice.

She sighs.

"Of course, you did." I groan. "I can't believe you sided with him. Neither one of you trust me enough to let me be on my own."

"It's not like that, Grace," she argues.

But it is like that.

"I feel like all the concessions were just a farce. Seth doesn't have a bodyguard. Nathan doesn't have one either. But I do because I'm the girl. A fragile one for that matter."

"No, you're our little miracle, Grace," she says. "After James, we didn't know if I'd be able to have children. You gave us hope. Your dad has tried his best to include you in everything. We hated the idea of letting you go to college so young."

"Instead, he sent me with bodyguards. Dad used my best friend as my shield," I snap. "He could've at least told me. He didn't trust me."

"He wanted it to feel normal. Beacon's idea of having your friends watch over you sounded good at the time," she continued. "I hate when your dad uses you as bait. It kills me knowing that either one of my children is part of some dangerous mission. He doesn't have an issue with that. That's how his brain works, Grace. Mason trusts you enough to let you do it. He knows you're capable, just like him."

"That doesn't make sense. It is like you're telling me that he's afraid of me being in the real world."

"That's where people get hurt the most," she answers.

"Don't justify his actions."

"I'm not invalidating either one of you. You are right. He should've trusted you. I just want to make sure that you know that this is his way of saying you're our little girl, and we can't lose you."

We're both quiet for a long time. "This should be the part of the conversation where you tell me you know someone who had a big fight with her parents and regretted not speaking to them in years."

"You know that I do." She sighs. "Whatever I say might not be enough. Just remember that you'll regret all the time you missed being around your family."

"Why would you say that?"

"What you told him when you hung up the phone." Her voice is loud. "You're cutting ties with us?"

"Ugh…No, I don't even know if I'm going to have children. I just need time," I protest, quite sure that Dad told her what I said, and she blew it out of proportion. "I know your family tends to be a bit dramatic. I'm more practical, like Dad, in that regard."

Grandpa Gabe is an actor. I swear some of my cousins crank up the drama so high they are a walking soap opera.

"He's concerned."

"Tell him," I pause because I can't say anything to make him feel better when I'm still so mad, "that I need time to cool down."

"I love you, Gracie."

"Love you too, Mom."

MY OPTIONS ARE to stay and brood in a strange house or go to my friends' place.

Grace: *Where are you?*
Mane: *At Beac's*
Grace: *Ugh. Why not at your place?*
Mane: *Because we don't have a cool game room or food at our place. Come over.*
Grace: *I'd rather not.*
Mane: *Are you going to start making things weird for us? Don't be a Lang.*

I laugh when I read the text. He's right. Lang is the dramatic one of us.

Grace: *Fine. I'm on my way.*

It's not like I have many places to go to at this time of the day in this small town.

I could gather the Aldridge wives. They are surprisingly good listeners, except they can't listen to what I have to say.

So, my father had a bodyguard babysitting me for eleven years. By the way, your brother-in-law is a secret agent for... Nope, I can't say that.

I can be a mature adult. Things won't be awkward. I change my clothes before I make my way to the Aldridge place. The evening is chilly, slightly dark, and quiet. There are a few stores still open. Unfortunately, the bookstore is closed. I could use a book or two.

They have old editions of books, handmade jewelry, and some souvenirs. Grandpa Bradley loves when I send him something from wherever I visit. I'm staring at the window of the bookstore when I feel Beacon's presence. I should've known he'd come to find me.

"Hey, gorgeous," he greets me when he's just a few steps away from me.

I turn to look at him.

Hey... I don't know what to call him. *Idiot, Beac, gorgeous man?*

I recognize that I feel so much better just by being in his presence. His devastatingly handsome face is all I need to relax after the conversation with Dad.

It's hard to admit how much I need him.

His green eyes are bright yet worried. He opens his arms. The corners of his lips stretch toward the sky. I adore that smile. It's one of my favorites. This is his "everything will be all right" smile. And you know what, he ensures that things work out for me. It's crazy that this enrages me a little. I'm sure it doesn't make sense that I love so many things about him—and I hate them too. The one thing that upsets me the most is that I can't be mad at him for long.

"I hate you," I mumble, walking into his warm embrace.

"I know," he answers, holding me tight.

"This doesn't mean I'm not upset," I continue, but I break down in seconds.

It's so hard not to cry. The emotions inside me are too strong to ignore. I shed angry tears, sad tears, even a few happy tears. Thinking about the eleven years of lies infuriates me. What enrages me the most is that I can't just be emotional and say fuck you to Dad and Beacon. I wish…I don't even know what I want.

"Dad should've trusted me," I say between sobs.

"Let's go to my place," he offers. "Did you eat?"

"Not yet."

He grunts. "G, you know what can happen if you skip a meal."

I want to yell at him for reminding me that my body is fragile. *When can it be my turn to be irrational and not care about the consequences?*

Chapter Twenty-Eight

Grace

HOLDING HANDS, we walk to the restaurant one more time, where the manager is outside waiting for us with a takeout bag. When we arrive at Beacon's place, I realize that it's empty.

"Where is everyone?"

"The guys left to give us space."

I want to argue that I wanted to be with them, but I don't. The truth is that I just need Beacon right now. We eat in silence. Once we finish, we go to the studio. The box with the new cello is already there, waiting to be opened, but I'm not ready for it.

"I wish you had a gym."

"We do," he says. "Who do you want to punch first, *him* or me?"

I snort as I take a seat on the stool and caress the piano's keys. "I wanted him to yell at me the way he does at Nathan when they're fighting about my brother's indecisions. The way he does at you when you get in his face and defy him."

Beacon raises an eyebrow. "He didn't?"

"Nope. He used that firm voice I hate. The worst part is he's right, even when he's wrong. He can't help himself because what if he loses me? I remember how sad he was when Mom and Nathan were still delicate after my brother was born. He wouldn't move from the hospital when I ended up in the ICU."

I pause and look at Beacon. "Why do I have to be so rational?"

"It's part of your beauty."

I snort. "That's such a lie."

"No. It's refreshing to be with someone who makes sense in a world where everything is chaos." He waves his hands fast. "There's this crazy cyclone in my mind all the time. When you're around, you're the anchor who grounds me. My grandparents never understood why I could be so calm when you were nearby."

"I like your chaos." I curl my index finger, calling him to me, and pat the empty space beside me. "It creates some of the best songs in the world."

He smiles, taking a seat right next to me. "You're the only one who understands it."

"Sometimes, you only need one person to appreciate you for who you really are, Beac," I say, resting my head on his shoulder.

When I say that, I feel like there's a deeper meaning within those words. A lot more emotions are involved. Emotions I don't want to analyze because what if I can't handle them?

I understand why he did it, but can I trust him?

Who am I supposed to trust?

My best friend, my bodyguard, or the guy who swears he's been in love with me for years.

Head exploding in five, four, three—

"I'm not sure when I'll get past this. I should go back home."

"You're giving up on us already?" The tone in his voice breaks my heart. "At least, give me a fair trial."

"It'd be best if we—"

He huffs. "Too many emotions?" He shakes his head. "We'll deal with them together. You're not doing this alone. I'm not leaving you hanging. Sometimes I think that I'm responsible for that part of your personality. The one that would rather not deal with feelings."

"I kept telling myself that what I felt for you was only a crush," I mumble. Maybe I should confess to him it was more than a crush. "Eventually, I got over it."

I think?

"It feels like eleven years of lies that we told to each other, to ourselves, and what am I supposed to do now? Trust you blindly?" I slam my hands on the piano, closing my eyes and confessing, "I loved you so much, and you broke my heart."

He exhales harshly at the same time that I gasp in surprise. This is the first time I admit openly that I was in love with him. That it hurt when he called it off.

"I had no idea," he says, standing up from his seat. He walks back and forth. "If I had known—but you wouldn't have admitted it, would you?"

"What does that even mean?" I argue.

"You never tell people how you feel, Grace!" His voice echoes through the studio. "You didn't stop me."

"Because what if what happened to Mom and her first love happened to us? They were best friends…" I stop for a second, trying to remember if she ever told me about her relationship with that guy. She didn't. I don't even know his name. "I think."

He groans. "Of course, it was your mom and her fables."

I could argue about Mom, but the part that's making me furious is that he said I never tell people how I feel. "Are you calling me frigid? Emotionless? What is it that you implied by I never tell people how I feel?"

I'm so mad. I stand up and walk toward him. My chin tilts up, and I dare him to tell me the truth. "Is that what you think about me? That I'm devoid of emotions?"

The way his eyes transform takes my breath away. They darken with anger and need. He lifts me by the waist, pushes me against the wall, and presses his body against mine. Our noses almost touch. I can feel his shallow breath caressing my face.

"No, you confine all your feelings inside your music," he says, nipping my ear. "I know your soul, your heart. I feel your music—every note. That's the only way you handle them. This mess is my fault, but you are responsible too. If you had told me…"

I shiver as his teeth pull my earlobe gently. "There's no point in discussing the shit that went wrong between us. It's killing me to know that I broke your heart. If it makes you feel any better, I broke mine too."

Who do we blame for this?

My father, the circumstances, or our ages. Maybe we were too young, inexperienced, and afraid.

We're usually pretty daring.

He's bold, courageous, and spirited.

I'm not as audacious as him, though. He's one of the few crazy people I know who'd walk toward open fire to catch the bad guys. Our biggest fear is to lose each other.

"What now?"

"Don't leave," he begs me. "I need this time. You want to know why I was hammered for three days? I thought you had found the guy, and that was it. I had lost you forever."

He wouldn't lose me. It takes me a second to realize what he's saying. He's not afraid of losing me as a friend. My heart is confused. I'm sad because he spent two days mourning a loss. Upset because he could've avoided it if we had talked—but it's not that simple, is it?

"So, what's going to happen when your sabbatical is over? When you have to go back to your fans? When I go back to my life?"

"I'll quit everything that comes between us," he assures me, slanting his mouth on top of mine, running his tongue along the seam, parting my lips. A spark ignites, starting a wildfire burning through us while we kiss deeply, passionately.

"You are my life. Nothing else matters to me but you. Let me show you, Grace. Let me make up for what I did."

He kisses the center of my chest. "I'll gather all the shattered pieces and put them together. I promise never to break it again."

Forgiveness is so complicated. I don't think it's going to happen instantly. I don't even know who I have to forgive—or to blame. There's my father, Beacon, the circumstances, and I'm the cause of my own pain.

"I choose to stay and to grow," I answer. "To learn from the circumstances that kept us apart while our hearts heal. Also, I'm staying because I made a commitment to Leyla and your brothers."

"Thank you for never giving up on me, even when I always fuck up."

My heart hurts so much because this man always thinks that everything is his fault.

Chapter Twenty-Nine

Grace

"WHY DO YOU DO THAT?"

"Apologize?" he says.

I glare at him. He's infuriating when he pretends to be dense.

"I—"

Before he continues talking, we get interrupted by Dad's ringtone. I silence it and focus my attention back on Beacon. It rings again.

"You should take that."

"He can wait."

Beacon laughs. "Yeah, right. If you don't answer now, he's going to call me. If I ignore him, he'll send whoever is closest to this location—or fly to us."

I sigh heavily because even when he's right, it irritates me that Dad can't just give me space. "Two hours isn't enough time," I say instead of greeting him.

"To an extent it is," he argues. "There have been times when I only have thirty seconds to dismantle a bomb or an entire place, city, or country could disappear. If I wait, thousands or millions of people could die."

"Drama doesn't look good on you, sir,"

"The point is," he continues, "that I understand your anger, but you never asked me about my motives."

"You explained everything," I remind him.

"No, I told you I couldn't afford to lose you. Then, you began to give me all the reasons why you loathe me. You think I'm misguided and overprotective, yes?"

"Seriously, Dad, you're ready to invalidate my feelings and tell me that I should be thankful for your services."

"You're putting words in my mouth, Grace Aiko!"

"Fine. Enlighten me, father."

"It's a well-known fact that you're Gabe and Chris' granddaughter. We always try to ensure that you guys live a normal life, but there are some limits," he explains. I stay quiet. "Most of your cousins have security—unless they are well trained."

"Is that why you trained us? So that we could protect ourselves?"

"In part. It wasn't the original idea, but once everyone was learning, we all thought, what if..." Dad confirms. "You left home at sixteen, Grace. You know what can happen to a single woman on campus. You've witnessed it. Put yourself in my place. My underage daughter was heading to New York—by herself. That's not everything, though. I've been careful since I started this company, but my entire family is in danger if someone ever figures out my real identity. I just added a layer to what I taught you."

"You used Beacon to do it. My best friend."

"He volunteered," he presses. "He came up with the idea."

"Dad, I need time to work this through," I say with a calm voice.

"Listen, I understand your 'misguided ways.' They make sense even when I don't like it. You should've talked to me about all of this eleven years ago. We could've agreed, worked this out together. Now tell me, what's going to happen in a year when Beacon's sabbatical is over. Let's not go that far. Are you already setting up a team to babysit me without telling me? Just because you think I can't take care of myself?"

Dad growls. "They don't watch over you *all* the time."

"That doesn't answer my question."

"If I feel like you need a bodyguard, I'll contact you first, like we do with Too Far from Grace. You'll get to choose your team," he compromises.

I almost laugh if it wasn't because I realize something. "So, all this time Beacon has been setting the security for me, not him. It's not about his groupies but keeping me safe."

Beacon flinches and nods.

"You two are exasperating," I screech, staring at Beacon while I speak to Dad. "From now on, I have a say about my security. I'll make the decisions. You two are allowed to make suggestions. Beacon is no longer my bodyguard. Do we understand each other?"

"I'm sorry," Dad says.

"Sorry because you won't allow it or sorry for undermining me?"

"For not including you when I made the decision," he says. "For not trusting you at the time. I think you're capable, but I also want to protect you. At the end of the day, you're the three-pound baby girl I met twenty-eight years ago. The same I swore to protect."

"Dad." I sigh because his low, broken voice squeezes my heart and almost makes me cry.

"Why don't we talk next week? I'll come to visit you," he suggests.

"That's a good idea. Love you, Dad."

"Love you, too, Gracie."

I put my phone away and focus my attention on Beacon. Today I'm re-writing history. Putting together clues of a puzzle I had no idea existed. I don't even know if I want to finish it. "Were your groupies ever dangerous?"

"They are," Beacon says, shrugging. "If my house wasn't under your name, I'm sure they'd be trying to break in and steal my stuff. It happened to Fish's LA home. I have two layers of security. The first stops anyone who could get close to you, and the second is for my groupies. When the time comes, I can explain to you how everything works so you can take over if that's what you choose."

"What's the alternative?"

"We make the decisions as a team."

Tonight, I don't want to go back to an empty house. I also don't want to be alone. If I stay, he might want to continue this discussion. All I want is to head to his bed, snuggle next to him, and forget that I lost eleven years of Beacon because my father couldn't trust me.

"As I said, I need time," I repeat. "I'm angry because of what happened and also because I have no idea where to put that anger. Who can I blame when everyone has a logical answer?"

I can't fix my issues because really, what's there to fix? I have to get over it and make sure these men understand that I can take care of myself. It's hot that Beacon is always watching over me, but not when my dad is paying him to do that.

"I'm sorry, G. I'll do anything to make this better."

"You need to stop blaming yourself for everything." I bring back our earlier conversation. "This was my father's fault, and he used you as a pawn."

"True, but I could've stopped it."

"I don't understand why you didn't tell him, 'Hey, she's going to be pissed. You might want to talk to her.'"

He shrugs.

"When?"

"When what?" he asks.

"Stop being obtuse. When did you tell Dad to tell me about it?"

"Please, don't drag me into this," he pleads. "I swear I'll make it up to you."

"Ten years? Five years? Yesterday?"

He chuckles. "I don't recall. You know the guy. He likes to think that he knows best."

"You know how you can make it up to me?"

He lifts an eyebrow, crosses his arms, and says, "As long as it doesn't involve my family, I'll do anything."

"Ha! You have to talk to your brothers about what happened when you were young. I think it's time to erase that guilt."

"Let it go, G."

"It wasn't your fault that the paparazzi caught your father. Maybe we should start digging more into your parents' pasts to figure out what happened. It might give us an answer to why you guys are here—it could help you."

"I don't need help."

"You blame yourself for all the shit that happens in the world because you think you're the one that caused the situation your father created. It might tear down the wall between you and your brothers. A wall that *you* built."

"Now you're analyzing me," he says, annoyed, and looks at the time. "Can we go to bed?"

"Promise me you're going to work on that," I press.

"If I do, can we go to bed?"

"I'm still upset at you."

"Do you still hate me?

"I could never hate you, Beac."

He smiles and steps forward until our feet almost touch. "I'm sorry. You've no idea how much I wanted to tell you, but I couldn't. I was afraid he'd fire me, and I can't trust you to anyone else."

"You're a little possessive, aren't you, Mr. Aldridge?"

"You've no fucking idea," he says, slanting his mouth on mine.

Chapter Thirty

Beacon

THERE'S a theory among the Aldridges: Once you give your heart, you never claim it back. It's true. Grace and I are living proof. That makes me want to research what is wrong with the family that we can't stay with the one person we love forever.

My grandfather left my grandmother in Baker's Creek and moved to New York without giving her a second glance. It seems that we always do something that makes our true loves stay away.

Who did my father love and leave? I doubt it was my mom.

If anything, it makes me wonder if William was trying to teach us a lesson by shoving us into one place, like getting back to the one you love or recognizing you are in love. Maybe he was trying to get his family together. But why now and not when he was alive?

Dad grew up in this town. Someone in Baker's Creek might know about his past and who he left behind. They're pretty vocal about what they know, but no one has mentioned Dad's past. With Grace here, we might be able to figure out more.

Will figuring out his past give me any answers about my present and maybe my future?

I look at Grace, still sleeping. She's my destiny. Everything else doesn't matter as much, except I don't want to make my father's mistakes.

I'm so fucking lucky because she's going to give me a chance. I know she's upset, and I have to grovel my way into her good graces. Still, I'm happy about having her close. And how fortunate I am that she loved me once. It shouldn't be hard to find out where she buried those feelings and make her fall harder.

Why didn't I know you loved me? I think, kissing the top of her head and pressing her closer to me.

This woman is good at hiding her emotions. She's a great poker player, not that anyone lets her play. She counts cards. Her quirks and tells remind me that she has to have breakfast. I smile like a fool, happy that this time I can serve her breakfast in bed. We can follow it with fooling around in bed.

Fuck, I'd give up everything just to get this, Grace, in my bed every morning.

Before I go to the kitchen to prepare some food, I kiss her temple and put on a shirt. Maybe Vance prepared something more than instant oatmeal. If he didn't, I'll just cook for Grace and me.

"Morning," Leyla greets me. "Just the man we were expecting."

I frown. "There's a family meeting I didn't know about?"

"It's your turn to prepare breakfast," she declares, pointing toward the chore board.

"No, I switched with Vance," I remind her. "Did he skip town because one of my friends came onto him?"

Mills chuckles and shakes his head. "He went to Portland. There's some emergency he didn't tell us about."

"Ugh," I grumble and open the refrigerator. I grab mushrooms, spinach, and onions to prepare a frittata. That's the easiest, fastest thing to do. I chop the ingredients, beat the eggs, and pour the mixture into the skillet. Thankfully, our oven has a feature that sets the temperature to however we want, no need to pre-heat.

Once I set that, I go to the pantry to extract two boxes of muffin mix. If it weren't because I want to serve Grace a delicious breakfast, I would just take a box of cereal, hand them a gallon of milk and wish them luck.

Fucking Vance. He better have a good explanation.

"He's making muffins?" Pierce, who is carrying Carter, asks, kissing Leyla's forehead. "Can we keep him forever? I promise to feed him and clean after him."

"Ha! Your wife would keep me because I know how to feed you better than you can feed yourself."

I'm in the middle of pouring the batter when my phone starts to ring. I ignore whoever is calling, but they aren't letting this go.

Pierce reaches inside my pocket to grab it.

"Don't molest me."

"You're an idiot," he says, glaring at me. "Beacon's phone."

"He's busy at the moment. May I take a message?"

I turn to look at him, and he frowns. "I'll let him know."

"Who was it?" I ask after he hangs up.

"Janelle Fitzpatrick," he stares at the phone. "Her ghostwriter is scheduled to start next month, and you haven't responded to her calls."

"Fuck!"

"Language," Mills calls from the other room.

"So, your mom is writing a tell-all?" Pierce asks.

"My people haven't been able to confirm that," I explain to him.

"I'll have my lawyer work on that," Henry, who enters the kitchen, says, winking at me and looking at Pierce. "Dude, fix that."

Pierce flips him the finger. "What do you want me to do, Beacon?

Should I contact your PR, agent, manager, or can I just sue her because I didn't like her effing tone?"

"Or you can set the record straight and give your version, Beac," Grace says as she enters the kitchen. "Morning, everyone."

"She forgave him too fast," Henry complains. "And what did your father forget to tell you that got him in the doghouse?"

"As if she had just let it go," I say, walking toward her and giving her a peck on the lips. "She's going to make me work for it. I'm still in the doghouse."

I go back to the mixer to continue pouring the ingredients.

"You were saying something about setting the record straight," Pierce cuts into the conversation. "What would that entail, and how would it help?"

"He can easily post a picture of him and his grandfather on social media, write something touching about missing him, how he and his wife raised him as his own after his mother abandoned him," Grace explains something her aunt—my PR—has suggested a few times. "That tells the world the real story in only a few lines."

"I don't want the attention." I put the muffin tray in the oven and pour the rest of the batter into the second one.

Everyone laughs.

"Really, you don't like attention?" Mills says, mockingly. "I can see that since you keep to yourself."

"Can we ever get through a conversation without a thousand jokes?" Pierce asks, looking at me. "What does she want?"

"I think she's trying to have some sort of comeback. The easiest way is to say I'm her son and have us perform together. She's tried that already. I refuse to do it. According to my sources, she's broke. I could just give her Grandpa's money, but Grandma made me promise I wouldn't give her anything. Her last wishes were that I preserve his legacy."

"He hates the attention," G sets the record straight. "Which is why he doesn't want to add that to his social media."

"She wants to cash in on her relationship to him," Pierce concludes. "When did this start?"

"The tell-all? When Dad died."

"She wants William's money?" Henry's voice booms inside the kitchen.

"If she does, it'd be just my cut," I explain. "She might want part of it. I haven't spoken to her."

"Is that even possible?" Henry questions.

"Dude, my mom wanted a cut too," Pierce confesses, and we all look at him. "I guess she felt entitled to some of it because she had to deal with him. It's irrelevant. She's not getting anything from us."

"Can we forget about my mother?"

"We have to stop her." Henry looks at everyone. "You can't just give her money to her shut up. If you do it once, she'll never stop."

"Who are we giving money to?" Hayes enters the kitchen. "Good, I thought no one was going to make breakfast today."

"Beacon's mom is blackmailing him."

"She is?"

"No, yes…I don't know," I say, exasperated because I swear, they just made a bigger mess out of this.

I explain to Hayes what's happening with my mother while I check on the food. Henry and Mills start setting the table. Arden helps them.

"Sometimes I wonder if William had a type. When I hear about our mothers, I confirm it," Pierce says. "He liked high-maintenance women."

"His mom was not the love of his life," Henry concludes.

Dad left a letter to each one of us. Some of us haven't received them yet, and the ones who have are waiting until we all have them in our hands. However, Leyla received one when she and Pierce separated.

The letter had a hint that he had lost the love of his life. They are all trying to figure out which one of the six women he was with was it. On the other hand, I will be doing some research of my own because I'm sure he had someone before those six women, and that's the love of his life.

Maybe it's a mystery woman from Happy Springs, the town next door. It could be his high school sweetheart.

"I agree with Henry," Hayes says. "If you give her money once, she'll keep coming back. You should take away that power by doing what Grace suggests. It's up to you, though."

"It might bring a lot of publicity to you and the town," I warn them. "It'll be just like what happened when the paparazzi first discovered me."

"We can take her."

"Let me figure out how to handle her."

Chapter Thirty-One

Beacon

BREAKFAST IS uneventful after we agreed that I'm going to look into how to stop Mom from creating a three-ring circus. I live a private life. Maybe it doesn't seem like it, but no one knows the real me. I doubt she understands that. The last time I saw her was when Grandma died.

Grace helps me clean up the kitchen—which happened to be Vance's chore. Afterward, she leaves with Leyla and Sophia. They're spending the day in Portland. I, on the other hand, volunteer to clean the barn. It's not my favorite chore, but the horses are cool. Ally, the alpaca is a hoot. She likes it when I take her out for walks around town.

"What's the plan for today?" Mane asks.

"Learn how to crochet?" San asks.

I glare at him and turn on the hose.

"Why the fuck are we here?" Fish protests.

I swear, I want to direct the stream of water toward him, but I don't because if any of the animals escape, Pierce will kill me.

"He brought us to clean his shit," San jokes while cleaning Poppy's stall.

"Shut up. You volunteered to help," I remind him. "You could be sleeping, like Sir Byron Alasdair Langdon."

San bursts into laughter. "I swear he has a pompous-ass name. His family hated him before birth."

"Someone should tell him it's past noon," I suggest.

"He was up all night. One of his bands is having *issues*," Fish says, drawing air quotes. "I told him not to start a boy band. Those kids think it's all just looking pretty and learning cheesy choreographies."

"Divas!" San grunts.

"Talking about divas, why is your brother approaching us like he's about to attack?" Mane tilts his head.

I turn my head to where his attention is focused and spot Vance. He fucking owes me.

"You left me hanging, asshole!"

Vance's eyes have a shade of green I don't see often. There's a huge fucking storm brewing inside. I swear they are almost black. He's charging toward me, arms by his sides, and hands fisted.

"Stop!" I warn him.

"Nah, I want to see how he hands you your ass," San jokes.

"You know how this is going to end." Mane sighs.

"With my fist in Vance's face?" I mumble under my breath.

"Yes. Beac's going to lose his shit, and Vance will end up in the hospital, and everyone will find out he's not *just a musician*," Mane concludes.

My body tenses when he gets in close proximity to me.

"I'm going to fuck up your pretty face," Vance warns me.

"Promise?" Fish jokes, putting himself between us. "I like it rough, baby."

"Listen, I don't want to fight with you," I say calmly.

"Did you forget to save him a muffin and that's why he's upset?" Mane asks jokingly, standing right beside me.

"You need your friends to defend you?"

I shrug. "They're more likely trying to protect you. You want a go, try it. Just know that once you throw the first punch, I'll reciprocate and won't stop."

Fish nods. "It's hard to stop him once he throws the first jab. I like you, but I wouldn't stop him. Grace is the only one who can do it."

Vance points at me. "How the fuck did your girlfriend get a password and fingerprint access to my security room?"

San rolls his eyes. Mane flinches. They caught us. I don't react, but fuck! I forgot about the CCTV. He could see everything that happened yesterday.

"What?" I feign ignorance.

"Your girlfriend," he repeats, pulling a piece of tape out of his pocket. Then he shows me a second one. "I have her fingerprint from the scanner. The second is from a glass of water she drank last night. She's the last person who opened the security room."

Then he pulls out a USB. "Who the fuck are you?"

"The Beacon," Fish jokes.

"The recording inside the security room has audio too." He throws the USB to the ground.

"Aw, Beacon's first sex tape," Fish continues. If he's hoping to distract either one of us, he's failing miserably.

"I thought you trusted me. Who the fuck are you? What organization do you work for? Most importantly, I'm telling Henry. You're using his hotels to feed a terrorist organization."

San huffs. "That's rich coming from you."

Vance's scowl is now directed to him. "What the fuck does that mean?"

"San, shut up," I warn him.

"No, I need to know because, since yesterday, you've been insinuating that I'm disloyal to the family." He points at the USB on the ground. "I have proof that it's the other way around."

"Your fucking buddies currently work for a Mexican cartel. A year ago, you were in the Indian Ocean escorting a cargo ship with dozens of kidnapped women," Fish growls at him.

Vance steps closer, grabs me by the front of my jacket, and pulls me closer to him. We're eye to eye. He's about to lose his shit. I could easily knock him with my forehead and then strike him in the jaw. I wait. Whatever happens between us, I'm not going to be the one swinging the first punch.

"Did you run a fucking background check on me?" His raging voice booms through the barn.

"Yes, I did, asshole. The Organization has the pesky tendency to run a background check when they are interested in an asset. We invited you to join us," I respond. "It was for the best that you refused. What we learned is alarming. So far, I've given you the benefit of the doubt."

"Join you?"

He looks at each one of us and releases me. "I fucking knew there's something wrong about you. You don't look like fucking musicians."

"We are the best fucking musicians in the world," Fisher corrects him. "I could rock your world if you wanted me to—"

"Fish, are you fucking serious?" Mane chides him.

"What can I say? I like my men flustered." He shrugs.

Vance takes this moment to connect his fist to my jaw. I squat, extend my leg, gyrate my body, and kick him in the legs. He loses his balance and falls on the ground. I pin him and threaten him. "That's the first and only time I let you hit me."

"Look at you, kicking the ass of our scary brother." I hear Mills speak. When I turn toward the door, he's not alone. Pierce and Henry are with him.

"This is where we say goodbye," Mane says, walking toward the door. "Call if they don't ground you. If they do, see you in a couple of weeks."

"Let me go," Vance warns me.

"No, you wanted to play rough. We're playing rough," I say.

"I just want a fucking explanation about what I saw and heard. You have to come clean to Henry. The equipment will be returned next week. Who are you mixed up with?"

"What equipment?" Henry asks.

Pierce grins, walking toward us. "So, we finally get to see you practicing some of your ninja moves. You ready to tell us what the fuck it is that you do when you're not playing music?"

"He'd have to kill us," Mills jokes.

I glare at him. "You want to take his place?"

"Dude, I like you more when you play buffoon." Mills lifts his hands.

"Release me," Vance orders.

"Not until you calm the fuck down. I can be here all day."

"What equipment?" Henry asks again, picking up the USB.

"He sold—"

"Shut up, Vance."

"Beacon." Pierce says my name with authority. "I've been cool about your secrets, but your time is up."

Chapter Thirty-Two

Beacon

TRUST BEGINS with giving my brothers a warning before I tell them.

"You can't tell anyone about this. You put me and yourselves in danger," I forewarn them, looking at each one of my brothers.

"Why is Beacon staring at you with a murderous glare?" Hayes says when he enters the living room where everyone is sitting, except me.

"He's explaining to us why he had Vance pinned to the ground."

Hayes raises an eyebrow. Mills brings him up to date. My brother nods and looks at Vance and then me.

"That's a nice change of pace," Hayes says, taking a seat. "So, after this you're killing us?"

"It's not about killing anyone for knowing the truth. This is a serious matter. I'm trusting you to keep my secret."

"I can't promise I won't kill you," Vance warns me.

"You try to hit me, and I won't stop this time."

His nostrils flare, but he says, "Just don't give me a reason."

"H-I-B was formed long ago. It has a few subdivisions, and I work for one of them…"

They listen without interruptions. When I finish, Henry chuckles. "You work for them."

I nod and grin. His bodyguards are part of H-I-B. Even though he pays them, since they arrived in Baker's Creek, they've been working for me in a capacity.

"Do I at least get a family discount?" he asks.

I snort. "No."

"I don't care who they are. They can't use our equipment for their gain," Vance protests.

"How so?" Henry asks. "I am confused about that part. Why didn't I know it was a H-I-B product?"

"Listen, I can strip our credentials from it," I say, avoiding Henry's question.

Henry shakes his head. "If you need them, I guess they can stay. So, you can take this one down?"

"Focus, Henry," Vance insists.

"He's starstruck," Pierce tells him. "His baby brother can take you down. Let's remember he's scared shitless of you."

"Bear in mind that this has to stay between us," I remind them.

"Are you telling the wives?" Hayes asks.

I stare at them and shrug. "I trust them, but the less they know, the better for everyone."

"The equipment," Vance insists. "I'm not comfortable having other people accessing it."

"Because then you can't access it for your people?" Henry is the one who asks. "Listen, I've been speculating why we have the new set up. It's great, but do I really need that much for my hotel? I swear I thought you were handling some operations from there."

"I'm not," Vance growls. "I told you, once I quit, that was it. We set up everything because the company who sold us that shit recommended it. It sounded like a good idea at the time."

"It is a good idea. Even if we can't use it, you get to see what's happening all over the world," I remind him. "Well, within the premises of the hotels. That's something that as the chief of security you should be proud of doing."

Henry points at me. "Are you running an operation from there?"

"It's an asset, but there's nothing running from there," I explain. "I can take it down if you prefer."

"No. As long as you're using it to help, I'm cool with it. I trust you," he says, and all of us stare at him.

I'm not sure what confuses me the most. His cool demeanor or the fact that he said, "I trust you." Two days ago he was chiding me because I asked to borrow one of his cars—I'm not responsible enough to drive them.

"What?" he asks. "I can be reasonable. As I said, I know the company. They're the best in the business. Now, tell me what you know about Vance."

I scratch the back of my neck and go to my small office where I have a copy of his file. Instead of handing it to Henry, I give it to Vance.

"The guys you work with aren't particular about the cases they take," I state, staring at him. "Who scores the jobs?"

He grins. "Classified."

"Vance, this is serious," I say. "Do you have any idea who you worked for?"

He opens the folder and starts scanning the documents inside. He frowns and shakes his head. "This is wrong."

"I didn't make up that shit," I argue, pointing at the folder. "You can read the report. What did you use to do for them?"

"Once they secured the contract, I'd gather the necessary information to do the job. I scouted the places, created a plan, and made sure it was executed properly."

He was the brains. How are they handling the new contracts without having him in charge?

"You planned the missions, but you didn't know who you were helping."

He nods, cringing as he continues reading the file.

"Are you a hockey player, Mills?" Pierce questions.

He nods and looks at me. "So, this is the shit you couldn't tell me."

"Yeah."

Vance stands up, fans the folder, and says, "This is bullshit. I'm going to prove you wrong."

He storms out of my place.

"Do you think he's going to leave?" Henry stares at the empty space, scared.

I nod because if it was me, I would be figuring out a way to reach my people and demand an explanation.

"Should we stop him?"

"On it," I say, texting the guys. They can intercept him if he tries to leave.

Since I used The Organization's server and used my team's chat, Grace responds.

Grace: *What happened?*

Beac: *I'll tell you when you're back.*

Mane: *They caught him.*

Fucking, Mane. Does he have to disclose everything all the time?

Grace: *Who caught who?*

Fisher: *Vance has a recording from the security room—of the two of you. I didn't know you like it so dirty, Lady G.*

Grace: *Fuck off, Fish.*

Fisher: *It's okay, everyone has a sex tape. It's the rite of passage to celebredom.*

Grace: *That's not even a word.*

Fisher: *Just imagine your future. #Gracon*

Grace: *What happened, Beac?*

Beac: *I got into a fight with Vance. He genuinely didn't know what he was doing while working for his pals.*

Lang: *I knew he wasn't dirty. So why are we watching the town exits and your house?*

Beac: *He doesn't believe that what we gathered from his team is true. He might want to leave the state in order to get some answers.*

Grace: *Do you need me to head back?*

San: *We're all in position.*

Beac: *G, stay in Portland. You might be the one stopping him there if he gets through all of us.*

Lang: *Don't break his nose.*

Grace: *I'll try not to, but I can't promise anything.*

"Everything okay?" Henry asks.

I nod.

"Do you think I should follow Vance?" Mills asks.

"Vance has a lot to deal with. Give him time."

"Anything else we should know?" Pierce asks.

I shake my head. "Everything is under control."

"Who knew Mr. Chaos would have everything under control?" Henry says. "I said it once, and I'll say it again: This place is like the twilight zone."

"You never said that, but whatever, Henry." Mills rolls his eyes.

Chapter Thirty-Three

Beacon

A COUPLE OF HOURS LATER, Vance finally comes out of his room.

"Can I have a word with you?" he asks, tilting his head toward the door.

I grab my jacket and nod. We head to the fire pit. While I'm turning on the fire so we don't freeze our asses, he asks, "Why didn't you tell me you were part of this H-I-B group?"

"I was going to do it, but decided to wait until we recruited you. You said no and with all that crap they found on your guys…" I shake my head. "I couldn't risk it."

He runs a hand through his hair. "What am I supposed to do with that? I believed that what we were doing was helping people. I did a lot of good deeds during the time I spent with them."

"How do you know they were good?"

"Because I was the one who would come up with the assignments. Those were called pro bono missions. I funded them—and paid the salaries of the guys who worked during those assignments. It wasn't all mercenary shit," he argues. "Why would they do that?"

"I don't know what you can do," I answer. There are a few options. Things that can't be done while we're here. Once we're out we can help him, but it's up to him. "As for why they were doing that, we've been thinking about it."

He glares at me. "We?"

"My team and I," I clarify.

"Your band?"

"They are part of it, but I have more people working under me," I explain further. I'm slightly uncomfortable giving him more information. "We tried to see it from their points of view. Working as a mercenary is an easy job. You go in and out, no questions asked. It pays better than the retirement plan from the government."

"I care," he protests. "They should've told me."

"Why weren't you part of the decision making?" I ask, because this guy is too dominating to let others choose his destiny.

He shrugs.

"It didn't matter to me," he answers. "I wasn't doing it for the money. Fuck, they were my brothers. I trusted them."

"It's different, Vance. You have a fucking trust. You quit West Point to join the army so you could be a Delta Force," I remind him. "If you hadn't done it that way, you'd be on your way to becoming a General, like your grandfather."

"You know that?"

I grin. "Do you think we let just anyone in?"

"Why did you want me to join you?"

"Because I can see that you miss it," I explain. "I could use my brother by my side, not that I'm working with them anymore."

"Did you have to quit too?"

"No. I'm taking a sabbatical," I lie, because really I have no idea what my status is with The Organization. For all I know, I'm out since this time I chose *her* over the job. "As you know, I'm stuck in this forsaken town, like you."

"I miss the action. That's why I accepted to join them when they offered," he answers. "I thought I was doing something good, like when I rescued Blaire, or I set up a security detail for her because she traveled to places where she was in danger."

"Why do they have the rule of once you're out you can't go back in?"

"I never asked," he answers. "I know this might sound stupid, but while I was a Delta Force, I belonged somewhere. I had my people. Some of these guys were part of that unit. I thought it'd be the same. It was in some ways, but not all ways."

"No. I understand you perfectly. I've been the odd person everywhere," I say. "G's family accepts me, and I fit in well, but they aren't mine. I always wished we had this." I tilt my head toward the house.

"Every time we had to go home, I wanted to take you guys with me. That's what brothers do, you know, but I couldn't, and I never heard from any of you until the next year."

"William fucked us," he concludes.

"Adults suck, and now we're adults fucking up our own lives," I agree with him.

"I'm so fucking upset at myself, at them. I have this anger I can't release. Calling and leaving a message saying, 'Fuck you, I need an explanation' doesn't do anything. I have no fucking idea on what to do. If I could, I'd jump on a plane and search for them and kill them one by one."

"Not a good choice." I grin. "I can help you once we're out of here."

He shrugs one shoulder. "As I said, I called Bennett, but I doubt he'll call me back."

"Were you two together?"

"It's complicated," he answers.

I arch an eyebrow. "It's a yes or a no. I'm not asking if you had a title."

"Listen, because of the General, I can't be with anyone. We fucked often, but that was the extent of it."

"Dude, you're in your thirties," I argue.

"I left West Point. I retired early. The General calls me a fucking loser. I'm the black sheep of the family. He reminds Mom over and over again that I'm a fucking failure. She pays for my mistakes. He hasn't forgotten about her affair with William. If I had a male partner, he'd disown Mom, my stepfather, and my siblings."

"That's why you and Bennett fought?"

He nods.

We stay quiet for several minutes until he says, "For a guy who likes to control everything, I fucked up pretty bad, didn't I?"

"You trusted them."

"Do you trust your team?"

"Always," I answer immediately. "Maybe the difference between what we do and what you do is that we all have to agree on which cases we take, who we're working for, and if it's a good cause."

"So, it's free?"

"Nah. If a guy like Henry wants our services, we'd charge him a hefty amount," I answer and grin.

As if I had invoked *the boss*, my phone buzzes. I grab it, and I grunt. It's a text from Bradley. *Call me now!*

No, dude. I'm not doing your daughter, yet. Leave me alone.

Though I'd love to ignore him, I can't. I'd rather have him yelling at me for five minutes straight over the phone than have to deal with him for days because he had to fly to me.

"Yo," I answer.

"When you ask for a sabbatical, you don't request your team to babysit your brother," he exclaims. "It's like I have to repeat the fucking rules to you every two minutes because you can't follow them."

I flinch. Fuck, I forgot this guy monitors everything. Okay, we need to set up our own server until we get back to The Organization —if we get back to them.

"It was important," I debate.

"I'm listening."

Oh fuck, why does he have to be rational? Can't he just tell me not to do it again and move on?

"Vance didn't know about the jobs he did with his unit until today," I mumble. "By the way, my brothers know that I work for you."

"You think those two sentences give you a fucking pass?"

"No, I don't have much to report—since I don't work for you."

"Beacon, I need you to take a moment to regroup and take this seriously," he orders. "I understand that yesterday I wasn't professional. I called you in the capacity of a concerned father. Today, I'm your fucking boss, and you used a server because you're worried about your brother—the mercenary. I need to know if there's more to it."

I clear my throat and walk him through everything that's transpired since yesterday. I'm impressed that he doesn't call me out on my fucked-up shit. I forgot the CCTV. That's so stupid on my part.

When I finish, he asks, "Are you concerned?"

"No. I...I'm not sure," I mumble, but then say out loud the one thing that alarmed me while I was speaking to Vance.

"LISTEN, he left a voicemail with one of his buddies. The guy he used to date. I might be off, but what if he wasn't supposed to know any of that information? Does that put him in danger? What about our family? I don't know if there's going to be any consequences."

"I bet there might be some. These jobs are classified. It seems like only a few knew exactly what they were doing. These people are the type who really will kill you if you find out who they are," Mason concludes. "I'll ask again, are you concerned?"

I fidget with my chin while I try to figure out how to prevent a tragedy. "Yep."

He grunts. "Your sabbatical just ended," he informs me.

"Nice try. I'm still dating your daughter," I joke, trying to lighten the situation. We both are thinking the same. If we're not careful, something can happen. My family is on the line. "But maybe she should go back home."

"If she knows what's happening, I doubt she's going to agree with either one of us. Plus, you need her." He sighs heavily. "I hate you, Aldridge."

"You Bradleys have a funny way of telling me how much you love me," I joke.

"I'll be there tomorrow so we can work on a contingency plan. Figure out how you're going to house the rest of your team," he orders. "I'll bring Ainse, so it seems like a family visit. Keep this airtight. Only the team can know about what's happening. Do you understand?"

"Loud and clear, sir."

"And tell your team to be on maximum alert."

My gut tightens. This is one of those times when I should bring up Pierce and the stupid lawyer. My family should be out of here and somewhere safe until I know nothing will happen to any of them.

"What if I get them out of here?"

"We'll cross that bridge later, okay?"

Easy for him to say. His family isn't in danger of being killed by heartless assholes.

Chapter Thirty-Four

Grace

"I WAS PROMISED FUN TOYS–FOR me. Not shit for my nephews," Beacon complains when he closes the trunk of my SUV. "That tricycle is too small for me."

"Why are you here again?" Sophia asks, then glares at me. "We agreed, no Aldridges during this trip."

I raise my palms and shrug. "I didn't call him." I point at Vance. "Or him."

"We thought it'd be best if we get there in thirty minutes. We have a family meeting," Beacon declares.

"I'm not leaving my car in Portland."

He extends his hands. "I got that covered."

"Of course, you do." I hand over my keys because it's not a request. It's an order. Something happened. I can see it in his eyes. I also got a text earlier saying there's a meeting at the cabin later today.

He owns a secluded cabin that he only uses to hold meetings with The Organization, switch cars so he can leave the town, or disappear from his brothers.

Leyla frowns and looks at me. I shrug, feigning ignorance. Something terrible must have happened that my father asked Beacon to forget his sabbatical. With Sophia and Leyla by my side, I couldn't text or call anyone. I assumed that if they needed me before, they'd call—or pick me up in Portland.

I gulp. Okay, so something is happening, and we have to leave.

"We can skip next week's festival and come back again," Leyla suggests.

Sophia rubs her belly and shakes her head. "With these two passengers, I'd rather stay home. Asking where the restroom is in every store was an experience I don't want to repeat anytime soon."

Beacon drives us to the airport. When we arrive, one of the guys is waiting for us.

"Seth should be here in twenty minutes," Beacon announces. "Wait for him and then head to Baker's Creek. See you at eight."

"Are you organizing a party and not inviting us, Beacon?" Leyla asks as we make our way to the helicopter.

"You're welcome to join us," he invites her. "Just don't bring your stuffy husband along."

She laughs. "I'm more concerned about leaving my baby behind. It's been hours since the last time I held him. We should've brought him with us."

"We said no children," Sophia reminds her.

"Yet, Beacon is with us," I joke.

He winks at me.

The ride from Portland to Baker's Creek doesn't take long. Everything happens too fast. One second, I'm at a parking lot shoving all the clothes and toys we bought for the Aldridge boys 2.0—that's how everyone is referring to Arden, Carter, and the babies that are arriving within the next few months. The next, I'm sitting in the living room, eating tacos, and listening to Beacon talk about his undercover job.

I don't pay much attention. My mind is trying to figure out what exactly is happening. We have a team meeting later tonight. Seth's team will be here too.

"You work with him?" Blaire directs her attention to me.

I smile. I could say yes, and that my father is our boss. I don't.

"Of course, she does," Leyla confirms. "Why do you think she has that innocent look but can swat a fly if provoked?"

"I've never swatted a fly," I correct her.

"Or so you say," Leyla huffs.

"Are you or are you not?" Sophia stares at me.

I burst into laughter and shake my head. "I'm not admitting anything, but you have to be careful with this information. Like, don't tell it to anyone outside the house. I'd prefer if the kids don't learn about it—ever."

We didn't know about Dad's company until we were old enough.

Everyone starts talking on top of each other, and Beacon claps. "If you don't mind, we have to leave."

"We have questions," Blaire says.

"That's all I can disclose," Beacon responds. "I play with the good guys. You're safe around me. I can't tell you more."

Once we're in his truck, I ask, "What happened?"

"Maybe nothing, but I want us to be prepared." His answer doesn't make me feel any better.

When we arrive at his cabin, it's empty.

"Was that a ruse to get me alone in the woods, Aldridge?" I joke as I watch him lock the doors and set the alarm.

He makes a low, deep sound. It'd sound sexy if I didn't know it's his way of saying we're fucked.

"What's happening?"

He brings me up to date then says, "If I have a say in it, I will send you home until this is over."

"The team needs me."

He opens his arms. "I know that I need you, but I also need you to be safe."

"It's better when we're together," I remind him.

He bends his head, I lift my chin, and our lips meet. There's no tenderness to this kiss. It feels as if he's stealing all the air from my lungs. He's trying to absorb my essence as he dives in deep. His hands rest on my ass, pulling me to him. The taste of him is becoming my new favorite.

There's nothing gentle about this kiss. He takes everything, demands more from me, and gives me all of him. As the bulge in his jeans presses against my pelvis, I become excited, maybe even needy. I've been fantasizing about him for too long. The burning desire is overtaking me when the alarm goes off.

I jerk out of his embrace.

"I'm going to take a cold shower."

"The alarm," I remind him.

"I set it up, in case the guys came before the time we agreed. I didn't want them to catch us…making out." He winks at me.

"Can I shower with you?"

He shakes his head. "Nah, we haven't had a date yet."

"What are you two doing?"

"Go away, Byron." I groan.

"Oops, am I interrupting?"

I glare at him.

"You don't get to eat any of this delicious food." He shows me some bags.

"Where are the guys?"

"Mane is giving instructions to Henry's bodyguards. It's just a precaution since we're all going to be in a meeting."

I look at Beacon. "Do you think they're coming?"

"As I said earlier, I don't know if I'm overreacting, but I'd rather cover my ass."

Lang tilts his head and whistles. "He has a fine ass."

"San and Fish?" Beacon ignores him.

"They went to Happy Springs for water, soda, and beers. I suggested hard liquor, but it seems like we can't have a big party."

Beacon places a kiss close to my ear and whispers, "We'll finish our conversation after the meeting."

"Looking forward to it."

Chapter Thirty-Five

Grace

AT THREE IN THE MORNING, we're in Beacon's room, playing our hearts out. We brought a few instruments from the studio. He's too stressed. I doubt he'll be able to settle down tonight. I, on the other hand, am about to fall asleep standing while playing the violin.

Knowing him, he'd rather be in the field looking for these guys and settling things with them. I'm not sure what settling would entail.

I stop, placing the bow on top of the desk. Once he stops strumming his guitar, I ask, "You want to be wrong, don't you?"

Beacon nods.

"I'm glad you soundproofed this room, or your brothers would be banging on the door."

He grins. "I like to say it's to avoid listening to them having sex with their wives. It's to ensure I have some privacy in case I need to make calls or lead a mission from here. Fuck, I can't believe this is happening—and I don't even know what *this* is."

"Stop worrying," I insist.

"This is one of those instances when I can't even plan to avoid the outcome," he answers. "What the fuck is the outcome?"

"I wish I could say it's going to be okay, but what if it's not?"

"Exactly," he agrees. "If your dad approves my idea, we might be fine."

"We don't hunt people," I remind him.

"We'll be keeping an eye on them," he corrects me. "The way I see it, they can easily come to Baker's Creek and try to kill Vance. What if they think we know something? Then maybe they'll just get rid of the entire family. They wiped out an entire town in Mali. You saw the pictures."

I cringe. They were horrifying. I set the violin down and sit on the bed next to him. "Let's get some sleep. We can make more decisions tomorrow."

He nods, kissing the top of my head. "We should talk about the kiss we didn't finish." He presses his lips on my bare shoulder. "Have a late-night snack."

"I thought you said sex was off the table."

"I'm just planning on making out with you before I fall asleep."

Shrugging, I say, "Well, you lost your chance."

His features switch from playful to serious. "Okay. There's no pressure on my side. I'm going by what you think you need."

The way he says it, with determination, warms my heart.

"Do you have any idea how adorable you are?" I ask.

"I'm not sure if I like the term, but tell me why you are comparing me to a teddy bear."

"I never realized you'd do anything for me."

It's like someone took off the eye mask, and I can see how this man lives to make me happy. I clung to the idea that we are just friends so desperately that I never noticed how he treats me. Yet, it makes sense why not one guy was good enough for me. They weren't Beacon. I'd be lying if I said he's stealing my heart little by little. I think he's had it all along, and I never noticed.

"You anticipate my every need. Still, you respect my wishes. How you manage it is a mystery, but I think I love it."

He nuzzles my hair. "I have a PhD in all things Grace," he jokes. "Do you want me to stay in the bedroom with you? If not, I can sleep on the couch if you want me to."

"Stay," I request, kissing him. We fall into the bed and stay entangled—lips, limbs, and hearts—for a long time.

THE NEXT MORNING, we go through the day as if nothing is happening. Mom and Dad arrive around eleven. They are waiting for us at the rental house. We put a leash on Mozzy and walk to meet them. Several bystanders stop to take pictures of him.

When I open the door and take off the leash, he goes running to Mom. I hug her and then look at Dad. "Hey."

"Can I have a word with you, Gracie?"

I nod and follow him toward the small office at the end of the hall. After I enter, he closes the door.

"Are we here to talk about the Aldridges or what you did—eleven years ago."

His gray eyes stare at me for several seconds. The silence is deafening. I argue for either one of the subjects, but I can't start the conversation until he makes the first move.

"As I told you on Friday, I did what was best for you. I apologize for treating you like a child when I am aware that you're mature for your age. We could've handled it better. Your request to decide your security detail is difficult to process. I hope you allow me to help you make the right decisions when the time comes. With that said, I don't know what we're facing, and I suggest you leave with us."

"Why?"

"These men are dangerous."

"This isn't my first rodeo, Dad. If I wasn't your daughter, would you ask me to stay back?"

He shakes his head. "I don't know why I don't feel comfortable with this case."

"A hunch?"

"This is new to us. We go in, do the job, and leave. This is unprecedented. I don't even know if there's a real threat," he explains. "I was talking to Harrison and Anderson last night. The possibility of this becoming a clusterfuck is high. We can't stand down and wait for things to happen. Knowing that not only one but three of my children are involved is fucking scary."

"Is Nathan going to work with us?"

He shakes his head. "I mean Beacon. He's family."

I smile. "You like him."

"He's annoying, but yes. I do." He waves his finger. "That doesn't mean I'm happy knowing you two are together."

"We're still working on that," I inform him. "The guy lied to me for eleven years, and even though it doesn't look like I'm upset, I'm still angry about it."

"That's your prerogative. Just remember life is short. Don't keep him in the doghouse for too long."

"So, you approve now?"

He shrugs one shoulder. "If I have to choose, I guess he's better than any of the losers you paraded. At least, he has good reflexes and might move fast enough when you try to break his nose."

I raise an eyebrow and cross my arms. "Really, Dad?"

"What can I say? It's still funny."

"It was never funny," I say, but hug him. "You're the best dad in the world."

"I doubt that, but I have the best daughter in the world." He hugs me back. "Let's get to work. We have a lot to plan, and I promised your grandparents I'd be back in time for dinner."

MY PARENTS LEAVE AT FOUR. Mom promises to come back the weekend after. She loves to come down during the festivals. Plus, she wants to spend more time with Arden and Carter. She adores babies and toddlers.

During dinner, Beacon updates his brothers. It's not a full explanation, but he tells them enough so they can cooperate. The next morning, Beacon calls the team for another meeting. This time, Seth's team joins us. These are extraordinary circumstances. A team never overlaps missions, but Seth says that the Bryant case is under control. We can't do anything until the end of March.

"Are we taking them down?" San asks once we are all gathered in the cabin's living room.

"It's not that simple," Beacon answers. "We're being proactive, not reactive. Next week, we're going to install security all over town. Every establishment is getting an upgrade. Henry is visiting each business as we speak."

"Is that even legal?" Mane frowns.

"My family owns the buildings. We had Pierce look into the lease contracts. They have a clause that allows us to make any improvements without the permission of the tenant."

"Do your brothers know what we're doing?" Langdon inquiries.

"Only the basics," I explain. "We don't want them to worry about any speculation."

"And Vance?" he questions.

"He knows more because he's concerned about it too," Beacon answers. "Listen, while you're working here, be invisible. I don't want the town to notice any of you. If I see anyone on the fucking Twitter feed, you're going to be sent to the H-I-B bodyguard division and work with celebrities. I'll make sure they assign you the most annoying asshole."

"You?" Seth jokes.

"Fuck you!"

"The equipment arrives tomorrow," Seth takes over. "If you have any questions about your role, ask now. For those staying at The Lodge, this isn't a vacation. Everyone else, make sure to follow protocol."

Half of his team is leaving Baker's Creek immediately. Their mission is to spy on these guys and get back to us with their whereabouts—or give us a heads up if they're heading to Oregon.

"The most important thing is that we finish this with zero casualties. Meeting adjourned," Beacon says.

Chapter Thirty-Six

Grace

MONDAY IS the day Mills takes Arden to Happy Springs, where they have a Mommy and Me class. He spends the rest of the day with him. His schedule is flexible enough that Arden doesn't miss him. But now that his knee is better, thanks to Hayes, he wants to go back to skating.

That's why he's happy that I'm going to be here. I'm not sure how to tell him that I don't plan to stick around for the rest of the year. It might be easier to break the news to him than to Beacon, though.

Leyla only works in the morning. Since I wouldn't be able to be with Carter until noon, Pierce said he'd take the day off to be with him.

"I feel like a slacker. I came to take care of your nephews, and I had to excuse myself on the first day." I laugh.

"No, you came to be with me. You're doing them a favor," Beacon rectifies my statement. "But since it's for their protection, I think it's fine that you took the day off."

We're approaching the Baker's Creek exit when he asks, "What do you want to do? We could go to Portland."

"No. Why don't you walk me through a day in the life of Beacon? When I visit it is usually over the weekend, or you ask someone to cover for you."

He grins. "It's around eleven. That means I texted you about five times already. It's Monday, and today I'm scheduled to work at The Lodge."

"What do you do there?"

"I usually work at the front desk. When I piss off Henry, I get sent to one of the restaurants. I usually end up washing the dishes since I'm not allowed to cook, and I'm a shitty waiter—according to the manager."

"We used to waiter at that restaurant close to Central Park during college. What gives?"

He chuckles. "That was fun. I don't miss the stuffy uniform. That's not the point. I don't want them to know that I can do it."

"So, you're always washing dishes instead," I say, laughing.

"What can I say? Henry gets irritated easily. It upsets him that I'm not willing to learn new things. How am I supposed to manage The Lodge if I don't know the difference between a fucking salad fork and a table fork?"

He pauses, looks at me briefly, and says with a grumpy voice, "Do you know there are fourteen kinds of forks? I'm lucky we only use two types."

"You need to stop teasing your brother."

"Well, if you want, we can work at The Lodge for the remainder of the day. I promise to behave. But hear me out, there's a second option."

"Ooh, goodie, what else can you offer other than pissing off your brother so we can wash an unlimited number of dishes?" I laugh. "Do you have any idea how ridiculous that sounds?"

"How many times do I have to explain to you it is about having fun? Life is short. I'd rather look back and say, 'I had a fucking awesome life' rather than 'I wasted it in nonsense.'"

"It's a bit crazy that your nonsense is logical."

"Which is why option number two should be our goal of the day." He pauses. "We're going through your list."

"You'd like that, wouldn't you, Mr. Aldridge?" I say in a sultry voice.

"You've no idea, babe." He grabs my hand and kisses my knuckles. "I'm wondering what a guy has to do to get to number five."

I snatch back my hand. "That's personal."

"I'll make it personal to figure out what you need in and out of bed." His intense voice shoots a dose of desire along my body.

"There are four items before that one," I remind him, trying to control the lust.

"Kissing is a top priority. You're improving, but we definitely need to keep going with the list."

"I'm improving?" My voice comes out appalled.

"*We* are improving," he corrects himself. "My theory is that kissing has to do with both parties. I don't think I've ever kissed anyone the way I do you. Then again, I've never wanted anyone as I want you —ever."

The feeling is mutual. Last night while we kissed, my mind worked hard to stay in the moment while my body wanted a lot more than just kisses and caresses.

"We're practicing flirting," he continues. "I think dirty talk could be included during those 'search for the G-spot' sessions. You can tell me how you want me to touch you. Maybe between your long, toned, beautiful legs. I bet you'll be so wet and hot for me. Fuck, I can't wait to mark you as mine. I'll be deep inside you ordering you to come for me."

The way he says those things, with a low, commanding voice, makes me hot. I want to reach between my legs and touch myself until I come. Better yet, I want him to do it with those long, calloused fingers of his.

"Tell me what you're thinking, G," he orders.

"I..."

"You want me?"

"Yes." I almost moan.

"Say it. Tell me how you imagine me touching you. Do you want my cock in your mouth?"

I lick my lips and groan. "Yes, I want to feel it in my mouth, inside me."

"If you're a good girl, I'll let you suck me dry."

This is driving me crazy. I want him to park the car so he can touch me. Make the ache disappear and replace it with pleasure. I want to mount him and ride him.

The phone rings. It's Henry. "Yo?"

"We need you at The Lodge," he answers. Beacon grunts. "Kid, we need help with the lunch rush. I only have one waiter. Can you do this for me?"

"I can teach him how to do it, Henry. I used to wait tables back in college."

Beacon glares at me.

"I owe you one, Grace. Thank you." Henry hangs up the phone.

"G, I'm hard as a rock. I was hoping we'd go to my place and do something different. Not serve tables for the next couple of hours."

I grin. "I could offer you a blow job, but it's not on my list. Sorry."

Chapter Thirty-Seven

Beacon

HAVING Grace in Baker's Creek makes it harder for me to separate my life in Seattle and my life here. I learned to do that when I was a teenager. It was easier to convince myself that the brotherhood only lasted a week. Grace is forever.

The lines between one and the other become a total blur as the minutes pass. It's like now I'm living in one reality that includes the life I couldn't have and the one I was gifted. When I was a kid, I didn't realize what my grandparents had given me: a big, loud, and loving family.

"Look at Henry. He's smiling," G says as we wait for our orders to be up. "I think he likes teaching you. Maybe he feels like he has a second chance to take care of you. You should give him a chance."

"I love you, but you're a pain in the ass, Bradley." I kiss the top of her head when the chef says, "Order up."

The lunch rush lasts until three. Henry doesn't leave until there are only a few customers in the dining room.

"So much for 'It's Monday, it won't be that bad,'" Grace says, taking off the black apron with The Lodge logo that Henry gave her when we arrived.

"It's ski season," I remind her. "This was quiet compared to what we get on Thursday or Friday. Let's not talk about the weekend."

Between the festivals, ski season, and the fame the restaurants are acquiring, the place is full from the time we open until midnight when we close. I have to give it to Henry. Without changing the name of The Lodge, the place has become a success.

Around four, when the shift ends, I send a message to the group chat.

Beacon: *Taking my woman on a date. Don't bother me.*
Pierce: *We have to have dinner together.*
Beacon: *Pretend I'm there.*
Henry: *It's too quiet to pretend.*
Mills: *Aw, look at Henry trying to make a joke.*
Henry: *:middle finger emoji:*
Sophia: *Can you make sure Grace is here tomorrow morning? We have a board meeting at the factory.*

I groan.

"What's the matter?" G asks, eyeing my phone. "We don't want to have a meeting?"

"We don't," I admit. "What should I say?"

"I'll be there first thing in the morning."

"You'll be there late at night too." I wink at her. "You might need coffee to stay awake because I might not let you sleep."

I open the door of my truck and help her get inside.

The phone rings a second later. It's Leyla.

"Yep?"

"You left your cat in the house."

"Mozzy," I correct her.

"You left an unattended cat in the house," she rectifies.

"Okay?" I frown, opening the driver's door and looking at Grace. "Is Mozzy okay?"

"Your cat scratched Buster," she says. "Daisy ate from the litter box. I…we can't have a cat in the house."

"Did Mozzy scratch Buster before or after your dog tried to eat him?"

"There might've been some chasing," she confesses. "I just think we should've introduced them before leaving him to wander around the house."

"I told you that on Saturday. You said, 'We'll do it later.'"

"That meant, 'don't to bring him until we're ready.'"

"What do you want us to do?"

She growls. "I don't know. Let me research because it's not fair to kick the cat out because Buster thinks he's a big rodent."

"Fuck, I forgot your dog likes to hunt."

"As I said, let me research, okay?"

"You're a queen," I say, hoping she doesn't suggest we take our cat somewhere else.

Mozart can't go to sleep by himself. I could move him to the studio, but I'd have to stay with him, and I can't. My family doesn't know it, but I have a few agents staying underground.

"I know you want to skip dinner," Leyla continues, "but you have to be a responsible parent and come watch your child."

"If I needed someone to cockblock me, I'd have invited the Bradleys to stay."

Leyla laughs. "Have I told you that you're a brave man? If any of your brothers had an in-law as scary as Grace's dad…well, none of them would be married. Anyway, get your cute butt and your gorgeous girlfriend back home. You can organize a date night when your cat knows how to behave."

"My cat knows how to behave. Your dog needs to learn the difference between an intellectual feline and a rat. See you in five," I sigh.

"Everything okay?" Grace asks.

I nod, turn on the engine, and catch her up on everything that happened at home while driving to the mansion. Between Mason Bradley, Vance fucking up, and Mozzy attacking Buster, I'm never going to have a fucking date with Grace.

I park in the garage, swoop her from her seat, and place her on my lap, kissing her hard. "Are you okay if our date plans have changed to family dinner and pet watch?"

"There's plenty of time, Beac," she assures me, wiggling her ass on top of my very hard cock. "This isn't a marathon. Dating is not at the top of my list."

"Grace, don't tempt me because I won't be able to control myself tonight."

She opens the car door, jumps out, and asks, "Is that a promise?"

WE SPEND the evening with my family. When it's time for everyone to head to bed, Grace and I go to my room. This time I carry the cello from the studio to my bedroom. She's so fucking sexy when she plays it.

I choose to play the violin since I can't have a piano or a drum set up here. The atmosphere in the room thickens as the intensity of the music we play increases. As time passes, we begin to undress. It's slow. First my shirt—it's too fucking hot. Grace takes off her sweater. Her white tank top is loose, and she's not wearing anything underneath.

Fuck, I want to grab her, pin her against the wall, and thrust inside her.

Grasping the little self-control I have, I continue to play. It's the first time Grace is conscious about what the notes between my instrument and hers are doing. They're making love with one another, fusing, bonding.

We could do this all night, but I get to a point where I'm burning on the inside. This is the first time she's bared her soul to me. I want to get tangled inside her body, her soul.

My desire for her is consuming me. I can't hold on any longer. I put down the violin, grab her cello, and pull her toward me. I hold her by the waist and kiss her hard, so fucking hard I'm devouring her.

I push her against the wall. Gripping her wrists, I lift her arms and press them above her. I proceed to retake her mouth. This is overdue. I'm not sure if I'm speaking about the kiss, the music we just created, or this moment.

"Beac," she moans my name, rocking her hips against mine.

"What do you want, G?"

"Everything. I swear if you say we should stop, I'll kill you."

I chuckle, nestling my face down the side of her face, kissing her as I make my way along the delicate skin of her throat. "But you have a list."

"Fuck the list," she says. "I've been thinking about having you in my mouth since you mentioned it earlier. The ache you provoke has lingered since this afternoon. Make it go away."

"Your wish is my command," I tease her, nibbling the top of her breasts. This tank top has been fucking teasing me since we started playing. I want to rip it off, just like I want to do with all her clothes. "Are you fucking sure about this, Grace?"

"I've never been surer about something in my life," she assures me. "Don't make me beg. It's been too long."

I don't know what she's talking about. The time we've been apart or since the last time she was with anyone? I refuse to ask. I assume it's about me—us.

"Make the ache go away."

Bending, I press my mouth against hers. My teeth fidget with her bottom lip. My hands slide down to her waist. They push through the elastic of her leggings. Fuck. The surge, just from touching her flawless skin, makes my cock hard as granite.

This wasn't part of the plan. Woo her, make sure she wants to be with you, and then you can feast on her.

Does it matter the order?

This is what she wants. Now. I'll take my time getting to know every inch of her gorgeous body later. We have a lifetime to do everything on her list and add more to it. We'll get to know everything we don't know about each other, in bed and outside of it too. I want to share everything with her.

Today, I'll ask her to be mine. Soon, I'll ask her to become my wife. There's no other way. After today, I won't be able to let her go. With all the patience I can muster, I start undressing her. Everything I do is with a slow rhythm, like a love ballad.

"You're gorgeous," I whisper after I'm done unwrapping her like a present given by the gods.

The best, most exclusive gift a person could ever claim. Her eyes look at me expectantly. She's biting her lower lip. I can't resist and nibble it too before kissing her. As our lips latch onto each other, we move toward my bed—tongues dancing. They hustle in a tango that ends with Grace in the center of the bed.

Her intense gaze locks with mine. Fuck, I'm not going to last. It's been too long. One thrust and this is going to be over.

"What are you thinking?"

"I'm admiring your beauty." I wink at her.

Leaning closer to her, I use my pinky finger to pull down her panties. I'm extra careful, making sure her insulin pump doesn't disconnect. I kiss the clef tattoo on her left hip, and feather kisses on each musical note around it. Once I'm done, I look at her. This is a dream come true. Grace in my bed, legs spread, and wanting me.

I kneel in front of her and slide the tips of my fingers up her thighs, following them with my lips. I am about to reach her core but move backward.

"Beacon, don't tease me, or I swear you'll pay for it."

"I'm not," I say playfully. "I just want to make sure that every inch of you gets the right attention."

"Just remember, tit for tat," she threatens me.

"Really?" I laugh. "So, I get your tits in exchange for what tat?" I mumble against her skin as my thumb slides up and down her core.

She pushes her hips against my hand. I take it away. "Patience, G," I whisper, replacing my fingers with my tongue.

The taste of her is addictive. I want her so fucking much. I devour her delicious pussy while I slide a finger inside her. It's so fucking hard to control myself. I want this to last, for her to enjoy every second as I enjoy her.

Her melodic moans get louder as I lick her and nibble her clit.

"Faster," she orders.

I want to continue with the pace, but I can't wait any longer. As the seconds pass, I get harder and harder. It's when I feel her inside walls squeezing my fingers that I lose control and thrust faster, lick faster, suck harder.

"Beac, now, please," she moans my name, and it's close to an angelical sound.

I stand up, push down my pants, and reach for the condom fast. I unwrap it, cover my length, and kneel between her legs.

I lean forward, pressing my cock against her entrance, and slowly enter her. Inch by inch. The warmth enveloping me fogs my mind, and I thrust myself deep inside her. I crush my mouth against hers as I roll my hips in and out. We find a rhythm. It's nothing like what we've played before, but it's so perfect.

There's chaos, calm, fire, thunder. Everything inside us is in flames.

We burn.

We melt.

We fuse.

The sound of our hearts finally colliding against each other is the culmination of a sonata I never thought we'd compose.

"Gracie," I groan her name as she bites my shoulder. "I fucking love you so much. I doubt I'll ever let you go."

"Promise you won't do it again." Her voice is so small, fragile.

"Never, baby. I—never again," I repeat her words as I hold on to her.

My lifeline, my music.

My everything.

Chapter Thirty-Eight

Grace

THE NEXT MORNING, I wake up next to Beacon. Our arms, legs, and bodies are tangled with each other. I'm tucked safely next to him. My head rests on his chest. The thump of his heart is steady. Mine beats at the same rhythm. Who knew there could be a calm like the one we're sharing?

Last night I felt like we traveled to a far-away galaxy. One where only we belong. I trace the lyrics on his chest. They go along with the notes of "Call You Mine." It's Too Far from Grace's biggest hit. One of my favorite songs.

Beacon is a poet. His lyrics always hit right to the heart. I never looked into them closely, but as the song plays along in my head, I feel the heartbreak, his pain.

His fingers catch mine. "What are you doing?"

"This song...who is it about?"

He kisses the tips of my fingers. His focus is on the tattoo.

"Beac?"

"All my songs are about you, Grace," he answers.

I close my eyes because it's obvious that I wasn't the only one in pain, and maybe he hurt for longer than I did. He never stopped loving me. Did I stop loving him?

What if that's why I couldn't be with anyone else?

I had my Beacon already.

"Forgive me," he says. "I wasn't trying to wound you but to make sure you were cared for."

"There's nothing to forgive. We were too young. It wasn't an easy choice." I kiss his chest, then his heart.

He pulls me toward him and says, "Why are you sad, gorgeous girl?"

"You hurt, and no one was there for you to make it better."

"Being with you makes it better—always," he assures me. "Call me a dreamer, but I always thought we'd find a way back to each other. Even if it happened in the afterlife."

"You'd have waited that long for me?"

"An eternity," he whispers, his lips caressing my jaw. "I think I've belonged to you since before I was born. Not sure if that's even possible. If anything, I know that one day, you cut all the way down to my soul, grabbed my heart, and kept it."

I lie on top of his chest. Our gazes are locked with each other's. His hands cup my face. "I love you."

"That song is wrong."

He laughs, "Really?"

"I don't think you ever lost me, or let me go," I explain to him, as my lips dust kisses on his torso. "No, we just pretended for years that we weren't together. I can see it now."

"You do, huh?"

"I love you, Beac. More than I ever thought I could love anyone."

I feel his length harden, growing, reaching toward my center. I slide my body down, position myself, and moan as he fills me all the way inside. Being with this man, sharing this moment, and loving him is the best feeling in the world.

"I SAW you're subleasing the house already," Pierce says while we're cleaning up the kitchen.

The chore board doesn't care if these guys have a meeting or are wearing a suit. If it's their turn to cook, clean, or wash dishes, they do it.

"What?" I ask, confused, as I dry my hands.

"I went out for a run and I saw a couple of men coming out of the house," he answers.

"It could be my brother, a cousin…" I pause, shrugging. "It's hard to tell."

"Would they come in without telling you?"

I nod. "Yeah. Before Beacon had a place here, we always crashed at Tucker's," I answer, trying not to lie more. "Remember that time you flew to Seattle and Beacon just handed you the keys to his house? It's the same."

It's true that we never ask to go to each other's vacation homes—not that I own one.

"Well, if you're ever in Colorado, you can crash in my apartment," Leyla informs me.

Pierce frowns. "You still have it?"

"I told you last week," she says. "We should go to Colorado to get that packed. I need my books. You said, 'Let's save the days we have left for when this is over. Maybe we should keep it so we don't have to stay in a hotel.'"

Pierce yawns. "I'm sleep deprived."

Since it's time for me to take charge of Arden and Carter, I ask, "Where's Carter?"

"He's in the nursery," Leyla answers. "My son likes to nap during the day so he can save all his energy to stay awake all night long."

We all laugh.

"I remember Arden doing the same," Mills adds, staring at his son who is playing in the living room. "It goes away as they get older."

"It does?" I smirk and look at Beacon. "Yet, you still have it."

Henry high fives me. "Keep this one around."

Beacon puts his arm around me and hugs me tight. "I plan on it."

Everyone leaves for work, except Mills, who gives me a list with Arden's schedule.

"He has a schedule?" I stare at it. "Lucky me, it doesn't have hockey practice at five."

"We'd need the ice arena to be finished. That's not happening until April," he says.

"You're building an arena?"

He nods. "It's the first step. I don't even know if I'm going to be able to play again. The Orcas released me from my contract."

"Just buy the team with the money you receive from the inheritance," I joke. "Then you can do whatever you want, even move them to Portland."

He frowns. I've seen that look. Beacon has it every time I joke, and he thinks I just solved world hunger.

"It's something to consider," he says.

"Do you want me to teach him how to play music while I'm here?"

"He's too young to understand."

"It's more like an introduction," I amend. "We could always start speaking to him in French."

He looks at me and smiles. "As long as you don't teach him how to conjugate the word fuck, I'm fine."

"That's ridiculous."

"Is it? Because last year Pierce taught him how to say, 'What the fuck' and the kid says it more often than I'd like to listen to it."

"It's 'Du'fu,'" I correct him. "Probably French, for you don't make sense."

He shakes his head and waves at Arden. "I'm leaving, sport. Be nice to Aunt Grace."

"G!" he exclaims, pointing at me.

"Okay, buddy, let's get to work. We have a full day with activities that include bubble making, finger painting, and most importantly, nap time."

Chapter Thirty-Nine

Beacon

IN MY LINE OF WORK, a day is a long time. A week can be considered a year. One can plan an entire operation in a week. It's been almost three weeks since the Vance incident. We still have a team searching for his old unit.

Do I want to kill my brother for calling his ex?

Sure, but Grace forbade me from doing it. She said it's my fault for being careless when I showed her the security room—or what she loves to call my game room.

Is she right?

I prefer not to dwell on that small detail. The woman is always right.

Baker's Creek was secured when I came to live here full time. It's just a precaution. As the boss always says, we wipe our tracks, but we have to be careful.

It's dinnertime when my phone rings. Sophia glares at me. I ignore it, but it rings again.

"It might be important," I say.

"We have a rule."

The phone rings again, and this time it's Grace's phone. "It is an emergency," she declares, pulling her phone out of her pocket.

She shows it to me. The screen has a picture of Seth.

"Hey, little brother."

Her eyes open wide, she nods. "Dad's with you?" There is another nod. She looks at me and sighs. "Let me transfer you to Beacon."

"Yeah?"

"These guys are idiots," he states.

"Who?" I stand up from the table and go to my room.

"Vance's people," he answers.

Speaking of the idiot, I'm about to close the door when I notice my brother right behind me. I let him inside. Once the call is over, I might have to talk to him.

"What did they do?"

"Talk about a job gone wrong," he states. "They tried to play a cartel and get away with the drugs and the money."

"You don't fuck with those guys unless you plan on killing them," I state. So, they're not our problem anymore. Unless... "Does it matter?"

"It wouldn't," he pauses, "if two of my guys weren't held captive along with them."

I run a hand through my hair as I pace along my room. "Fuck!"

"Yep, fuck is about right. We have the blueprints of the ranch. If you come along with your team, we might be able to rescue them tonight."

"Where are you?"

"On a plane. I should be in Portland soon. I need you at the airport in thirty. My father is with me. He plans on staying in Baker's Creek with a team, just in case."

"In case what?"

"Bennett, Vance's guy." He grumbles something. "He isn't with them. I haven't been able to locate him."

I rub the back of my neck as I stare at my brother. "Are you serious?"

"It's like the earth swallowed him. They either killed him, or he's somewhere searching for a way to get to Vance—and maybe the rest of the family," he speculates. It's a hypothesis, but we can't take chances. Before I can think of what to do, he adds, "If you ask me, your family should move to the cabin, at least until everything is safe."

"If the lawyer catches us, this is over."

"If we don't take precautions, their lives might be fucking over," he concludes.

I take a big sip of air and let it out slowly as I think of a solution. "I got a report earlier that Jerome Parrish is in town. I'll have the guys bring him over."

"Get moving. I'll meet you at the airport in thirty."

I send a message to everyone alerting them that we're on the move, then request Mane to bring Jerome Parrish ASAP. When I finish, I go to my closet and pull out my armor. Vance patiently watches me as I dress. Once I'm ready, he says, "Pockets and a utility belt, wow. It's like you're Indiana Jones."

"Fuck off!"

"Tell me what the fuck happened."

I stare at him, not sure how to deliver the news. *Your guy might be dead or coming to kill you. Pick your poison.*

"Listen, I know shit is happening because your woman just jetted out of the house." He glances at me. "And you were on an important call."

I sigh, hunch my shoulders, and tell him what we know. One of his hands rests on his waist while the other pinches the bridge of his nose. His eyes are closed. "I'm sorry. I promise to find out what happened to him."

"Unless he's spying on us and trying to kill me?"

I shake my head because I don't like that option. That makes me want to leave Seth's men behind and stay here to take care of my family. "If he were anywhere near, we'd know."

"He could be hiding anywhere. We can camp in zero-degree weather—without being detected. Even with all the security details you have around."

"You've noticed them?"

He nods. "Just because I know what I'm looking for," he explains. "They're cautious enough to go undetected. So, what's the plan?"

I tilt my head toward the door, and we march to the downstairs area.

"You going to a concert and didn't tell me?" Pierce asks when he sees me.

I roll my eyes and shake my head. "Listen, we have a problem. Grace and I have to leave immediately. We won't be back until tomorrow—if we're lucky."

"We need authorization from Jerome Parrish—in advance," he claims.

No, I don't. It'd be so easy to just leave without telling them shit, but I have to. Mason Bradley is going to be here soon. He might evacuate them from the town—or at least shove them in my bunker.

"He should be here soon. Then I'll debrief you."

"He's going to debrief us." Henry chuckles. "Those are big words for my baby brother."

"I'd give you a comeback if I didn't need to make sure your ass stays alive."

Henry goes pale. I love the man, but his timing is shitty. Suddenly, I feel everyone's eyes on me.

"What's happening, kid?" Hayes asks.

At that moment, Jerome steps into the house. He wears a cream trench coat and a matching colored hat that makes him look like Dick Tracy. *Dude, the fifties are over.* Grace and Mane are right behind him.

"He was outside the house."

"I came to visit." Jerome looks at all of us, taking off his hat. "What happened? Is everything okay?"

"No. I need permission to leave the country, now. I won't be back until tomorrow—or when things are back to normal." I pause, look at everyone, and sigh before I explain what I can discuss with them.

Jerome is pale, and he shakes his head when I finish telling them as much as I can of what's happening. "That kind of work isn't allowed in the will."

Pierce points at Vance. "For him, not for Beacon. I can fight you, and I will win, Parrish."

"Your father put that clause in because he didn't want Vance to get hurt again. He hoped he'd retire," Jerome explains. "I'm sure he'd feel the same about Beacon—he's a kid."

No. I'm not a kid. When are these people going to stop seeing me as the toddler who got caught in the middle of the paparazzi storm with his father?

Before I can protest, Pierce says, "I thought you and our father weren't friends."

"We weren't. I just know it." Jerome uses a harsh voice. He studies me and sighs. "Two days. You have two days to do this, or this is over."

I grin. "I knew you were more than a stuffy suit."

My family is freaking out more than I anticipated. Bradley is going to make them shit their pants. I hate the choice I have to make, but I know it's for the best. "Grace, if I ask you to stay with your father so you can keep an eye on them?" I look at my family, whose panicked faces are making me nervous.

She glances at them and nods. "Count on it."

I pull her to me and kiss her hard. "Thank you."

Her hands hold my face, our eyes lock, and she says, "I'll be waiting for you."

Chapter Forty

Grace

BEACON LEAVES with most of his team, leaving me with some of Seth's guys. I'm in charge until my father comes to take over. Dad texts me that he should be here soon with his team. I had no idea he was bringing what we call *the originals* with him. That's Dad, his partners, and the team they've always worked with.

Lang drives to Portland, where he'll have access to the security room at Merkel's corporate office. We only have so much time to move. My orders are to take care of the family. I message Beacon to get approval to move them. It's easier to divide them and put them in places where no one would think they'll be.

Grace: *Can I set them up in different locations?*
Beacon: *What are you thinking?*
Grace: *It'll be best if we move them far from the house. I can set two men for each couple—or father and son.*
Beacon: *That's a good idea. Keep them calm, okay.*
Grace: *Don't worry about them.*
Beacon: *Take care of yourself.*
Grace: *Same. Love you.*
Beacon: *Love you more.*

It doesn't take much to convince them to leave the house. We use the underground tunnel that goes from the house to the outside of the property. It leads to a small shed Beacon had built close to a wooded area. There's a well-illuminated trail leading to a back street where no one notices who comes or goes.

"It makes me wonder if the kid ever used it to ditch us and we never knew about it," Pierce growls as we walk through the hallway.

"He wouldn't do that," Hayes assures him. "Plus, it is new. I'm sure he hasn't been able to use it."

"Jerome Parrish will hand us our asses if he even suspects that Beacon left town at any point," Henry concludes.

Mills looks at me and smiles. I'm sure he knows more than he'll tell his brothers.

"Okay, how are we doing this?" Henry asks.

I explain to them where they should go. Henry and Sophia go to her parent's vacation home. They take Arden and Mills. I send Hayes, Blaire, Leyla, Pierce, and Carter to Tucker's house. I'm not sure where Vance will go—probably the Heywood's home. Then again, if I were him, I'd want to be part of the operation.

Mom: *Gracie, call me when this is over.*
Gracie: *I love you, Mom.*

She hates when we go on missions. If Seth, Dad, and I handle the same operation, she's a nervous wreck. I'm glad Nathan is part of the Nerd Herd, along with Lang. It'd kill Mom with a panic attack—or a heart attack—to have everyone in the field at once.

While I wait for Dad, I make sure the house is secured. I lock Beacon's bunker, setting the alarm too. If anyone enters the studio, they won't be able to access the underground floor. The tunnel's doors are locked too.

My father and his team arrive forty minutes later. I had plenty of time to hide knives in most of my armor.

"Hi, Dad," I greet him, hugging him and waving at everyone who is behind him. "How did everyone make it here?"

He shrugs. "We have our ways."

"You've known this for hours," I say.

"We thought it'd be best to wait until we were close to let you know what's happening. Aldridge gets wired up and has trouble waiting for instructions. I assumed it'd be worse if his family was on the line."

He's not wrong, but this is annoying. I wait for him to give instructions to his team. "Walk me through the property while we secure the perimeter."

"It's secured," I inform him.

"How well do you know the area?"

"We've hiked plenty of times," I explain. "But Beacon and I haven't gone too far lately because it's winter. The surveillance team has been out daily."

As we walk, I point toward the security cameras Beacon installed when he first moved in. "You can access them through the system."

We're further north on the property when he stops and narrows his gaze toward one of them. He clicks on his earpiece and says, "Nathan, please check the cameras around the perimeter. I think a couple of them aren't working. Find out why, what was the last thing they captured, and when did they go off?"

"Yes, sir," he answers.

I wonder if anyone is flying a drone for surveillance. That's usually something Lang or Nathan would be doing.

"Anyone in the family come out here often?" he asks, squatting and touching the snow that's about four days old.

"Not that I've noticed. I've only been living here for such a short time," I remind him. "From what I've seen, they go as far as to where the ice arena is being built."

I point toward the construction with a couple of rooms finished, but everything else still needs walls and a roof. Dad looks around, nods, and we continue walking.

The place is quiet, too quiet. I've never walked around the property when it's so dark and cold. The only light comes from the reflection of the moon against the snow. I wish it was a full moon though.

Nathan calls. Dad turns off the earpiece and answers. He listens for several seconds while he shakes his head. "Can you see their faces? It can be Beacon getting away to piss off his brothers."

He exhales harshly. "Are you sure?" His voice comes out harsh. "No, I don't need Lang to verify it. I believe you. I'll have one of the guys replace them tomorrow."

"It's a blind spot," I remind Dad. "Tomorrow can be too late."

Right now might be too late. Someone is inside. Goose bumps cover my body. What if they saw everyone leave? No, they didn't. We did it through the tunnels, and there's no way they can know about it.

"What do you suggest?" Dad focuses his attention on me. I swear, I feel like he's quizzing me.

"Send a team to search the area. I think we missed something," I explain to him. "This guy knows how to be invisible."

"She's right," says Anderson Hawkins, one of Dad's partners. He's part of the original team. When he reaches us, he says, "We taught these guys to go unnoticed—the same way some of us learned from our training."

"You want to lead it?" he asks Hawk, who is great at searching.

"Yeah, but she's coming with me."

Dad glares at him.

"I trained her well. Plus, she's been here more times than any of us."

Before I can complain that my father has trouble letting me go, there's a loud boom sound. The ground shakes. Dad grabs me as I turn my body and see Beacon's studio burning. Flames are consuming what's left after the explosion.

Dad barks orders, asks everyone to take shelter. He gets a count of the team—no one was inside when it happened.

"Make sure all the Aldridges stay where they are. Tell security to be alert," Dad commands as he releases me. "We need to find out if there are more explosives."

I do as he says, then call Lang, "Do you have a drone nearby?"

"Ready to fly. What do you need?"

"Beacon's studio just exploded. I need you to search for any other explosives around the premises."

I sigh with relief. If I had sent his family underground, it'd be almost impossible to get them out of there until we remove all the debris.

"One of the guys is going to release a couple of land bots to search the area," Lang tells me. "In the meantime, I'll survey the perimeter, but I doubt I'll find anything. Is everyone okay?"

"Yes, no one was inside," I explain. "We don't know where to search. I have the feeling that whoever did that is camping on the northeast side of the property where the cameras were deactivated."

"They timed it well—too well," he explains. "According to Nathan, it happened today when the sun was setting, and the camera couldn't film the face of whoever did it.

"Start searching by air while I search by land," I order.

"Who's coming with me?" I start walking toward the arena.

"Where are you going?" Dad asks. "We need to stay under."

"They're trying to get everyone out of the house—they don't know it's empty," I tell him. "We can go to the arena first. I have a feeling that they're hiding there. It's under construction—no one would notice. I think they want us to be sitting ducks in the dark and shoot everyone they see."

His eyes stare at me for a second before giving instructions to Harrison, "Go to the barn, be careful because they could be hiding there." Tiago is the next one to get orders from him. "Check the arena."

"It was my idea," I tell him.

"You, Hawk, and I are going to the house," he explains. "If

they're trying to break in, we'll intercept them. As you said, they don't know the house is empty."

I never noticed how big the estate was until I realized that even with all the people who have been scouting and watching the premises, these men were able to move around. My blood is running hot. I'm not upset that we missed anything. My guess is that they caught up with what we knew and found a way to take at least half of the team away from here before they made a move. I shoot a text to Beacon.

Grace: *Trap, be careful. TTYS.*

I put away my phone, hoping that I'm wrong. Dad puts on his night vision goggles and I do the same. As we approach the house, I notice them. Two men climbing up the house. Black hoods cover their heads. They're unrecognizable. I can make out the gun harnesses under their jackets.

Dad and Hawk slow down when I point at the men. This isn't new to me. I go into autopilot, pulling out two knives from the pockets inside my combat boots. Usually, I don't have any emotions when I'm on a job. This time I'm raging and worried. They broke into our property, destroyed Beacon's studio to distract us, and are trying to possibly kill Vance if not the entire family. How far are they going and how many are in here?

Is Beacon walking into a trap?

They can't avoid going in because they have our men. We never leave anyone behind—ever.

"There has to be another guy," I mumble.

My body tenses when I hear a shot coming from the barn. At that exact moment, one of the men climbing the house reaches for his gun. I react and throw a knife, stabbing his hand. I realize he had an automatic gun hanging on his shoulder.

I aim the next knife at his shoulder. He loses his balance and falls to the ground. I reach for another blade and shoot it toward the second guy as he jumps down to aid his partner. I hit his leg, but he doesn't care. He's bending down, reaching for the M-70 his partner is carrying.

"Stop, or I'll shoot you," Hawk orders, pointing his gun toward the guy.

The guy straightens up and grins. He takes a step closer toward me. I approach him because this man might take the bait and believe I'm an easy target. He pulls out his gun and points at me. "Try it, and she dies."

"G," Dad yells. I squat, take out another blade, stab him in the side of the ribs, and punch him when my father shoots him in the leg.

"You fucking bitch!"

Dad fires a second shot that hits the guy in the shoulder. "Watch your fucking language."

I see movement from the corner of my eye and see the man who is still on the ground reaching for a second gun. He pulls it out and out of reflex I reach for another knife and aim for his neck at the same time Hawk shoots him. The gun skitters out of his slack grip.

"How many more?" Dad presses the gun to the wounded guy.

"Kill me," he begs.

Harrison is dragging a man with him. "We found this guy waiting at the barn. Two more are at the arena—well, just one. The other tried to kill Tiago, and that didn't go well."

He tilts his head toward the guy Hawk shot. "I guess he didn't cooperate either. So much for not having any bodies tonight."

"I aimed for his shoulder. Grace is the one who couldn't hold the knife or kick his ass," Hawk says apologetic. "You know how the Bradleys like to show off—all the time."

Before I can laugh, another guy approaches us. He's aiming a high caliber gun toward us. Even though we have armor, if he shoots us in the head, we're gone.

"Where are they?"

"Who?" I ask.

"The Aldridges," he asks. "Where the fuck is Vance?"

"You won't find them," I answer and smile. Then, I bluff, "Put that down, or you'll regret it."

He laughs. "You're cute. I thought you were just a pretty face. I might dispatch them all and then have some fun with you before I kill you—with my bare hands. I'll let your boyfriend know how that went...if he comes back."

"So that's your plan, killing everyone?"

"It's a rule. No one knows who we are, what we do, and more importantly, no one talks about us, or they die. Vance knew about it. He chose the wrong side. I sent his little brother to the slaughterhouse. I hope he learns how he dies before I find him and kill him."

I'm praying that Lang sees this and shoots him. My prayers are heard because there's a loud bang. The guy falls to the ground. When I turn, I see Vance staring at him, gun in hand.

My blood runs cold when I notice the grimaced expression. "You okay?"

He nods. "Beacon. Someone should alert him."

"We're already alerting the team," Dad assures him.

"Do you recognize any of them?"

He points at the guy he shot and nods. "That *was* Bennett."

Chapter Forty-One

Grace

WE DON'T FIND any more men around the premises—or outside. The team made themselves scarce. They take the bodies and the men who are still alive away for questioning. We need all the information we can gather to help Beacon and the crew rescue our men. Vance goes with them.

We're glad that the fire department and the sheriff had to focus on the flames and the people trying to come onto the property first. That gave everyone plenty of time to move without being noticed. Unfortunately, they heard the shots.

"It wasn't just the explosion," the sheriff urges. "When we arrived, I heard a gunshot."

Dad shows him a gun and nods. "I thought a person was coming toward us. You can't blame me. I just saw that building explode."

"Mr. Bradley, are you allowed to carry a gun?"

He nods and gives him his business card. "In all states."

"Oh, you're security," the sheriff says and nods. "Do you know what happened? Where are the Aldridge brothers?"

"Sophia, her husband, Mills, and Arden went to the Aragon's place," I explain.

"I think Blaire and Hayes went to check on Mr. Heywood. He wasn't feeling well. Pierce joined them in case they needed help to move him around."

The sheriff sighs. "I hope he didn't have another stroke."

Pierce and Henry arrive at that moment. I jog to meet them. "Stop. I just told them you were visiting your in-laws, and you were at the Heywoods."

Pierce nods. "What happened?"

"It's a long story that I'll tell you later."

"Is everyone okay?" Henry stares at the studio. "Beacon is going to shit himself. All his instruments are inside."

I don't tell him that he has plenty of instruments and his favorites are at home. That's a problem for another day.

"Let's talk with the sheriff," Pierce says.

While the conversation is happening, I look toward the gates where the police are blocking the unauthorized people. There are a lot of people watching. I'm sure we're featured on the town's social media speculating what they think happened here?

Among the crowd is Jerome Parrish. The fire department is doing its best to contain the inferno consuming Beacon's studio. There aren't any trees close to it. Still, they want to make sure it won't spread.

The land bots found explosives around the house. My biggest concern at the moment is Beacon and the mission. Nathan and Lang will be with them—via drones. They are aware it's a trap. Leaving someone behind isn't optional.

When the authorities leave, Dad says, "I'm staying until the team is back. We'll be at the hotel. The security room has the equipment necessary to oversee it."

Henry looks at him, then at me, and shakes his head. "I feel like you should give me my money back for letting you run your business from mine."

Dad grins. "Just think about it as a good cause—we're not charging you for monitoring your properties. That's usually a lot extra."

"What's next?" Pierce asks.

"Stay where you are at until we have neutralized the threat," I order.

"There's still a threat?" Henry asks, looking at the angry flames trying to reach the sky.

I nod.

"Is Beacon okay?" he asks, concerned.

"He'll be fine," I assure him.

I'm not sure how my voice comes out because Dad grabs my hand and squeezes it. Okay, so I'm worried about him. The guy is walking into a trap. I trust him—all of the team. Still, a lot of things can go wrong. I'm not there to help. I feel useless—powerless.

"We have to discuss this with the lawyer." Pierce clears his throat. "Fuck, how do I explain that we were out."

"Easy. You went to hang out with the Heywoods, and Sophia went to check on her parents' place."

"You must've skipped curfew several times," he jokes, then looks at Dad, who growls. "Or not. I'm sure she's a great kid."

We approach Jerome, and Pierce says, "A word, please."

I don't hear what is said. I can only see a couple of nods from Parrish and the worry on his face.

"It's all good. We are allowed to stay away until the security team allows us to come back in, and it won't affect the stipulations."

Dad looks at me. "Where do you want to be?"

The security room, with Beacon… "I don't know."

"You should come with us," Pierce suggests. "Mozzy is there along with the kids."

"That's a good idea," I say and hug Dad. "Call me when you have good news, Dad."

ALL NIGHT I pace back and forth. I haven't heard anything from Beacon, Dad, or anyone for that matter. Around six in the morning, Henry arrives at the house.

"You woke up early," he says.

"I haven't gone to sleep yet."

"You should," Blaire, who is climbing down the stairs, prompts me. "I don't like to be *that* doctor, but it's best if you follow the simple recommendations to stay healthy."

"I eat well."

"Your sleeping habits aren't that…" She pauses and smirks. "They leave me wondering if you're following the medical advice."

"Often," I answer with a word that makes no sense. I often disregard it. I usually follow it, but it all depends on the day.

"What do you have there, Henry?" she asks, staring at the box he holds.

"Casseroles," he answers.

"You're a married man," I remind him.

Since they moved in, the single women have been dropping off food at their home every day. Well, they only do it to flirt with the single Aldridges.

"It's actually for the family."

"For us?" Blaire asks, confused. "That's nice, but why?"

He arches an eyebrow. "You don't know about it?"

"The studio?" she asks. "Everyone knows. I felt the shake and saw the flames. I am glad no one was inside when it happened."

"I just wish someone can update me on what's happening with Beacon."

Henry looks at me. "They didn't tell you?"

My stomach drops, and I shake my head.

"Your dad called around midnight asking if we could set up him and his team with some rooms—he offered to pay. I didn't accept it, though. They saved my family. I owe them a lot."

"Why would they want to stay?"

"There's a change of plans about the operation. Something about waiting for the right time," Henry explains to us. "Vance stayed up all night. He's been in the security room, monitoring the area along with other people from the nerd something."

"Okay, let me go and see if they can update me."

I make my way to The Lodge and enter the room where Vance is, staring at the screens.

"Are you okay?"

He shakes his head.

"Can I help you?"

He turns around and stares at me for a few beats before he speaks. "Your dad had me talking to a therapist for an hour. She said, 'Call me when you're ready for your next session.'"

"What is wrong with that?"

"I was hoping she'd say I'm good to continue with my life and we won't meet again," he answers. "I don't think she believes I'm fine."

"Are you?" I arch an eyebrow. "You killed the man you loved."

"No, I didn't. I thought I loved him." He pauses, taking a big breath. "I had a choice, him or my brother. When I pulled the trigger, I knew the answer. Beacon comes first. There was no hesitation, only anger. He was trying to kill *my family*. Yes, they're fucking annoying, and most of the time I want to punch them, but they're mine."

"It seems like he wanted to finish Beacon before he finished you. Why?"

"Beac is my baby brother. I'm protective of him, even when it looks like I can't stand him. Mom always said, of everyone, he got the worst hand. His mother and father abandoned him."

I want to tell him that maybe he could've reached out to him years ago. It's not the point, though. A lot of things were done that affected them all. Bringing them up doesn't make sense. That's something they have to fix between them.

"What's happening?" I signal toward the monitors. "They are moving in today?"

He nods.

"Nathan and Lang have been scouting the place from the air. Beacon and Seth will plan their move based on the data we gather."

"I'm sorry about what happened last night," I repeat.

He gives me a sad smile. "Maybe that's why the therapist wanted to see me again. I'm either numb or I really don't give a fuck about it."

"Maybe it's both. You're compartmentalizing everything."

His inquiring gaze reminds me of Beacon. I smile and explain to him, "Sorry, my grandfather and my aunt are therapists. You learn a term or two along the way."

I yawn. He shakes his head.

"Go to sleep. Everything will be fine."

"Call me, okay?"

Chapter Forty-Two

Grace

THE ORGANIZATION'S cleanup crew arrives around nine in the morning. They sweep through the entire estate, clean the scene—and the spattered blood—and secure the area. Dad hires a crew to clean the debris of the studio. There's nothing to save.

Vance and I go through the tunnels to check on the bunker. Other than some fallen objects, including frames, everything is fine.

We try to have a normal day, but I can't be still. Not knowing what's happening to Beacon is killing me. It's around eight when Blaire hands me a pill. "Here, take this."

"I don't want anything."

"Listen, either you take it, or I'll try it cartoon style," Leyla demands.

"How is that?"

"You know, I bang your head with a pan and hope for the best," she says.

"I'll sleep when he's back home."

Blaire gives me a glass of water. "You're too stressed to try to sleep. You've been awake for more than twenty-four hours. I'm three weeks from popping out this child, and I can't be nurturing you while focusing on my current patients and worrying about this little one."

"That's low even for you, Blaire," I say, but take the pill. "If I can't sleep, it's your fault. If he arrives before I wake up, it is your fault."

"Go to bed, Grace."

I head to one of the guest bedrooms at Tucker's house. Mozzy follows me and snuggles himself against me.

"Meow," he says.

"I know, he's coming back. They were going to start in a couple of hours. He might be home after midnight."

We both close our eyes and fall asleep.

"GRACE," Dad's voice comes from somewhere, but my eyes are so heavy I can't open them.

"Gracie," he insists. "It's Beacon."

I open my eyes immediately and spring out of bed. My heart is racing fast. "What do you mean?"

Vance is next to him, ashen-faced and worry-eyed.

My body freezes, and I feel as if all the air in the room has been sucked out, and I can't breathe. "What happened to him?"

"He's going to be fine. They're flying him to Saint Francis Memorial in San Diego," he explains.

"What happened?" I insist.

"He got into a fight on a roof. It was a one-story fall, but he's badly bruised. We're heading to San Diego."

"Let me change," I say, going to the bathroom, washing my face, brushing my teeth, and putting on a clean set of clothes.

We leave promptly in two separate helicopters since all the brothers are coming—along with the lawyer. I don't understand why we're bringing him, but I didn't ask. After Dad gave me the news, I haven't been able to speak. I'm focusing on Beacon. He has to be all right. The flight to Portland feels eternal. When we board the plane to San Diego, I text the guys.

Grace: *How is he?*

Mane: *I don't know, G.*

San: *He's sleeping. The EMT gave him something for the pain and fixed him up the best he could so we can transport him to San Diego.*

Grace: *How far away are you?*

San: *Thirty minutes.*

That's too long. I don't want to think about what can happen during transport. Maybe if they tell me how he got hurt, I can deduce if he'll be fine—not that I'm a doctor, but I've seen my fair share of accidents.

Grace: *Was he wearing his armor?*

Fish: *Great, she's trying to solve a mystery. It was a casualty. He did everything right. He's going to be okay.*

Grace: *I might feel better if I know what happened.*

Mane: *He got into a fight, fell from the roof. The armor couldn't protect him from the blade—or the fall. I think he lost blood—and he couldn't move.*

Grace: *What do you mean he couldn't move.*

San: *We don't know, G. As you know, we're not trained medical professionals.*

Grace: *Any other casualties?*

Mane: *No, only him. We tried our best to cover him, but I swear he was the fucking target. I can tell you that they paid for what they did. Also, there's nobody left to tell the story of what happened. Seth's going to need a fucking therapist.*

Grace: *Why?*

Mane: *He feels responsible for what happened to Beac. I keep explaining to him that it wasn't his fault.*

Grace: *There's more to it, isn't there?*

Mane: *One of his guys was playing double agent. I bet they offered him a lot of money while they had them captive.*

San: *I know this is a fucking hard time for you because it's killing us too. However, I want you to stay positive. He'd say just go and party until he's out of the hospital before he joins you.*

Mane: *He would say that.*

Lang: *Turn off the fucking phone!*

Grace: *Look after him. We should be there soon.*

Mane: *You got it.*

"HE'S GOING TO BE FINE," Hayes announces when we arrive at the hospital, and he marches toward a door with a big sign that reads, *Personnel Only.*

During our flight, he was in one of the office spaces on the phone. Unfortunately, he was in the soundproof area. I couldn't hear anything.

"You think they'll let him inside?" Pierce asks no one in particular.

"I made a few calls," Dad answers. "Plus, he's one of the best orthopedic doctors in the world. It'd be stupid not to let him at least assist."

"Isn't there a rule that says doctors can't treat their family?" Henry asks.

Vance glares at him. "Stay fucking positive for once."

Everyone stares at Vance for a second before Mills asks, "Why does he need an orthopedic doctor?"

"He might've broken his back," Dad answers. "We don't know much. For now, we're heading to the reception desk to ask where you'll be donating blood. He lost a lot."

Henry squeezes my shoulder. "He's going to be fine. Did he ever tell you about that time when he fell from the tree?"

"No," I whisper.

"Fuck, he scared us." Pierce sighs. "I thought Dad was going to kill us."

Henry's hand gestures how Beacon fell from one of the tallest trees and landed on his back. "Like a flipped pancake," he says. "He didn't open his eyes for a long time. Hayes ran to get our grandmother and father. We were all staring at him, and suddenly Beac opened his eyes and started laughing."

"He's made out of rubber." Mills grunts. "I swear he'd fall, bump into things, and do so many stupid things. Nothing happens to that kid."

"It's going to be like that," Pierce's voice is almost broken. "Fuck, it has to be like that."

Vance nods, holding the bridge of his nose.

Everything at once finally hits me, and I begin to cry. Dad takes me into his arms and gives the brothers some instructions before taking me away.

"He'll be fine," Dad assures me. "We called all the best specialists I know. They'll be here soon."

"Dad," I hear Seth's voice.

"How is he?" I ask.

"I haven't heard anything," my brother answers and gives me a hug. "I'm so fucking sorry. This…I should've let them die."

"Tell me we did something good," I ask, sniffing.

"We weakened a cartel. I probably have to go back and finish them all. We erased our tracks, though. For all we know, they think it was the assholes they hired who tried to play them."

"It wasn't your fault," Dad suddenly says.

"Why does it feel like it?"

"Because you're a perfectionist," Dad answers. "I need you to call the therapist soon."

I look at Seth. "Beacon would be upset if he heard you."

"I'm praying that he gets up and kicks my ass." He runs a hand through his hair. "I couldn't handle it if…"

Just when I thought the waterworks would stop, I start again.

"He's going to be fine, Gracie," Seth assures me.

THE ONLY UPDATE we get from Hayes is that Beacon will be in surgery for several hours. Dad always has a way to make sure that everyone is taken care of during an emergency like this one. A few hours after we arrived, we're in a private waiting room. My family, including Mom, is here.

I don't like what she says when she hugs me. "Your grandfather called Janelle."

"Why?"

Grandpa Chris glances at me and opens his arms. "Come here, Gracie." He hugs me. "I'm sorry this is happening. We're all praying for him. He's a strong man. He'll come through."

"You called Janelle," I say in an accusatory tone.

"No, it was Gabe who did it."

"Throw me under the bus, rock star," Grandpa Gabe complains and takes me into his arms. "I'm sorry, Gracie. I don't know what to say. Just, we're here for you."

"Thank you, but why did you call her?"

"It might be a good time for them to get closure," Grandpa Chris explains. "If one of my kids had an accident, I'd like to know, even if we were estranged."

This feels surreal, like a funeral. I shake my head and leave the room. I can't deal with closure, grief, or pain.

"He's going to be fine," Mane assures me as he catches up with me. "It's Beacon fucking Aldridge."

"He's right." Seth hugs me.

When I turn around, I notice that the guys and my brothers surround me.

"I know you want to run away, but it'll be best if we all stay in the waiting room—waiting," Seth suggests.

"His mother is coming. She's going to make a scene." I blow out some air as I try to calm myself. "He doesn't like when people air out his private life."

"I'll make sure she behaves," Seth promises.

"Just picture it," Nathan says. "In a couple of hours, you're going to see him, and his first joke is going to be about his broken back and sex."

"Don't be crass."

He grins. "At least I made you less sad and a little raggy."

I wish I could joke like them. They don't see the big picture. According to the guys and the EMT, Beacon couldn't feel his arms or legs. He couldn't move his hands. How is he supposed to create music? His life is making music. It's what he loves the most.

"Come on, Mom is worried about you. She has lunch and snacks, so you can munch while we wait," Seth says, pulling me toward the waiting room.

The moment I enter, I smile. Beac would love this. His family is here. The band, Dad, my brothers, and my grandparents. Some of my cousins came earlier. Tucker has been texting Seth, asking for updates. Jacob and Aunt Pria were in New York when they heard about the accident. They're taking a plane, and some of my cousins are coming with them.

Most importantly, his brothers are here.

Dad approaches me. "You should take a nap."

"What went wrong?" I ask one more time.

He shakes his head. "They did everything right."

"But?"

"You don't expect that the people you are trying to save will turn on you." Dad lifts his gaze, focusing on Mom, then Grandpa Chris. He takes a big sip of air. "He'll pull through. He's a fighter."

"I wish I could be with him."

"Do you want me to request access to his room so you can take a nap?" He sounds like Blaire. She hounded me until I took that pill, and now…I woke up to the worst news ever.

If I go to sleep and—*Don't think about it, Grace. He's going to be okay.*

He has to be fine.

I want to scream to everyone, to no one in particular, "How could you let this happen?"

Of all the people in the world, he's supposed to be the one to stay —forever. Out of all the people in the world, he was meant for me. He's meant to be my exception.

He promised me he'd never leave me again.

"He can't leave me," I sob again.

"He'll be fine."

"Why is it that I feel like he's leaving?"

"Grace, you need to rest," Dad insists. "I don't want you to get sick."

I stare at him with watery eyes. He looks blurry, but I can feel his worry—for me, for Beacon. "If Mom was in the operating room, would you be able to sleep?"

He shakes his head. "I'd try to be in the operating room," he answers sincerely.

"If it was me, Beacon wouldn't be napping."

"No, he'd be pacing outside the doors trying to figure out how to get in and make sure the doctors are doing everything right," he answers, and I hear some regret in his words. "He's always wanted to make sure you're all right."

"I can't just take a nap," I conclude.

"He loves you. I don't think I realized how much until he said fuck it and was done with my rules. I was talking to your mom about everything he's done, and…he'd give his life for you."

I send a silent prayer to God, to Beacon's grandparents, to his brother, to anyone who can hear me. Save him.

Hold on to my fingers, Beacon. This time don't let me go. Hold onto my heart and soul, Beac.

Chapter Forty-Three

Beacon

THE LAST THING I'm going to remember is begging Mane to call Grace and him saying, "Dude, hang on. It's going to be okay."

He could be right or not. I felt nothing. I wasn't in pain, so maybe I was dying. I can't find any other explanation as to why I'm back in Baker's Creek, sitting in the tallest tree next to the lake.

"Fucking Beacon. Get down from there," I hear the voice and look down.

I smile at Carter, "What are you doing here?"

"Someone had to come and find you." He points at the branch.

"Didn't you get it the first time? You're going to fall down and get hurt."

I pat the spot next to me. "We're older. It'll be okay."

He shakes his head, climbs up, and sits beside me.

"Every time I hid, you were the one who found me."

"It wasn't hard. You chose the least obvious places. I just had to think, 'Where the fuck would Beacon go?'"

I laugh. "Such an enlightening philosophy."

"Remember that when you have children," he suggests. "Think, 'what would I be doing if I was his age and my parents or siblings annoyed the fuck out of me?'"

I look at him. He looks less…sick than the last time I saw him. "You look good."

"Better than you."

I look at my body. It's fine. I can wiggle my fingers and move my legs. Then, I remember that I have to go back to Grace. I don't know where she is—or where I am at. "I can't be with you. I need to leave."

"Who invited you to stay?"

"Why am I here?" I ask, confused.

"You missed me?"

"I always do, fucker." I push him, but he doesn't move.

"I'm still around. You just don't see me."

I snort. "So, what? You're spending your eternity haunting us?"

He laughs. "Not at all. Again, you shouldn't be here," he insists.

"So, where am I supposed to be?"

He shrugs. "I…I don't know."

"I thought you'd know everything since you know, you're dead."

He laughs. "I'm busy watching over you assholes—not haunting you. I haven't had time to learn more because my stupid brothers keep fucking around. Do you have any idea how long it took me to get Blaire and Hayes back together?"

"Stop meddling," I order. "We're not some fucking reality show."

"It's been entertaining. It got better once you had to move to Baker's Creek," he confesses.

"Do you know why he did it?" I ask, and add, "Our father. Do you know why he shoved us together like that?"

He nods.

"Are you going to tell me?"

He laughs again. Fucker, he's having a blast. "Have you thought that I might be just a figment of your imagination? A part of your psyche keeping you occupied, so you don't have to face reality?"

"Are you telling me that you're not a ghost from my past taking me away?"

"Why would I want to take you away?"

I scan my body, trying to find the wounds. Nothing. I healed, or my spirit doesn't bring any injuries from the living world. "The last thing I can remember, I couldn't feel my legs or arms. I might never walk or move again—if I make it," I explain to him.

"And that makes you think I'll take *you*?"

"If you needed to take one of us, who would it be? I bet it would be me."

He smirks. "You're still the most creative of us. I'm not the ripper, Beac."

"Can I at least go say goodbye to G?" Fuck, I promised I wouldn't let her go.

"Again, you're not dying," he insists.

"No?"

"Nah, Hayes is in the operating room barking orders. He's good at that shit. You know what's funny?"

"That I get to see your ugly face before I die?"

"Again, you're not dying." The fucker is persistent, or I can't believe him for shit. There's a reason I'm here. Carter looks at me and says something that almost makes me shiver—if I could feel. "Hayes is thinking, 'Carter, find Beac and make sure he's fine. We can't lose him.' Just the way he used to do when you were little."

"Is that laying out the work before I see the light and shit?"

He shakes his head. "You still have a lot to do. Grace is waiting for you. You still have a long life with her, your children, and music. You heard the guys. They can't lose another brother."

"We miss you. I wish—"

"It was my time to leave. I don't have any regrets. Life is about living it—it's that simple. Don't complicate it with useless shit. Tell our brothers I said that." He pats my shoulder.

"They're not going to believe me that I talked to you."

"Probably not," he confirms, looking at the horizon. "Henry will insist that it was a dream or whatever drug they gave you for the pain. Hayes is going to go all scientific on you and explain to you how your mind retreats into a place where it feels safe. Pierce will try to believe you, but he'll have his doubts. After all, you lied to him for almost a year. Mills is going to say, 'I hope you said hi to him.' Vance might grunt, or he might tell you that yeah, he's seen me a time or two."

"Have you seen him?"

He nods. "He's had his brushes with the afterlife too."

"Blaire?"

"She'll smile, look up and say, 'Thank you for watching over the kid.'"

"Were you in love with her?"

"Nope. I loved her, but not that way. She's always going to be the person who saved me from a miserable ending."

"I wish you could come back with me." I pat his leg.

"Again, I'm with you when you need me. Plus, someone has to keep company with the old man."

"He's not in hell?" I ask, confused, surprised, and I even look around to see if I catch him.

"Who told you I'm in heaven?"

"I just—"

He chuckles. "The guy was human. A man who fucked up a lot. He didn't know how to say fuck it, it's my life. Just dig deeper. You might find some answers."

"What he did—"

"He's insane. I'm not excusing him, but it wasn't only him. The adults who were in charge of us made a lot of mistakes. We paid the price. Our father died, regretting his life."

"You forgave him after what happened when you were dying?"

He closes his eyes and nods. "In a way, he loved Mom enough to try to save her son. I let it go, and maybe you guys should let it go too. Forgive him."

"So, your mom was the love of his life?"

He laughs.

"What did I say that's funny?"

"I feel like I'm in the middle of a tactical interrogation." He snorts. "You surprised the fuck out of everyone. It's cool. You do you. Well, stop doing this double life shit."

"I can't. G won't quit this life."

"Her guy almost died. I'm sure she'll do anything to ensure that you stick around longer. Your bandmates are there because they are loyal to you and Grace. But have you ever asked if they are happy doing it?"

I shake my head. If I get out of this one, I have to talk to them about it.

"It was cool when you were eighteen. Now, it might be time to retire."

More like back then, it made sense to become a part of The Organization. I was good at it; G was going to be a part of it. The guys were going to be my team.

"I was great at football, and you didn't see me joining the college team."

"It's not the only thing I do. Maybe I can change the way I do everything?"

"Just remember when you questioned if this was your future. There's always an expiration date for some jobs. This might be yours, and today could be a big sign that all of you have to rethink your priorities. Music is your first love."

"No, it's Grace."

"Grace is music, so it's all the same," he responds.

"You sound like a wise big brother I wish was still around."

"There's no do-over for me." He gives me a sad smile. "There's a second chance for you. It's going to be fucking hard, but I trust you'll do it without being an asshole."

"This is it when I see the light?"

He laughs. "Yep, the bright fluorescent light in your room. Until then, enjoy the sunset."

Chapter Forty-Four

Beacon

WHEN I FINALLY OPEN MY eyes, I can't move. There's a tube inside my mouth, machines beeping, and Hayes staring down at me.

"You're the first patient I've had that's opened his eyes when I said, 'He should be waking up just about now,'" he says, smiling. "I'm going to get a nurse to pull the tube. Don't try to talk, okay?"

I blink because what else can I do. I want to ask him about Grace. That's when I feel someone squeezing my hand.

I feel her—her touch. I breathe, relieved that the numbness is gone. I try to move my neck, but I can't. My eyes open wide.

"I immobilized you," Hayes warns me.

So, this is how it ends?

"You have a long way to go. We repaired your whole fucking body. I assume that you can feel touch. That's why you're agitated, because you felt Grace squeezing your hand, but you can't see her. Can you wiggle your fingers?"

I do as he says, and that's when I hear her voice. "He can."

Grace stands up and smiles at me, then kisses my forehead. "Hey, stranger."

I try to smile, but the fucking tube doesn't allow it.

"You had me worried." She caresses my face with the back of her hand. She smirks. "I'm going to play nurse when you come home."

She's trying to be brave, making a joke, but I can see her worry, the sadness, and all the pain in her soul. I wish I could hug her, have her pressed against me.

A team of nurses arrives. Hayes says, "Sorry, Grace, you have to wait outside."

She bends over and whispers, "Thank you for not letting go."

I want to beg her not to leave me. A tear rolls down her cheek, and I wish I could wipe it away. I follow her with my gaze until the door closes behind her. They take out the tube, Hayes feeds me a few chips of ice and says, "Don't try to speak just yet, okay."

I take a deep breath, looking at him. I hope he says more than that.

"It's been almost three weeks since the accident," he starts. "We put you into a medically induced coma. There's significant swelling of the brain. I wasn't sure if you had any damage or how severe it was. The neurologist and I concluded that it'd be best to shut you down until your body began to heal. Now that you're awake, we begin the healing part. It's going to be hard, but you have a great team behind you."

Is this what Carter meant?

The work I was going to have to put into the future. Am I never going to walk again?

"While you've been sleeping, we had the construction company build two extra rooms in the gym for your physical therapy. For now, we're going to use the pool at The Lodge, but we have plans on building an indoor pool. We hired the therapists to come and help you. Will you walk again? Yes. Is it going to be hard? Yes."

He puts a paper cup on my lips. "Okay, let's try to swallow some water."

I do as he says, and he smiles. "At least you can do the basics. Can you talk?"

"How long?" I ask. My voice is raspy, and my mouth still feels like I swallowed a bunch of sand.

He grins. "Good, you can speak."

"Why do I feel like you weren't sure if I would speak?"

"I had no idea if you had cerebral damage. We're going to have to run several tests before you can go home. Maybe you're all right," he answers, "or you're fucking fine. For all I know, you were faking it like the time you fell from the tree. This time you have a broken back and a few stitches."

"I never faked it," I tell him. "I swear, I fell, and then everyone was looking at me as if I had died."

"You were unresponsive," Hayes repeats. "I couldn't feel you breathing."

I roll my eyes. We're never going to agree about that day, are we? "So, when can I move back home?"

"It's going to be a slow process," he says, touching my hand. "Can you feel this?"

"Stop pinching me, asshole!"

"I'm going to do it with all of your body. I need you to complain every time you feel it."

"Fuck, fuck, fuck!" We continue for a long time until I say, "Is this some kind of torture?"

"No, I just want to make sure there's no nerve damage or paralysis."

"You'd know if you'd release me from these weird needles that seem to be holding my body," I complain. "Is this a doctor's kink?"

He shakes his head. "Your brain functions seem to be the same."

"Hey, you said it's been almost three weeks. What's going on with Blaire and your little spawn?"

"She hasn't gone into labor yet," he answers, taking my vitals. "I'm hoping that we can transport you to Baker's Creek before the baby comes. If not, your in-law has a plane on standby for me."

"Can I speak to Grace?"

"I'm almost done. There's a long line of people waiting to see you, so make it fast. You can't speak much, or you'll get tired. Let's see how many smart comments you have to keep to yourself." He chuckles.

"Hey, were you asking Carter to take care of me?"

He looks at me weirdly and smiles. "Yeah, I told him to find you and stay with you while we saved you."

"He did."

Hayes closes his eyes for a second and says, "I fucking miss him."

"I told him that too," I assure him, then I add, "Thank you for saving me."

"Anything for you, kid. I'm just glad you're with us." He squeezes my hand and leaves the room.

Grace comes back. Her eyes are red and puffy.

"You okay?"

"I am now." She brushes her lips against mine.

"Don't you think I deserve more than that?"

"The doctor said I have to be careful," she explains, holding my face. "I was scared."

"Because you thought I wouldn't walk again?"

She shakes her head. "You were in a coma because he had no idea if there was brain damage. That could mean many things—I just can't imagine a world without you, your voice, or your laugh."

"I held on tight to your soul," I say.

She gasps, touching her lips.

"What?"

"I...I said that while you were in surgery. Then I had a dream of you where you promised you'd never let go."

"If I could, I would hug you." I look at her, at her fading pink hair and her sad face. She's hurting so fucking much, and I have no idea how to make it better.

She shrugs a shoulder. "I guess I'll be the one hugging you until you're better. That can be an incentive to make you work harder. You can hug me when you regain your strength."

"I'll do anything to have you back in my arms," I tell her.

She scrunches her nose.

"What is it?"

"My family thought it'd be a good idea to tell your mom that you're here," she mumbles.

"Are there cameras outside filming her crying over her almost dead son?" I sigh, because the last thing I need is to have a show outside this room.

"No, it's just her. She's come every day to check on you. Unfortunately, she arrived when I went to the waiting room to give the good news to everyone."

I remember what Carter told me. I have to let go of things. Forgive. Make things simpler for everyone—including her.

"What do you think?"

"I hate her," she says. "But as I mentioned, she's been dropping by daily to check on you. I'm not saying she's the runner-up for the mother of the year, but she wants to see you, and maybe it's a good idea."

"Getting closure?"

"Something like that," she explains.

"You know what I owe you?"

She smiles and shakes her head. "Nothing, I only need you." She pauses. "Maybe we owe each other the rest of our lives."

She kisses my lips. "You're not supposed to talk much. Hayes might not be happy if you're tired out by the time he comes to check on you."

I want to remind her that I owe her a date. I want us to fall in love again. There's a list we need to revisit. This time I listen to the advice because I can't set back my recovery.

She kisses my nose. "Let me get your mother."

I want to reach for her hand and ask her to stay. All I need is her.

Chapter Forty-Five

Beacon

WHEN MY MOTHER enters the room, I expect the fashionable starlet who can't leave her house without makeup, her long hair styled, and the latest fashion. The woman who enters wears yoga pants, a sweatshirt, and her light brown hair pulled into a ponytail.

She looks at me from head to toe and gasps. "They didn't warn me. What happened to you?"

"I fell," I answer vaguely.

"Yes, something about being on a stage and falling." She waves her hand. "Maybe you should stop drinking before your concerts."

"Why are you here?"

"I understand why you're upset with me." She sighs, pacing. I want to tell her that she fucking needs to stay in one place because I can't move. "You've been dodging my calls."

I stare at her. I'm definitely not wasting my energy on explaining to her why I'm not going to sing with her or approve her book. More so when I can't even fucking move.

"I'm not the bad guy. I was young." She stops, staring at me.

"That's your excuse for leaving your eighteen-month-old child?" The machine begins to beep.

Hayes enters right away. "Is everything okay?"

I raise an eyebrow. He points at the monitors. "Your heart rate increased." He then looks at my mother. "Please keep it simple and don't upset him."

He closes the door and leans against it.

"I need to speak to him." She stares at Hayes.

He crosses his arms. "Well, either you talk while I'm here or your turn is over."

"You were giving me your excuse," I prompt her.

"I never had an excuse. I legitimately didn't like children. When you were born, I didn't know what to do with you," she explains. "My parents said it was my problem. I had money to hire a nanny. I did. Your father didn't like it."

"You cared what my father thought?"

"Listen, I was a kid. A twenty-year-old woman who liked to date older men. They didn't do drama like the guys my own age. They treated me like a queen. In my circle, the men my age were stupid idiots who liked to pass the joint and the women they fucked. William was different. He was in his thirties and handsome."

"That's your excuse? You were young. Why not just give me up?" I look at Hayes, who shrugs.

"William wanted you. I liked to please him. But the asshole disappeared on me often." She gives me a wicked smile. "When he realized I had a nanny watching you, he tried to take you away from me."

"Why not let me go with him?"

"Just because I didn't want to change your diapers doesn't mean I didn't love you. I do. You're my kid." She says it with conviction.

Hayes scratches his head. "It doesn't make sense. So, you had a custody battle?"

"Your father served me with the papers. I hired a lawyer who researched everything about your dad. He found a way to keep my son."

"How?" I ask.

"As you know, William had five mistresses and a wife," she answers, eyeing Hayes. "Before we countered the custody request, my lawyer, my manager, and I made sure he got caught with you. It served him right. All the lies crumbled within a day."

"It was you?" Hayes stares at her, not upset but more like confused. "Why?"

"The man had six women—seven children. If he had been honest from the beginning, I might've been okay with his polygamy, or not. He didn't give me an option—he wanted to take my kid away from me."

"So, you forbid him to see me after that?"

"No, that was the crazy lawyer. Sarah, I think that's her name. She suggested a hefty trust, paying child support, and…I really can't remember what else she proposed. We all ended up with different arrangements. His wife is the one who proposed that you spend a week with him—so you could grow together. Mine included giving custody of you to my parents."

I'm confused. There are so many questions swirling inside my head. "So, Grandma and Grandpa didn't want me?"

"They did, but they also wanted me to be responsible. When the custody battle for you guys began, they accepted to take care of you. I wasn't going to leave you with him."

"But he wanted me," I insist. Something about it makes things slightly different. It changes the narrative on how I used to see him.

"He did. We made sure he didn't get any of you," she says with an air of victory I don't like.

"Why would you do that?" Hayes asks.

"I think it was the best way to make him pay for what he had done to us."

"So, he didn't abandon us?" I ask again.

"No, he was actually a good dad when he was around."

"What is wrong with you?" My voice comes out harsh and the machines beep again.

Hayes looks at me and shakes his head. "I understand, but your health is more important. Maybe she should leave."

"Listen, I can only speak for myself. I was in my early twenties, Beacon. Imagine yourself at that age trying to mend your broken heart while dealing with much older women. I…maybe I would've done things differently if I had been older. Marie didn't like the idea at all, but she got onboard when she realized that she could lose custody of her son and have to move to New York. Addison wasn't much older than me. Her dad was harsh and didn't want Vance to grow up with a father like William. In a way, we were trapped."

I take a couple of seconds to think about what she's saying. It's too much to digest. I can't deal with any of it—or her.

"Why are you here?" I ask before I request her to leave.

"I want to make sure you're all right."

"Is this going to be added to your tell-all story?" My tone comes out more sarcastic than I intended.

"No. I'll send you the book. I want you to read it to see if it's something your grandparents would approve of. I don't want to add you. I…I'd like to sing with you because I think it'd be good for my career, but I'm not heartless."

"Why did you stay away for so long?"

"Your grandparents requested it so I wouldn't confuse you. I'm undependable. That's not great for a developing mind," she explains.

"So, what now?"

"I don't know." She shrugs. "I wish we could be closer. Like a strange aunt who comes to visit you?"

"I guess we could try that. Can I see that custody agreement?" I ask, because I want to know more. There's a story behind it.

"Your grandpa had it," she answers. "Since he became your guardian along with Mom, they had to have proof that they were responsible for you."

Hayes taps his watch. "Time for you to leave."

She nods. "I'm glad you have people who love you, Beacon. I'm sorry for not doing the right thing."

"What was the right thing?"

"William would've been a good father if I had let him have you… and maybe you wouldn't hate me. I feel responsible for what I did," she concludes. "It's been almost thirty years. I handled everything poorly, but there's nothing we can do to fix it. Is there?"

I think about my life. Grace comes to mind. "I'll always choose my fate if it takes me right next to G."

"Still, I'm sorry."

"It's fine," I repeat. "When I'm better, maybe we can share a cup of coffee."

She gives me a sad smile. "I'd like that." She looks at Hayes. "Keep me updated on his condition."

She turns back to me. "Call if I can do anything for you."

"Thank you for coming."

"You okay?" Hayes asks after he shuts the door.

I sigh. "Can you find those custody agreements?"

"This doesn't make sense," he says. "But it does. I remember my parents fighting about where we were going to live. Dad wanted us to move to New York. It was weird since they were getting a divorce. Then one day he never came back."

He gives me a long look. "Are you up for more or do you want a break?"

"Can I have G? I promise not to talk."

He nods. "She barely left your side. You can't see it, but there's a bed on the other side of the room. It's the only way to get her to sleep. I'm sure she'll be happy to keep everyone away and be by your side."

"Thank you."

"I'll talk to Pierce to see what he can find about the custody."

"Is he around?"

He shakes his head. "No. Parrish only let me stay. They had to leave two days after your accident. By the way, you were on a poorly built stage and fell."

That explains what my mother said. Nice lie, Bradley. Fuck, he's going to kill me when he sees me. Maybe even fire me.

Chapter Forty-Six

Beacon

BLAIRE GOES into labor five days after I wake up; Hayes leaves immediately. My nephew, Machlan Carter Aldridge, comes into the world a day before my birthday. Jerome Parrish allows my brothers and Leyla—who is the only one who can travel—to visit me that day. A lot of things happen while I'm hospitalized.

Seth finally has the last piece to get the Bryants into jail. There was a teenager who was having a child and reached out to them. We hired her to go along with the process, promising that we'd find a good place for her child.

When we had proof, Pierce offered a deal to his mother. She accepted it at first, but then things spiraled out of control.

His own mother tried to incriminate him. Thankfully, the authorities had proof that he hired us to investigate and about everything else the firm had done. She's serving time along with several members of her family. I'm sad that I missed it, but glad that it's over.

I stay in the hospital for three more weeks. Hayes wasn't kidding about having a kick-ass team to help me. They are fucking kicking my ass. Grace and the guys are with me every day, helping with rehab. Seth is the one who flies me to Baker's Creek. We have a landing strip now. Apparently, my brothers will do anything for me.

Not that I plan to cash in on it, but it feels good to know that they genuinely worry about me.

"This is the last time I'll carry you," San says, as he helps me get off the plane. "The next time, you better be walking."

"You wait and see," I assure him. "I'll be running faster than you before the year is over."

Grace, who is at the bottom of the stairs waiting with the wheelchair, smiles at me. "One step at a time, Beac."

"You saw me walking yesterday." I kiss her once San settles me in the chair.

"Ready?" she asks.

I hold her hand and nod. "Take me to our next destination, kind sir," I joke.

San grunts, but he pushes me toward the main house. Lang, Fish, and Mane are right behind us with Seth. I turn my attention to where my studio used to be and noticed that some workers are pointing from left to right while looking at a blueprint. Henry and I were on the phone the other day, and he promised he'd build me a better one.

It's going to be a long time before I can step into a studio. Only Grace knows that I'm having trouble holding a guitar, let alone strumming the chords. That's a fine motor skill I can't seem to grasp yet. It's the one thing that's fucking with my head. What if I never get to play again?

I stop and remember that I'm alive, and that's enough for now.

There's a ramp at the entrance. It's then when I notice there's a trail from the landing strip all the way to the main house. When Grace opens the door, I hear a loud, "Surprise!"

"So much for getting home and resting," I joke, smiling when I spot Blaire holding Machlan. "Can I?"

Blaire hands him to me. I'm extra careful. Grace is beside me, watching. She knows I might lose my strength and drop him.

"Hey, buddy. I'm glad we finally meet. Remember, I'm your favorite uncle."

Blaire kisses my cheek. She's crying. "You are still my favorite, kid. I'm so glad you're fine."

"I'm indestructible."

Hayes looks at me, rolls his eyes, and takes Machlan away from me. "Just don't do it again. I had a hard time putting you back together."

Grace takes me around the house. I notice the furniture is different. There's enough space for my chair. There's also a chair attached to the wall that seems to go upstairs. This is what the counselor and I discussed once I woke up from the coma. I might have trouble accepting my situation. It's temporary. I'm not the accident, the chair, or my current condition. I'm Beacon fucking Aldridge.

A guy with a new life who is finding his way in the world. It might take me years to walk again like I used to before. I might be lucky enough to only need a year to recover from that fucking accident. The biggest challenge is going to be adjusting my mind to what my body can do.

While the party is happening, Vance asks if we can talk.

I nod, and he takes me outside where there are fewer people and we can have some privacy.

"How are you?" I ask.

"Shouldn't I be asking you that?"

I shake my head. "Grace told me how you killed him."

He runs a hand through his hair. "It was a quick decision, him or my family. If I let him live, he would try killing us at a later time. I wasn't even sure if we'd be able to reach you and stop you from walking into the trap. What happened?"

"One of our guys," I answer. "We were about to leave when he attacked me. I wasn't expecting him. He knew the armor's weak points—knives. It just...who knew that we'd be betrayed by our own people."

"I'm sorry," he repeats. "If I hadn't made that call…"

"Before this, I never lived by the what-ifs. Now, I can't do it at all. Never say that again," I warn him.

He nods.

"It's going to take time for me to process everything," I explain to him, "because I don't know how things will look in five years for me. I have to adjust. But you…you're never recovering him. I need to know that you'll be fine."

He looks at me, then glances at the surrounding area and whistles. "I don't even know what *fine* is, Beacon. I'm with a therapist because apparently my issues are deeper than killing my ex-lover and almost losing my brother. I guess we both have to work hard to adjust to our new lives."

Chapter Forty-Seven

Grace

DAD and I watch Beacon while he talks to Vance.

"How are you handling this?" Dad asks.

I stare at Beacon. "It's hard to cope with his anger," I confess. "He's not an angry guy. It hurts to see how the accident changed him, but I have hope. When he realizes that things are steering to the dark side, he fights those new demons."

"Call me if you need anyone to talk to," he repeats.

I nod. "Other than that, he's Beacon fucking Aldridge, showing the world he can make things happen with hard work and the right mind."

According to his physical therapists and Hayes, he's made a lot more progress than many people in his condition. Beacon claims it's because he promised his brother Carter that he'd work hard. The silver lining from this accident is that he spent some time with his brother. Some don't want to believe him, I do. I want to think Carter held his hand when I couldn't. That he is who brought him back to me.

"Just remember that you don't have to take shit from anyone, not even him."

"No worries, Dad. My psychotherapist and I are working on my own issues," I mention.

Ever since the accident, I was asked to find a counselor who can give me support while I hold Beacon's hand. Also, to help me deal with the trauma of almost losing him. It was hard to wait and watch him do nothing for nearly three weeks.

Beacon has a therapist too. This is going to be hard, even more so because he can't just go home. He needs to stay in Baker's Creek for another seven months. His brothers might not understand him—or worse, they might be too condescending with him. At least the guys are staying in Baker's Creek too. If anything, Beac has us—his second family—to support him.

"The times I've spoken to him, he's asked me to extend his sabbatical. Maybe transfer him to the Nerd Herd, unless you and the team want to quit. Then, he'll quit."

I look at Dad. "What do you want?"

"For you to be happy," he answers. "You guys are a great team, but I want what's best for all of you. I can't see any of you working with another leader. He doesn't seem like he wants to go back anytime soon. You haven't mentioned work."

I shake my head. "I can't imagine being in the field without him—or on a stage. He needs me as much as I need to be with him."

Dad smiles at me and nods. "Should I buy a house around here?"

I look at Beacon. My entire body relaxes when I notice him

smirking as his other brothers approach him. "No, I'm sure we'll be back home when he's ready."

Hopefully, Beacon's perspective on his family dynamic will change soon from never seeing them again to coming and visiting often. I'm hopeful that his arms and hands will heal, and if not, he'll find another way to create music.

"WE NEVER DISCUSSED THIS," Beacon says, staring at the bed. "Are you staying or leaving?"

"Where do you want me?"

"Stop tiptoeing around my feelings, G," he says, sighing. "I can tolerate it from anyone but you. You don't take shit from me. Keep doing that. I need it to feel normal."

"I'm trying. It's just too hard. I almost lost you. You're closed up to me. I don't know what you're thinking half of the time. When you're angry, you retreat—only your therapist knows what's happening."

"I'm fucking adjusting," he says. "I don't want to be angry, but it's fucking insane that my body can't catch up to my brain—or maybe it's the other way around. My brain should understand that I might not be able to do shit. What if I can't play again?

"I want you to give me a solution. I want you to not say shit that will give me hope. I want you to leave because what if this is it. And yet I don't want you to leave me. And what am I supposed to say to you—but what if I don't say anything and we fuck this up?"

"We won't," I tell him, going to the box I had delivered a few weeks back.

I open it and take out the small drums. Setting them up on his lap, I grab my cello and sit on the bed. It's not the best posture, but they took away my chair when they reconditioned the room. I begin to play. It sounds strange; I haven't done this in so many weeks. I played for him while he was in a coma. Once he woke up, I stopped doing it and focused on his recovery.

"It's time," I say.

Closing my eyes, I let my feelings flow through my music—the pain, the anger, and mostly the love. I don't keep track of the time, but at some point, I hear him using his hands to follow me. We do it for a long time.

This isn't a love song.

It's a healing song.

I'm not sure what we're unbreaking—or fixing—but I know that we'll have to do this again and again until he remembers who he is.

He's an artist. The music he composes comes from his soul. He's not a guitar, nor his legs. He's an entire orchestra who can figure out a way to share his gift in many ways.

The drums stop. I don't. I continue playing, and that's when I feel the bed move to the side. Soon, his legs are hugging mine, his arms wrap around my body. His lips rest on my neck. He hums the melody while nibbling my skin. His hands run up and down my chest, his mouth begins to kiss me.

"They say there's a secret to having a great life," he mumbles. "Greatness comes from knowing what's worth holding on to. To let go of everything that's not worth your time."

He kisses my spine, dusting a trail of kisses along as he takes off my shirt.

"I don't care if I never walk or play again, as long as you're with me."

Opening my eyes, I stop playing and turn to look at him. "I'm yours. No matter what happens to us, I won't leave you—ever."

I put the cello on the stand and join him in bed. Slowly, we undress each other as we kiss tenderly. This is different from the last time I was with him. There's no urgency, but there's no prelude to our song. We just find our rhythm once we're naked. I sit on top of him, slowly sliding down his hardness. He fills me with his thickness.

This is us, fusing after a painful separation.

Making music again and dancing at the same rhythm. Maybe we didn't lose anything. We just needed to find the right song to play while he's healing.

"I love you," I mumble while we make love.

"I love you more, G. I'd be lost without you anchoring me."

Chapter Forty-Eight

Beacon

IT'S BEEN ALMOST three weeks since I came back to Baker's Creek. Grace and I are working on our issues through music. Well, that and making love. It seems like I have enough strength to do anything in bed—or in the pool. The only problem with the second one is that we got caught by Henry. It wasn't pretty.

Lang had to leave town. His clients are needy. Mane, San, and Fish have been helping with my rehabilitation along with my brothers and Grace. Hayes claims I need supervision because if I was left alone, I'd be overworking myself. Apparently, there's a thin line between working hard to achieve my goals and fucking up my body because I'm overdoing it.

Today, I decide to wake up early and try to at least do my chore—breakfast. Yesterday, I practiced preparing a meal with my occupational therapist. The entire session felt therapeutic. It reminded me of the happy times I spent with Mrs. Bradley learning how to cook. Taking care of others is a gift. It brings me peace, happiness, and comfort.

It's still a task to move from my wheelchair, to the stair lift, to the wheelchair downstairs, but I can do it on my own. That's one of this week's goals. I can check it off the list. The new list Grace and I decided to create. We included sexual positions to it. I need more incentive than swimming to the other side of the fucking pool.

When I arrive at the kitchen, Pierce is setting the basket of fresh eggs on the table.

"I heard you started selling them to Paige at the bakery because you guys kept having cold cereal for breakfast," I tease him.

He turns around to look at me. "You're up early."

"I'm always up early at the gym working out," I remind him.

Mozart, who is trying to eat from Buster and Daisy's bowl, looks at me and prances toward me. He leaps on top of my lap and meows. While we were away, Leyla trained the dogs and him to get along. Mozzy even goes with them to the barn every morning to feed the animals. So far, he hasn't toyed with the chickens. Feathers are his favorite toys.

"How are you feeling?"

"Better," I say.

"You must be since you're fucking around the house—and The Lodge," he teases me. "We understand there's *a list*, but stick to doing it in your room."

"I'm just saving all this for later," I warn him. "Wait until I find ways to give you a hard time."

"We have to take advantage while we can." He winks at me.

Looking at the counters and the kitchen, I ask, "So, when I can stand up for long periods, are you going to keep the kitchen this low?"

"Yeah, we thought it'd be great for the kids. We can teach them how to cook—like your grandma did with you when you were little," he explains.

I smile. Maybe I have to tell them the real story; perhaps someday. Then, I remember Janelle's first visit to the hospital.

"Did you find the custody agreements?"

He nods. "Is your mom still in touch with you?"

"She came a few more times to visit," I answer. "We exchange texts weekly. I think we'll have this weird relationship where she texts me on my birthday and holidays. I'll do it when Grace reminds me to check on her."

"It's better than my mother and me," he answers. "I'm dead to her. My entire family hates me—probably because they are disbarred and in jail."

"That would do the trick." I move around the kitchen, looking for ingredients. "So, the custody agreements."

"I can only find the finalized agreements. There aren't any drafts saved anywhere," he explains. "However, Hayes told us Janelle's conversation. Mills and Vance called their mothers. They actually came to visit."

"Why wasn't I told about this?"

He raises an eyebrow. "I assumed you were preoccupied with other shit."

"A conference call could've been scheduled around my therapy."

"Tough luck, kid. Either you play 007, or you stay at home—like we agreed from the beginning."

I wave my hand and focus on making breakfast. "You were saying about the visit?"

"Once the paparazzi caught on that Janelle had a kid and William was married, he filed for custody of each one of us. Addison said he didn't want to lose us. In fact, he wanted us to grow up together, in Manhattan. It was my mother and Henry's mom who began to dispute everything to make him pay. It was more about how they'd get back at him than looking at what was best for us.

"The battle could've lasted years. It began to get nasty, and William just let it go and accepted most of the conditions our mothers asked for—except for a few. He requested they send Henry to boarding school. He wanted him away from his grandfather and his mother. Hayes' mom wasn't allowed to get married until Carter turned eighteen. She's the one who proposed the one week a year with William. It's her weird way to ensure that we grew up together."

"Can you do that in a custody agreement? I would've said fuck it and married the first woman I found just to piss of my ex."

"She could've ignored it, but then William could've come back to fight her for custody of his children," Pierce states. "I'm sure she agreed to it just to get the divorce over with. Remember, they were legally bonded."

"What about you?"

"My mother was a fucking lawyer," he reminds me. "She made sure to get a lot and gave nothing in return—her child support was hefty compared to the others. Addison wasn't allowed to send Vance to any military school," he continues. "You had to stay with your grandparents."

"How about Mills?"

He smiles. "Oh, that one was low-key. The woman is a sweetheart. Marie said she wasn't going to fight him until he threatened to take all of us away."

"He was crazy," I conclude.

"Totally insane," he agrees. "How in the world was it okay to have different women, many kids, and keep everything secret? I don't know what he was thinking. There has to be someone who knows why he was a sociopath."

"Carter told me he's human but died with a lot of regrets."

Pierce shakes his head. "I want to believe that you saw him."

I burst into laughter and point at the hot skillet. "Slide it into the oven."

"Why are you laughing?"

"He said you'd say that." I go to the table to grab the watermelon. "You might want to help me cut it. I don't think I can do it sitting in the chair."

"You're just having fun about seeing him."

"Maybe it wasn't real and my mind just wandered. As Henry told me, 'I want to believe he was there while you were confused, waiting to come back.'"

He nods. "That I can see."

"By the way, I need you to do me a favor," I ask.

"You left our bed too early," Grace says, kissing me and taking Mozzy from my arms. "Morning, Pierce."

"Hey, Grace. Our cook is back. This time I might keep him."

She glances at him and shakes her head. "You can borrow him for a few more months. After that, I'm taking him home."

"This is home," Pierce insists. He looks at me.

"She's the boss." I give him a look that says, what can I do? "We'll come back to visit often. I'll have my kick-ass studio and a lake house. You promised to come and tour with me."

"I will," he promises. "What did you need?"

"For you to cut the watermelon," I say, hoping that he doesn't ask about the other thing. G is here, and we can't talk in front of her.

Chapter Forty-Nine

Grace

IT'S BEEN a couple of months since we came back to Baker's Creek. It's warm enough that we can swim in the lake. Henry banned us from The Lodge's pool. It was costing him too much to have the pool cleaned every time we fucked around. The studio is finally ready. The guys came for the informal inauguration.

They know Beacon might not want to play—or he might choose another instrument, like a tambourine. He's pretty good at shaking maracas.

"When did you start walking with crutches?" Fish asks.

"A week ago," I respond. "He's making progress. I think his hand-eye coordination is almost as it used to be. His legs are sustaining him a lot more than before."

Beacon gives me a wicked smile. We've made love a couple of times against the wall. He can last only few minutes. Not because he comes fast, but because his legs are still weak.

"Where is Lang?" Beacon asks.

"Stuck in London with his boy band—and not in a good way," San answers. "I think they're about to break up and become another one-hit wonder band."

"I told him not to get involved with those guys," Mane says.

I dare to ask, "Was he sleeping with any of them?"

"No. He doesn't sleep with clients or relatives of his clients," he recalls.

When we enter the studio, everything is different. It looks a lot like the studio we have in Seattle.

Beacon scans the place and finally asks, "Who helped Henry build this?"

"Lang did," Mane responds. "He had the connections, the people, and the blueprints from the original. We just recommended a few modifications—because the other one is an older model."

As we walk, they show me each room. The voice, recording, and production rooms have removable walls. There's a break room—and a music room too.

"What do you think, boss?"

"I love it," Beacon answers. "And I'm no longer your boss."

"Are we quitting The Organization?" Mane asks.

We all go silent.

Beacon shrugs. "What do you want? Forget about the accident and if I'll be able to go back, or not. What do each one of you want?"

San calls Lang and brings him up to speed before putting him on speaker.

"I'm part of the Nerd Herd—your nerd specialist," Lang answers. "I could do it—only with you. If you're out, I'm retiring too. I do it because it keeps me close even when I have to be far because of work."

"I do it for you," Mane answers.

San is the one who surprises us when he says, "If they need me to go in, watch from afar to make sure no one dies, I might volunteer. It's fun. I'm not in the field like you guys."

"I'm out," Fish says. "I'm done, I can't do it again. Not after I almost lost one of my brothers."

They all look at me. I smile. "I think I can still do some undercover work. Like go and play celebrity and get some tactical information—you guys could do it too. I just wouldn't do anything in the field."

"I'm with her," Beacon says. "You guys know the information they provide us after a few drinks."

"I could do that too," Mane says, and the other two nod. "So, from now on, it's just music then."

Beacon nods. "Only music."

"HOW ARE YOU FEELING?" Blaire asks.

We're sitting on the porch, drinking tea, and watching Arden play with Hadley—the new nanny. Or as we have to call her, our new friend. I'm not sure how Pierce worked around hiring her. All I know is that she's been here since Beacon's accident.

"And here I thought Hadley was a figment of your imagination," I joke, kind of. They keep mentioning her, but Beacon and I have never seen her since we arrived. "We wondered if you hid her in the bunker."

She laughs and shakes her head. "As you know, we set up a nursery-playroom at the factory. She's either in Happy Springs, at the medical practice with us, or at Pierce's office."

"That explains why we haven't seen her." I bob my head, studying Hadley. I don't believe I've seen her around town.

"You haven't answered me. How are you doing?"

I take a moment to analyze her question. "Great."

"This can't be easy for you," she states.

"Why not?" I ask, curious about her answer, but instead of letting her speak, I do it. "Beacon is alive. He's finding a new rhythm—we're finding our tune, so to speak. We're together. That's really what this is about, sharing everything. The good, the bad, and the fucked up. I had time to cry and be devastated. When he woke up from the coma, I knew the wallowing was over because we had to rebuild—together."

She squeezes my hand. "I admire your courage and strength. I'm glad he has you."

"We have each other," I mumble.

Chapter Fifty

Beacon

MILLS' ice rink is ready. He convinces Hayes to let me skate. At least, skate like a four-year-old holding an ice skating trainer. The one-hour sessions leave me exhausted. My prize is going to the coffee shop for a hot cocoa. You'd think that it'd be easier to make one at home. It could be, but the lady waiting for me at the shop is my real reward.

"You're doing great," Mills says as we make our way to Main Street. "I wallowed in self-pity for a long time before getting real help."

"I have Grace and all my family's support."

The word *family* is broad, it includes my brothers, my sisters-in-law, my band, and Grace's family too. I'm so fucking lucky to have all of them with me.

He grins. "It seems like they're serious about the family shit, doesn't it?"

I nod. "Maybe if we had reached out to them...but it's okay not to look back and just enjoy what's happening."

"I'm still not sure what the future is going to look like. We don't have much time left around here," he mumbles. "Are you staying?"

"Grace is too close to her family to take her away from them," I state. "It doesn't mean that I'm not coming back. It's just that I can't promise to stay. We'll build a house, next to the big tree by the lake."

"Your lucky spot?"

I nod. Ever since I came back from the accident, every evening I go there to watch the sunset. Sometimes it's just me, other times Grace joins me. Some days all my brothers are there, because maybe Carter is there with us watching the promise of the next day. I want to believe that's true.

"Listen, there's no rush about what's coming up next," I remind him. "The possibilities are endless. You can always start your own hockey team. The Timberwolves of Baker's Creek."

He gives me a weird look.

"I'm kidding."

"Grace mentioned it once, and I liked the idea back then. Now..." He shrugs. "I should do some research."

"It's a good first step," I offer.

"How about you?"

I look at my crutches and shake my head. "I'm still unsure."

Mason was here last Sunday. Actually, the Deckers moved the location of brunch and dinner so Grace and I could be there. Brunch was at my house and dinner was at Tucker's place. My brothers actually enjoyed the big gathering. It's the first time I made my famous French toast casserole for my family.

We spoke about my plans—I don't have any. My future—it depends on how I recover. And The Organization—we're changing roles when I'm better. Everything depends on when I can walk again.

"Did your boss fire you?"

I shake my head. "No, I'm taking a sabbatical. We'll reassess everything once I'm well enough."

The guys, Grace, and I decided to take different roles within the company. We're not retired, but we're not going back to the field. I guess none of us really thought about mortality until one of us had a brush with death. On the other hand, Vance might join The Organization once the Baker's Creek sentence is lifted.

As we're about to approach the coffee shop, I spot Grace chatting with Hadley. I've seen her only twice since we came to Baker's Creek. G and I have joked about her being a ghost. We know she's real only because Seth ran a background check on her before my brothers offered her the position.

"How's she working out for you?"

"Arden adores her," he states. The tone is a little off.

"So, we like her," I tease him.

"She's my son's caregiver," he mumbles under his breath.

"I mean, she's cute," I say with disdain. "If you're into the whole petite-curvy-honey-colored-hair-girl-next-door vibe."

He growls.

"Just give me a call. I'll teach them a lesson," Grace says as we're approaching them.

"Who are you maiming?" I ask, instead of saying, *your license to kill has been revoked.* This town takes everything too literal.

After the explosion in my studio, they're speculating about what happened. Some say I was trying to cash in on the insurance money because I'm broke. Also, I'm an alcoholic—thank you tabloids for posting and printing shit about me after my accident.

"Some women who think we're still in high school," Grace answers, pushing herself on her tiptoes and kissing me.

"Have you met Hadley?"

"Daddy!" Arden screams and extends his arms when he spots Mills.

"Hey, sport," he says, lifting him up and twirling him a couple of times.

"Hadley, I'm Beacon. It's a pleasure to finally meet you," I extend my hand.

She gives me a shy smile. "I hope you're doing much better."

I nod. "You know what we should do?"

Grace frowns. "Take a break?"

"I was thinking of going to the park."

Arden's eyes open wide. "Bark!"

"Park," Hadley says, emphasizing the *p*.

Mill glares at me. "Beac, I don't have time."

"I can take him," Hadley intercedes, reaching out for Arden. "Maybe we can go home for your tricycle and you can drive all the way to the park."

Arden nods a couple of times.

"After what happened, you shouldn't go by yourself," Grace intercedes, then looks at Mills. "You need to go with them, okay. I need to take this guy home to rest in bed."

"I'm all for missionary," I say.

"Well, then join me, handsome." She curls her index finger and I follow right behind.

"What happened to Hadley?"

She looks around and shakes her head. "Let's just say she doesn't have any fond memories of growing up in Baker's Creek."

"That usually does the trick," I agree and remain quiet until we reach the mansion. "Do you think they look good together?"

"Hadley and Mills?" She shakes her head. "I don't see matchmaking in your future."

"I've never tried it before," I protest.

She turns around and smiles at me. "She's nice. She likes Arden, but she's leaving soon. Our boy already has enough heartache to get through to add another one. Same with your brother."

Is she right? I want to see everyone I know happy. Mills said it before, he feels lonely. I want him to find what I have with Grace. He and his little boy deserve it.

"He'll meet *the one* when it's time," she assures me. "We just can't meddle with love. I had a lot of people trying to find me *someone* and it wore me out."

"You had *the one* right in front of you."

She wraps her arms around my neck and kisses me hard. "I did, which is why I never felt alone until you had to stay here, and I realized I was missing something—more like someone. My other half."

"One day, I'm going to ask you to marry me." I release one of the crutches and snake my arm around her waist. "Where do you want to live?"

"Do we have to choose one place in particular, or can we be gypsies who travel all over the world and visit our families when we aren't playing?"

"We can do anything you want," I offer. "The sky is the limit."

"I only want to be with you," she whispers, holding me tight.

Grace's Epilogue

Every night, we spend it practicing music—Beacon with a different instrument while I play the cello. He still can't play guitar. Mom and I have talked about this, and we believe it's a mental block. It's something he has to work out on his own.

Once we're all tired out, we get tangled in each other's bodies and make love a couple of times before we fall asleep.

"I was thinking," Beacon says as I rest my head on top of his chest. "We could travel around the world while I'm healing. This time will be just about visiting places, enjoying each other's company."

"Have you discussed your situation with the guys?"

He nods. "I told them that maybe they should look for a replacement—someone temporary. Neither one of them accepted my suggestion. Mane almost knocked me down. Fish stopped him only because I was on my crutches."

"We're a unit," I remind him.

"Would you play with us?"

"I owe you a tour, but remember I'm a cello nerd who likes her stuffy fans," I joke.

"You don't have to stop playing because of me."

"I wouldn't stop playing because of anyone," I remind him. "This break was planned a long time ago. I haven't found any offers for next year that are good enough to take me away from you."

He kisses my bare shoulder. "I can always carry your bags."

"Why don't you make love to me instead?" I ask.

It doesn't take long to convince him. He moves on top of me and thrusts inside of me. I can't remember what life was like before we became us. The only memory I have is of us making fascinating music.

Every morning I wake up to an empty bed. Beacon joins his brothers at the gym and then makes breakfast since it's the only chore that doesn't require him to be on his feet for a long time. Today, I frown when I find the crutches against the wall, the chair next to it, and Beacon nowhere around the bedroom. I dress fast and jet out of the room searching for him. He's not in the kitchen preparing breakfast.

Grace: *Where are you?*

There's no answer. I go to the barn where Leyla is feeding the animals. Mozzy looks at me curiously and continues staring at Ally. This is the first time I witness the sight of my cat hanging out with the rest of the animals.

I look toward at the lake, checking if his clothes are around. What if he drowned? My heart is beating fast when I don't find him in the gym. I walk to the studio and my lips turn upward when I hear the sound of his guitar. It's a prelude. The intro of a song.

She's an electrical storm,

A force that can move oceans,
And sometimes she stands still, controlling my chaos.
She knows my soul like she knows my heart.
She's my savior,
My reason,
My music,
And my life.

I haven't heard him play with this much heart in a long time. I listen to the entire song and when he opens his eyes, he stares at me.

"It's coming back." His cheeky smile melts my heart.

"I never doubted it."

He pushes himself up and walks toward me. No crutches, no help, no wobbling.

"How?"

"I've been working extra hard," he answers. "Those times when you're not around, I'm busting my ass. If I want to carry your luggage when you start touring, I have to be ready."

He then pulls out something from his pocket and drops on one knee.

"Grace Aiko Bradley, my first memory is of you. Of us on your family's playground, laughing carelessly, happy because we were in that moment sharing each other's space. We're not those kids, but I want us to become something similar. Two people laughing, loving, enjoying every moment. Walking through everything life throws our way.

"My therapist asked me why I thought my anger went away too easily. I told her, 'It's Grace. She reminds me that life is short. She's the one who makes it magical.' We have gone through so much more than this accident. How can I be mad, when I'm lucky to call you mine, and have your support?

"Also, how can I not ask the love of my life to share the rest of her life with me? We're forever. An eternal song. One that will play even when we're gone. Grace, would you do me the honor of becoming my wife?"

"Yes." I nod as I sob. This time it's happiness. My guy evolved. He's different and yet the same. This time, it's us.

"I love you, Beacon Aldridge."

"Love you more," he insists.

"How do you know?"

"I don't, but it's a good challenge. I say that I do, you love me more the next day, and I up the bets."

"You're ridiculous."

"Ridiculously yours."

Beacon's Epilogue

I work at The Lodge part-time. I work the front desk along with Grace. Although I love to make Henry's life difficult, I behave well enough. We don't have much time left in Baker's Creek, and I want to make this time memorable for everyone.

We will be back. Easton, the contractor, broke ground on what will be our Baker's Creek house. Grace and I are keeping our engagement low-key. Only her parents, her brothers and mine know about it. Instead of the ring I gave her, she wears a diamond pendant necklace.

The secrecy is to ensure that Jerome doesn't impose the will's stipulations on her too. She visits her family every other week. I can't imagine what would happen if Jerome Parrish says she can't travel anymore.

Yesterday it was her grandfather's birthday. I wish I had been there, but at least she celebrated with him.

As we sit at the table to have breakfast, I announce, "Jerome Parrish is in town."

"Are you ever going to stop following the poor man?" Blaire asks.

I stare at her for a couple of beats and shrug. "I don't know."

Grace and I are onto him. Hadley has been helping us dig some information about his past. I can't just stop the investigation.

"Why are you doing it?" Mills questions.

"There has to be more to why we're here," I explain to them.

"I want to know too," Henry agrees.

Suddenly everyone is nodding and throwing hypothesis. My phone buzzes. It's the alarm announcing that someone is approaching the property. I slide my finger along the screen and unlock the phone. Pulling up the app that allows me to see the cameras, I spot Jerome about to ring the intercom.

"Yo," I greet him.

He jolts and I grin.

"I have a delivery for you and *your* fiancée, Beacon."

"The letters." Leyla and Sophia both get jittery and noisy.

I don't see the point of getting excited when we agreed no one will open their letters until everyone gets theirs.

"It's open." I grunt as I open the gate so he can come inside.

I glare at everyone. "Who told him we were engaged?"

"No one said anything," Blaire assures me.

I look at the time. Grace just left Seattle. Vance is flying me to Portland to pick her up. How am I supposed to fucking fix this?

"We're getting caught over some stupid technicality. I fucking knew it," Henry growls and glares at me.

"No one is getting caught." Pierce clears his throat and points at me. "Deny any allegation. You're good at lying."

When there's a knock on the door, Vance is the one who opens it. Everyone still fears Vance. I guess he's the only one who could do any damage. I'm still not ready to arm wrestle against any of my brothers, let alone punch them if they fuck with me. That's my October goal.

"I'm here in time for breakfast," Jerome says.

We all glare at him.

"Why is he always inviting himself to have a meal with us?" Mills grunts.

I shrug.

"Mr. Parrish," Blaire greets him, while standing up to search for a cup and a plate, I guess. She brings back a to-go mug and grabs a muffin with a napkin. "Here. You give us the letters, and you can be on your way."

"Where is Ms. Bradley?" He scans the room.

"Why are you asking?" I stare at him.

"She's your fiancée. You know the rules about significant others." He sets a letter on top of the table that has Grace's name.

My eyes bulge at the meaning of this. William knew about her. How did he do that? Did he hire a private investigator and I didn't notice? I'll have Seth research since I'm not allowed to touch The Organization's assets.

"You're fetching for information, Parrish?" I taunt him. "That's low, even for you."

I push the letter. "You can drop it off to her when we make it official."

"It seems like you two are close enough to be *official*," he states, showing me the pictures posted on the Baker's Creek social media sites.

We all laugh.

"You can't base facts on what you see online," Pierce claims.

Jerome shakes his head and pulls out a letter size manila envelope. "This one is for you."

"Why does he get a big one?" Pierce argues.

We all stare at him.

Parrish grins. "I don't know. I'm just the messenger."

"It feels like you're more than that," I claim.

He grins. "And you'd be wrong," he states and leaves the house with his coffee and muffin in hand.

"Are you going to open it?" Henry urges me.

"No, we all agreed to open them at the same time," I remind them. I pick up the envelopes and go to my room.

I put them in the safe before leaving for Portland to pick up Grace. When we're back, I show her the envelopes. She looks at hers and grins. "I got mail."

"Are you going to open it?"

"No. I'm just happy because it means you really liked me."

"I love you."

"I love you too." She shows me her hand. She's wearing the ring. "I love you so much that I told my family."

"You won't be able to go back until the end of November," I remind her.

"They know. This family thing goes both ways, Beacon. They can visit us too. Just because we don't live next door to them, or in the same state, it doesn't mean they'll forget us. If we decide that living here is best for us, then we'll have to remember that we're not too far away from each other."

She's right about family. While growing up, I was taught differently.

A family doesn't end after the week is over, or after this crazy stipulation ends. Whatever William tried to do is insignificant compared to what's happening to us. We're actually connecting and becoming the Aldridge brothers.

"Thank you for being my family, my life, and for always being here for me." I kiss her with everything I have. "I missed you."

"I missed you more."

Dear Reader,

Thank you so much for picking up a copy of Call You Mine.

It's been two years of plotting and writing the Aldridge brothers. I can't express how much I love this family and these guys own my heart. In the beginning I was planning to write them in order, but that didn't happen because Beacon. This guy just doesn't like any rules. Also, he thinks it's unfair to be the last just because he was born last. I had to give this to him since we almost lost him.

Bringing back the Decker family and Mason was one of my favorite things about writing this book. You know who else I fell in love with? Manelik, Sanford, Fisher, and Byron (Lang). You'll probably get to know them a lot better soon. I have so many plans for him.

One last thing, if you loved Call You Mine as much as I did writing it, please leave a review on your favorite retailer, Goodreads, and on Bookbub. Also, please spread the word about The Baker's Creek Brothers among your friends. One of my favorite things about writing is sharing these characters with everyone.

Sending all my love,
Claudia xoxo

Acknowledgments

First and foremost, thank you to God because he's the one who allows me to be here and who gifts me the time, the creativity, and the tools to do what I love.

Thank you for all the blessings in my life. Thank you to my husband for taking upon the house chores so I can meet my deadlines. To my children and my family for supporting me in this journey. It's never enough to say thank you to my person, Kristi. Five years, a lot of patience and love that I will never be able to repay.

Marla, thank you for fitting this book in your schedule. I'm grateful.

Nina, Kelly, and all the team of Valentine's PR. To Kim, for keeping me organized, all her help in the background, and listening to my craziness from time to time.

Hang Le, my longtime friend and my cover artist. She always understands what my books need. Amy, Darlene, Karen, Melissa, Patricia, Caroline, and Yolanda for always responding to my incoherent questions. Their feedback is important just like their friendship.

To all my readers, I'm so grateful for you. Thank you so much for your love, your kindness, and your support. It's because of you that I can continue doing what I do. My amazing ARC team, girls you are an essential part of my team. Thank you for always being there for me. My Grammers, you rock! To my Chicas! Thank you so much for your continuous support and for being there for me every day! Thank you to all the bloggers who help me spread the word about my books. Thank you never cuts it just right, but I hope it's enough.

Thank you for everything. All my love,
Claudia xoxo

About the Author

Claudia is an award-winning, *USA Today* bestselling author. She writes alluring, thrilling stories about complicated women and the men who take their breath away. She lives in Denver, Colorado with her husband and her youngest two children. She has a sweet Bichon, Macey, who thinks she's the ruler of the house. She's only partially right. When Claudia is not writing, you can find her reading, knitting, or just hanging out with her family. At night, she likes to binge-watch shows with her equally geeky husband.

To find more about Claudia:
    website
    Sign up for her newsletter: News Letter

Also By Claudia Burgoa

The Baker's Creek Billionaire Brothers Series

Loved You Once

A Moment Like You

Defying Our Forever

Call You Mine

As We Are

June 2021

Yours to Keep

September 2021

Luna Harbor

Finally You

Simply You

Perfectly You

Madly You

Second Chance Sinners Duet

Pieces of Us

April 2021

Somehow Finding Us

May 2021

Against All Odds Series

Wrong Text, Right Love

Didn't Expect You

Love Like Her

March 2021

Standalones

Us After You

Almost Perfect

Once Upon a Holiday

Someday, Somehow

Chasing Fireflies

Something Like Hate

Then He Happened

Maybe Later

My One Despair

My One Regret

Found

Fervent

Flawed

Until I Fall

Finding My Reason

Christmas in Kentbury

Chaotic Love Duet

Begin with You

Back to You

Unexpected Series

Uncharted

Uncut

Undefeated

Unlike Any Other

Decker the Halls

Co-writing

Holiday with You

Made in United States
Troutdale, OR
01/12/2024